To Simon, Beth and Imogen.
May all of your roads be free from trouble and
may you arrive at all of your destinations safely.

Chapter 1

There are moments in life where you find yourself wondering what trick of fate led you to that spot at that particular time, when the consequences of being there were so dramatic. What if I had left five minutes earlier? Five minutes later? There are a series of random events that place people together by complete accident and, if only they had avoided that place, that route, that appointment, things would have been so different. Maybe they would have been able to carry on with their lives as normal instead of being transported into a life that was alien to them – one they neither wanted nor chose. When the event occurs, it is almost as if an unseen hand has picked you up and taken you from a route in your life and placed you on a completely different track. A track you did not wish to follow, yet cannot get off.

What if I hadn't taken that call? This was the question Andy Connolly found himself asking on February the 22nd. It seemed like any other day during the course of it, with no warning of the drama to follow. In fact, if anything, it had shaped up well at the garage – they had sold five cars, including the lime-green Volvo he had taken in three months before and couldn't shift. As the owner of the garage, his concentration was always on numbers: how many cars sold, how many service appointments made, how many parts ordered and then a comparison with targets for all of them. Running a garage selling new and used cars was a constant juggling act.

On this particular evening, his coat was on, his office light off and he was agonisingly close to being out of the building when the receptionist, Andrea, signalled from the front desk that he was wanted on the phone. Why hadn't he just put his head down and continued to his car? Maybe he thought his good fortune was to continue and he would pull off one last deal before going home. The car dealer's curse of perennial expectation. The call was, of course, a waste of time: it was Dave Maddison, asking if he wanted to buy a 'mint' four-year-old soft top sports car, hardly used. That was Dave, a trader, always selling the right car at the wrong time. Sports cars in the winter; lumpy great 4 x 4s in the hottest part of the summer. Andy pulled faces at Andrea and sliced a hand across his throat, much to her amusement, but the five minutes of unwanted chat interrupted his day and delayed his journey home.

It was that call that changed things by a crucial few minutes. He decided he would take a different route home to avoid the traffic; he'd use the back road for the twelve-mile journey. The main roads would still be busy so he used his local knowledge of the shortcut.

That particular night there appeared to be no traffic on the back road at all, until he slowed for a T junction and saw the rear lights of a Nissan Juke just ahead of him at the mouth of the junction. As a motor trader for many years, it was an occupational hazard for Andy to notice the make and age of every car and automatically guess its value. The Nissan stopped at the junction and indicated left as Andy pulled up behind it. There was a slight pause as traffic passed on the main road. He changed the station on the radio and in the second or two it took him to do it, his world changed.

To begin with, he didn't know what had happened. He recalled looking up from the radio to see the car in front leaping at him whilst he was thrown into an explosion that both deafened and temporarily blinded him. The next few seconds happened in slow motion as he heard and felt nothing, almost as though the sound system of his brain had been turned off and all of his nervous system had gone with it. Dust and glass flew around him as his involuntary movements danced along with them. He watched the objects as though looking through someone else's eyes as his disconnected brain sought to re-boot and catch up with events. All senses were disconnected but not shut off. He could see and was awake but the information being fed to his brain was scrambled. It was like an awakening from a dream when the noises and feelings of the experience joined him a few seconds after the visual effects. Noise first ... scraping, breaking and an explosion he later realised was the airbag. Then the feelings as the adrenaline subsided and reasoning returned. He was still slightly deaf from the exploding airbag and the collision but his hearing was trying to re-tune itself. Sensation was returning to his limbs as his brain tried to assimilate the information. It finally told him there had been an accident and he had been hit from behind and shunted into the car in front. Yes, that was it – that was what had happened and now he had to remember what you do in these circumstances. Who do you call? Is it the police or your insurers? Who are my insurers? Do I have their number? Who pays for what and is anyone injured?

3

Do we need an ambulance? How do I get home now? The questions were piling up and none were being answered.

The Nissan driver got out first and looked stunned. A well-built man in his early twenties, he appeared to be trying to work out what had happened as he looked at the rear of his damaged car. Andy tried his door but it was stuck and then it occurred to him he ought to make sure nothing was broken before he tried to get out. He moved various body parts carefully and everything seemed to be working; his arms and legs moved; there was no sign of bleeding anywhere. He tried the door again as a dark silhouetted figure walked past his window. The figure seemed to be confronting the Nissan driver. In the dim light and with his hearing still impaired he could hear raised voices and the body language of the dark figure seemed aggressive. Why would he be aggressive? Was it not his fault?

Two further hard shoves on the door and it was partially open in a creaky-gate sort of way but enough for him to get out. He struggled unsteadily to his feet and felt the cold bite of a winter's evening. There behind him was the badly damaged car that had rammed into him and sent him careering into the Nissan. The figure he had seen was a tall man who was now arguing with the Nissan driver. Andy cleared his head and wobbled towards them. His hearing and no doubt the shock were conspiring to lend him a sea-legs unsteadiness.

'Why the fuck were you just sitting there, you wanker?,' said the tall man dressed in a black shirt and black jeans as he glared threateningly at the Nissan driver, a few intimidating inches from his face. He had greasy black hair and a Donald Trump-style orange face. He looked about six feet tall, was slightly overweight and appeared to be the kind of man you would seek to avoid.

'What are you talking about, you dickhead? You crashed into the back of him. We were both stationary,' answered Nissan man. They were toe to toe as Andy reached them, instinctively drawing on his car salesman's charm.

'Come on guys, let's calm down and sort all of this out like nice boys, shall we?'

The Nissan driver turned to answer Andy and, with his attention distracted, the other man head butted him, knocking him on to his car. The head butt was followed by punches thrown wildly at his head and torso by the assailant, who was on him like an animal. Although shocked and alarmed by this, Andy moved to intervene. As he did so, the assailant broke off his attack to elbow Andy sharply in the stomach. The blow knocked every ounce of air out of him as he doubled over and fell to the ground. That split second and slight distraction allowed the Nissan man to regain his footing and punch back. Andy desperately tried to shout from his prone position at the fighting men in front of him, but found he could not force any air into his flattened lungs.

The ugly tangle between the two men continued until Nissan man appeared to land a clean blow to the head and the instigator fell to the ground. Whilst on the ground he fumbled in his pockets before getting up to renew his attack. In the scuffle that followed, the black shirted man's right arm pulled away and struck Nissan man's side, seeming to stop him in his tracks. The arm went in twice more before the two men disentangled and the black shirted man ran back to his car. Nissan man slumped to the floor. Andy was finally managing to force air into his lungs as the car behind reversed a short distance and sped off past both prone men. He stumbled to Nissan man's side.

'Are you okay, mate?'

'The fucker's stabbed me! Here. Look … look! Oh Jesus Christ … look at the blood … look what he's done to me!'

Tony did look and even in the dim light he could see the large damp patch forming on the man's shirt as the blood oozed from obvious wounds.

The man looked hard at Andy with wide-open terrified eyes,

'Am I going to die? I am, aren't I? Don't let me die,' he pleaded.

'Nobody's going to die. Let me call for an ambulance and get you sorted out.' Andy spoke reassuringly but the younger man looked very pale, almost grey in the face and was sitting motionless.

Andy phoned 999 and said he needed both an ambulance and the police as a man had been stabbed. The calm voice on the other end of the phone said they were on their way, but could he check to see what the injuries were without moving the man.

'Can I just have a look mate and see how bad it is?' Andy said whilst gently moving the man's hand.

'There is a lot of blood here,' he informed the operator.

'Can you see if it is dark or light blood?'

'Light I think, but it's hard to tell – it's dark out here. Yes, I think fresh red blood.'

'Good. See if you can apply gentle pressure to stop the bleeding and the paramedics will be with you soon. I will stay on the line.'

Andy really did not know what he was doing but put his hand where the wound was and pressed gently, causing the injured man to groan.

'What's your name mate?,' he asked as he tried again.

'Gary … Gary Newcombe.'

'Hi Gary. I'm Andy and we have this under control. You'll be in the hospital in no time and they will put you right, don't you worry. It's all under control now so just try and relax. Are you married, Gary?'

'No … but I live with my girlfriend Kate … Oh my god what will she say? We're supposed to be going on holiday next month. Jesus Christ …' Gary replied as tears formed in his eyes.

'You will, you will, don't you worry about that. I'll give her a ring when the ambulance gets here. Here they come now, can you hear the sirens?'

'I feel cold – that's a bad thing, isn't it? That means you're dying, doesn't it?' Gary said with a now panic-stricken expression as his energy levels were falling.

'No, it means it's February and you're sitting on the ground, mate. I'm bloody freezing myself and I haven't been stabbed. Just hang in there, the ambulance is nearly here.' Andy spoke reassuringly but without conviction; he really had no idea whether this man was going to survive.

'Just hang in there, Gary. They'll be here any minute now and they'll sort you out and whip you off to hospital so you can flirt with those pretty nurses,' Andy added as he looked around anxiously searching for the ambulance.

The operator was still talking to Andy and telling him to keep the injured man calm and make sure he didn't move or pass out. The noise of the sirens became louder until they were deafening alongside them. The paramedics jumped out and Andy stood back as they worked on the stricken man. He still could not assess the stranger's chances of survival, despite the professional assistance now at the scene but he was amazed at how calmly he had handled the situation, particularly as he had also been attacked. He was even beginning to work through what he would need to do about his car when the police car arrived a couple of minutes later.

So, there he was standing in the middle of a dark road at the time he should have been at home putting on the telly and asking what was for dinner. Instead he was without a car, had to deal with the police and a thousand other things. He had also encountered a dark and violent figure and although his instinct told him the encounter was bad news, he had as yet, no way of knowing just how bad. Andy's life would never be the same. And in the future, he would often reflect on his decision to take that last call at the garage. Fate had dealt him a card he didn't recognise – one he didn't want.

Chapter 2

Andy watched the paramedics calmly deal with their patient. They talked reassuringly, injected him with something to ease his pain and applied an oxygen mask. He remembered the call he had promised to make and went to the Nissan to search the front seats before finding Gary's phone in the glove compartment. Turning it on, he saw the screensaver: a photo of Gary with a pretty dark-haired girl, but the phone was password protected. Hesitating for a second or two he approached the paramedics and asked if he could make good on his promise to ring Kate.

'The police will do all of that when they sort things out,' answered a half-turned paramedic.

At that point one of the police officers approached him.

'Can you tell me what's happened here?'

'Yes. Some yob's just tried to kill the poor bloke they're putting in the ambulance.'

'So where were you then?'

'This is my car here,' Andy said pointing to his sad-looking Audi.

'I was rear-ended by this thug, who pushed me into the guy in front. At first I had no idea what had happened. The thug got out of his car and started a fight with the guy in front.'

'What did you do?' asked the policeman, who was also listening to his police radio.

'I couldn't get out at first but when I did, the thug elbowed me in the stomach and was then full on with the younger guy.'

'Is that the younger man they are putting in the ambulance?'

'Yes, that's him. Anyway the young man seemed to have fought him off but when the older guy got up from the ground, he stabbed him and buggered off.'

'Can you describe the assailant?'

'I would say he was a couple of inches bigger than me … I'm six feet tall. He would be a stone or so heavier than me. Maybe 14 stone or thereabouts. He was wearing a black shirt and black jeans and had oily black hair that … that … kind of made him look like an extra from Grease.'

'Grease?'

'Yeah … you know, that film with John Travolta.'

'Oh, I see. Was he white, black or Asian?'

'More orange really.'

'Sorry?'

'He looked like he used fake tan or had just come back from his holidays.'

'So, white but swarthy?'

'I suppose so.'

'Did you get his registration number?'

'No, but it was a beamer on a 16 plate.'

'I'm sorry?'

'It was a 3 Series BMW registered after March 2016. Blimey I didn't even know I'd spotted that until you asked! It was dark blue – imperial blue I think they call it. I'm in the motor trade you see, I have an eye for that sort of thing.'

Andy cursed himself for not taking out his phone and taking a picture of the car before approaching the two men. The police officer took his details and told him they would arrange a time to take a detailed statement from him. To his intense irritation they asked him to wait while they checked his car for valid insurance and to ensure there were no warrants outstanding against him or the car. He kept his irritation to himself however as he telephoned his partner Rebecca. It went to her answering service and he left a message:

'Hi babe, it's me. I'm going to be late home tonight. I've had an accident in the car but I'm fine … you should see the other bloke, as they say. Anyway, I'll tell you all about it when I get back.'

The next call was to Paul Bevan, his service manager, to get him to go back to the garage and come and collect him in the pickup and tow his car back. He told Bevan the whole story and began to realise how lucky he was not to be in the ambulance alongside Nissan man. He was beginning to feel a searing rage at what had happened to him and what he had witnessed. Who was this nutter, who had nearly killed somebody in front of his eyes and might have done the same to him? Despite his middle-class background, Andy was no stranger to conflict, even the physical sort; he had played football in the local league as a central midfielder. His job was to tackle hard and he often found himself squaring up to an opposition player or dishing out retaliation in an overzealous challenge. This was different though; this was a pre-meditated, extremely vicious act from a man who was obviously no stranger to violence of this sort. He played the incident over and over in his mind and kept seeing the right hand strike those three blows with the knife. Not one, but three. What kind of man does that? What kind of man carries a knife in his pocket? What kind of world had he accidentally encountered and what would happen next?

Bevan arrived about forty minutes later with the tow

truck pulling the replacement car for Andy and ready to tow the stricken Audi back to the garage. He wanted all the details, which Andy felt obliged to give him, considering he had interrupted his evening at home. The telling of the story felt detached as he gave his account. He could scarcely believe he was talking about something that had actually happened to him, and so recently.

Once he'd switched cars, he drove uneventfully to his house on the outskirts of Selby but his head was still spinning. His home was a Victorian terraced house with a lot of renovation under way and plenty more to do. Since his divorce from Hannah three years before, he had felt the need to rebuild his life and fortunes. Fortunes – that's what the divorce had cost him when Hannah found out about him and Rebecca. Hannah still lived in their executive five-bedroomed house with their three children and there was no prospect of them moving. He had drained his business account to buy the property he now lived in but cash was tight. Peter and Paul were regularly robbed to pay the bills on two homes, as well as school fees. Andy always tried to avoid thinking too much about his domestic situation, which was a mess of his own making. He and Hannah had been together for 12 years and married for nine of them. Their three children had arrived quite quickly and, indeed, the first before they were married, but Andy loved kids and the atmosphere his own family created in his home. He had stretched himself financially when Phoebe was born four years ago and bought their large house with a whopping mortgage. He hadn't worried about it too much as his garage business was very profitable and he could meet all the payments ... as long as he kept selling those cars. He had not, of course, expected or factored in divorce.

Two years ago, he'd advertised for a new sales person to assist in the expansion of the business and in walked Rebecca Gates. Tall, slim with long auburn hair, she exuded an air of confidence and would be the only female salesperson on the team. He had to admit that her physical attractiveness was a factor in her getting the job but then that was a plus for any sales staff, male or female. The punters like to talk to someone they find attractive if they're going to part with a lot of cash. He was sure he'd read that somewhere or saw it on the TV. Anyway, he gave Rebecca the job. It never crossed his mind that he would have an affair with her as he had been faithful to Hannah since they started living together, although he had a drunken fumble with Bevan's wife Corinne at a Christmas party a few years ago. Bevan had not seen it and neither Corinne nor he had ever mentioned it again. Andy always thought he had dodged a bullet on that one. The problem was that with Rebecca he could not blame drink, as he had acted spontaneously. There had been no real sign of anything between them. Andy was always careful in what he said and never indulged in flirty banter with any of the female staff. He was even careful what he said to the men. Fear of an employment tribunal always kept him focused after a bad experience a friend told him about. So, it was in all innocence that Rebecca and he went off to discuss providing a factory owner with a small fleet of cars on lease. The factory was just outside Epworth and involved them going on a 60-mile round trip. Rebecca had created the opportunity for the deal and Andy had gone along to close it. The deal involved ten cars and he found they worked very well as a team on the day. He had led with the friendly opening: a discussion on sport, the state of the economy and general stuff. Then he introduced Rebecca and she had run with the ball, saying how impressive the factory was and how good it was to see local industry. The factory owner was putty in her hands and Andy moved in at the end to close the deal.

In their excitement of the meeting's conclusion, they stopped off for a drink to celebrate. High on the adrenaline of success, they both held gazes a little too long in their conversation and ordered a second drink. Even so, Andy didn't plan to do anything but as they walked out of the pub, Rebecca pulled him into a corridor and kissed him full on the lips. The warmth of her body, and the scent of her expensive perfume caused the moment to overcome him and he responded fully. The kiss became passionate and they moved further out of sight to indulge in the moment. She was obviously experienced and confident as she opened his mouth gently with her tongue and rubbed her groin against his. She welcomed his probing hands inside her shirt as she pulled him to her but they were disturbed by another customer. As they pulled apart there was an uncomfortable giggle, but a line had been crossed. It was clear they both wanted to take it further. They chatted on the way back as if nothing had happened and Andy wondered if that was the end of it.

He found he thought about the moment quite a bit and often watched Rebecca glide across the showroom floor but he didn't heed the danger signals that were there. A couple of days after the Epworth trip, Rebecca was the last of the staff remaining at the end of the day, and she popped into his office.

'Okay Andy, I'm off now, unless there is something I can do for you?'

'Well, that's an interesting proposition!' He replied with a smile.

Rebecca closed his door and put both hands the desk, leaned forward to reveal a glimpse of her shapely breasts and, with eyes wide open and a smile playing around her lips, said,

'What would you like me to do?'

He got up and walked around the desk, causing her to straighten and turn to him. There was a moment's pause then he pulled her towards him and kissed her gently. She responded and they were soon locked in a passionate embrace which threatened to overtake them completely. Only worries over a customer drifting in or a member of staff returning stopped them short of tearing off each other's clothes.

The problem was a crossroads had been reached: instead of reversing away, the relationship had moved on. The time to admit the mistake and send Rebecca on her way was gone. He could have done that; he could even have told Hannah he had been attracted to Rebecca, but realised she and the children meant more to him. However, as so often in these situations, logic goes out of the window. There is a belief – built on the crumbliest of sand – that maybe you can have both. The gamble of the stability of a deep relationship with someone you love or a fling with someone who reminds you of the thrill of the chase; the uncertainty of the result. They both wanted to take it further but it was Andy who had most to lose.

They didn't have sex until a couple of weeks later, by which time he was infatuated with the younger woman who made him feel young and attractive again. He had decided to take the risk with his domestic happiness and lost. It was a friend of Hannah's who saw Andy and Rebecca together in a restaurant and realised there was more to it than just business. The friend hesitated, torn, but eventually told Hannah she had seen her husband holding another woman's hand and kissing her in his car. Hannah confronted him in a dreadful tearful scene at home and, although he denied it at first, he eventually blurted out the truth. Initially they tried to make a go of it for the sake of the children but the seal was broken. The love they shared leaked from the hole he had torn in the fabric of their relationship. He still loved his wife and maybe she still loved him, but the damage was too great.

They battled on for a while but soon found that the arguments were not the problem; it was the otherwise happy days with the kids that displayed what they had lost. All Hannah could think about was how she was with a man who'd betrayed her. In turn, all Andy could feel was a sense of overwhelming guilt and the acute loss of the easy pleasure of their relationship. It was over and he left.

He had stopped seeing Rebecca, other than at work, but when he separated from Hannah, he and Rebecca got together again. He moved from his friend's spare room to her flat. Despite the financial strain, and perhaps in trying to cement the relationship, they bought a property together and moved in. They were doing their best but it was a relationship hanging by a thread. Truth be told, Andy preferred having someone to go home to rather than returning to an empty flat and maybe that was the thread. What he didn't realise was that everyone he cared about would soon be in danger. Events would have a pace of their own.

Chapter 3

Rebecca was both shocked and sympathetic when hearing the whole story that night and Andy had to admit to himself that he quite liked the attention. Embers were reignited in the relationship as the drama of what had happened hit them both. There is nothing like potential loss to make you appreciate what you have. They even talked about pressures in their relationship and how they could address some of them and make a real go of it. What Andy didn't say was that whenever they had a problem, he just could not help himself looking at Rebecca and blaming her for the loss of his family, even though he knew they were equally to blame. In fact, he knew he was more to blame because he was the one with the family.

There was more attention the next day when he told the staff about his near-death experience to open-mouthed expressions and gasps. What he found was that when he wasn't talking about it, he was thinking about it, even when dealing with customers. It was an incident which was being played and replayed over and over as a backcloth to his normal daily tasks. His emotions were still raw but he had an ability to multi-task and he used it. He also expected a call from the police which did not arrive that day, much to his bemusement. He'd imagined feverish police activity and maybe squad cars at the garage but nothing happened.

As he got ready to leave that day, he phoned the hospital to enquire about Gary Newcombe but as he was not a member of the family, they could only tell him he had been admitted and was in the high dependency unit. He decided that he would try a visit and seek a little more information.

When he arrived, he followed the signs for the unit, which was on the third floor. There was nobody around to ask so he sat in one of the seats in the corridor and waited for a nurse. He checked his phone out of habit, read a few emails and sent a couple of texts. After ten minutes or so the double doors to the unit opened and he saw a dark-haired young woman, whom he recognised as Kate from her picture on Gary's phone. He hesitated but then got up.

'Excuse me. It's Kate, isn't it?' Andy said as he walked towards her tentatively.

She turned but didn't answer. She looked exhausted and had the bloodshot eyes of someone who'd been crying for some time.

'It is Kate, isn't it? I'm Andy Connolly, I was at the scene with your boyfriend Gary.'

'Oh, are you the one who called the ambulance?' She replied.

'Yes, I am … how is he doing?'

The question knocked down a paper-thin wall that Kate was building around herself and the tears came again.

'I don't really know, he's all wired up and has been down to the theatre twice,' she spluttered through the tears. She explained that her parents were on their way from Birmingham and that Gary's mother was not well and couldn't get to the hospital.

As she calmed herself, she added, 'I've spoken to him between his operations and he said you were very kind to him and that you were attacked as well. I can't believe it. I

19

really can't, he is such a nice person. Who would do a thing like this?'

'I didn't do much really and I got off lightly. I was just winded but I got a good look at the thug who did it.'

'Yes, so did Gary. He said he was all in black and looked like he fancied himself as some sort of gangster with his hair all greased back. He said he just couldn't understand it because the man ran into the back of him ... so it was his fault? You know – the accident I mean. The doctor has said that the next 24 hours are important for Gary. They couldn't stop the bleeding and he has had to have some transfusions ...,' and with that the tears returned as a cascade.

'He actually ran into the back of me, Kate and pushed me into Gary's car. Not that it matters of course because the guy is obviously a pyscho, but it is good that Gary can remember what he looks like. We can both give good descriptions of the attacker. I'm sure they'll catch him.'

Andy stayed another hour or so, exchanging phone numbers with Kate whilst offering his continued help, though he wasn't sure what that might be. She told him the police had been at the hospital but as Gary wasn't fit to make a statement they'd be coming back. As he left the hospital, he bought the evening paper and sat in his car to see if there was any mention of the incident and on page five there was a small article.

Car Incident near Carlson Village
There was an incident at around 6.15 pm last night near the village of Carlson when three vehicles were involved in an accident. Police say there was a serious attack on one of the drivers, which

lead to that driver being admitted to Goole and District Hospital. The condition of the patient is unknown. Police are appealing for witnesses who may have been on the road in to or out of the village at the time of the incident.

The report was short and cold. Andy wasn't sure what he expected but it was something more substantial than this. He had an odd sense of detachment from such a serious incident, almost as though he was in limbo, awaiting instruction as to what he should do, how he should feel. He read the sports news before folding the paper and throwing it into the back seat, then driving off in the direction of home. Perhaps because he was pre-occupied, he failed to notice the Mitsubishi Shogun parked opposite the entrance. As he passed it, it too started up and pulled in behind him. The car contained three male occupants who silently stared straight ahead as they followed. Every now and again, the Shogun would pull back and allow traffic to create a gap, but continued in the same direction as Andy.

Andy pulled up outside of his house and the Shogun pulled into the curb on the opposite side of the road, about 200 yards away. Andy hadn't noticed anything as he turned the key and went inside. He didn't see the Shogun start up again, slow down outside of his house and then pull away. Rebecca met him at the door.

'Hello love, did you have a good day?' she asked as she kissed his cheek.

'Not bad. I went to the hospital to try and see that guy who was stabbed. I was talking to his girlfriend – looks like he's in a bad way and they won't know if he is going to pull through until tomorrow – maybe even after that.'

'God that must be awful for her! How's she holding up?'

'Badly. Perhaps I watch too many detective programmes but I couldn't understand why there wasn't a policeman there and, for that matter, why I haven't seen one.'

'Well, it's only been a day, hasn't it? Are you saying you think the guy is still at risk?'

'Not really … well, I don't know. You just imagine that he would be guarded or protected or something. Maybe I'm overreacting, but it all seems so low key considering somebody was nearly killed. That's all I'm saying.'

'Maybe they've arrested him already, Andy.'

'Maybe.'

It preyed on his mind all night and he decided he would ring the police. He half imagined he would ring his local police station and maybe speak to the officer investigating. But having looked on the internet, he saw he couldn't do that but had to ring either 999 or 101. As it was not an emergency, he called 101 and was asked by an automated service if he wanted his local police force – North Yorkshire Police – or another force. Eventually, his call was answered by a civilian worker from North Yorkshire Police.

'Do you wish to report a crime?'

'No, I don't think so, I was involved in one last night.'

'Was that reported?'

'Yes, the police turned up.'

'Do you have a crime number?'

'No.'

'Where did it happen?'

'It was the junction of the B6544 and A768 just outside of Carlson Village.'

'Ah that's Humberside Police, would you like me to transfer you?'

'I suppose so,' he said, properly confused.

When he spoke to Humberside police, they told him that the matter was being processed and gave him a crime number for future reference. He was also told that a police officer would be coming to see him, but that the officer would be from North Yorkshire as that was where he lived. That officer would take his statement and pass it on to Humberside Police, who were investigating the alleged crime because it happened in their jurisdiction. Andy resisted the temptation to ask if there was now passport control in the short distance between his home and work. His frustrations were beginning to grow, but he was promised that somebody would ring him on his mobile. When he ended the call, he felt a little more insecure. It was as if there had been a seismic shift in police protection that he knew nothing about, until now, and a form of snakes and ladders that had to be encountered before a uniformed officer would appear.

When he was a child they had lived in a small village and the policeman had a house there with a small office attached. Everyone knew the officer who lived there and it was easy to discuss any criminal activity happening locally. He remembered an unusual spate of burglaries in the village and PC Dalton asking about them. His father told him that when PC Dalton was having a pint in one of the local pubs, a near neighbour had tipped him off about the son of the newsagent who had been seen with a quite a bit of cash. It turned out he was using the information his parents received about holidays, i.e. when people cancelled their newspapers for a week or two. He would tell a couple of rough lads from a nearby village and they gave him cash for the information, which also included whether or not they had burglar alarms – intelligence he'd garnered himself from his paper round. The boy was arrested, the burglaries stopped and the parents sold up in shame. Everybody seemed to know what to do when there was a problem and a uniformed officer was regularly visible. Now there didn't appear to be any village or local policeman. He was shocked.

No such territorial problems for the rear-seat passenger in the Shogun. He dialled a number and after three rings it was answered with a grunt. He spoke to the grunter:

'Man at the hospital lives at 27 Temple Street in Barmby on the Marsh. Drives a Honda Civic NX55 GFD. He looks about 40, six foot tall, medium build and darkish hair. Colin followed him up to the ward and saw him hugging our man's girlfriend. Maybe a relative but he could be the other man. What do you want to do?'

'Is he in for the night?'

'He's home. Do you want us to give him a knock?'

'No. We don't know who he is yet. Who else did you see at the hospital?'

'Just the same girl. The nurse said some parents are on the way but she wasn't sure who they were. What do you want us to do about this guy here?'

'Get there bright and early tomorrow and follow him so we know where he works. Use a different car. Even if he doesn't spot you, most routes have CCTV.'

'Will do.'

The Shogun started up and drove out of the street. They would be back. Storm clouds were forming.

Chapter 4

At a little after 6am the three men returned in a black Volvo and parked fifty yards away from number 27 Temple Street. A flask was opened and three coffees poured as they sat silently and waited for movement from the house. There was an eerie quiet in the street as daylight began to emerge to replace the cold darkness.

Andy had his breakfast at eight o'clock as he did every day, apart from Sunday when he and Rebecca had breakfast in bed. They would normally go into work together but recently, Rebecca had felt a cooling with other members of staff as she was now seen as the boss's spy. She had contemplated getting a job somewhere else but she was suffering from the mistress syndrome in her relationship with Andy: if he could do this with me, he could do it with someone else. Better to keep a close eye on him, especially with Anna the new trainee salesperson. Anna seemed to be looking for a more experienced replacement for her good looking but deadly dull boyfriend.

'Don't forget we're at Laura's on Saturday for dinner,' Rebecca said as Andy read the news on his iPad.

'Oh shit! Is it this Saturday?'

'Yes – it's been in the diary for weeks.'

'Do we have to go?' He sighed.

'She's your sister, Andy and yes, we do.'

'It's not Laura that's the problem, it's Charles I can't take.'

'He's all right when you get to know him,' Rebecca said lightly.

'All right to you if he can take his eyes off your chest, but I have to listen to how successful and powerful he is. If he asks me again to join the Masons, I'll have to strangle him.'

'Well he is a successful architect, isn't he?' She teased.

'So he keeps telling me,' Andy replied as he finished his breakfast and got ready to leave.

It was Rebecca's day off so she was still in her dressing gown as she kissed Andy goodbye at 8.30. She waited at the door to wave as he pulled away and paid no attention to the Volvo starting up and pulling in behind her boyfriend.

Andy was too pre-occupied with recent events and his concerns about the business to notice the car behind and in fact he noticed very little before pulling on to the garage forecourt having virtually driven the journey on auto-pilot. He certainly didn't see the Volvo slow down and the iPhone point at him from the rear seat, snapping pictures of him and the premises. Andrea looked up from the reception desk and called him over.

'Morning boss. Three messages for you. Andy King from Mitsubishi wants to arrange to see you and says you have his mobile number. Mr Robinson says he is expecting a call about his car that you promised him last Friday, and Dave Maddison says he has the very car that will make you a fortune.'

'Nothing from the police?'

'No sorry, that's it.'

Andy shook his head and walked into his office wondering if he should ring the police again but decided against it.

He checked his mobile to see if either the police or Kate had tried him but there was nothing. He was unsettled, unable to focus on the daily routine or normality. He had a desire to be proactive but, more than that, a foreboding that his life had changed track in an unwanted way. His unrecognised wish was to exert some control over events and feel his way back to his somewhat troubled but generally predictable life. The images of the black-shirted man and the knife piercing the young stranger's side were never far from his conscious thoughts. He kept seeing that expression on the victim's face at the moment he thought he was dying. Who was the knife man? Where was he now and how was he feeling? Did he suffer remorse or was this a regular event for him?

Just before lunch Andrea popped into Andy's office.

'Are you okay, Andy? You don't seem your usual bubbly self today.'

'I'm fine Andrea, just need to get the month-end figures together,' he lied.

'You might be in shock from that attack the other night. That can happen to people, you know. My brother had a bad accident and couldn't sleep properly for weeks. He said he got lots of flashbacks and he wasn't even attacked. Have they caught that bloke yet?'

'Not as far as I know.'

'It's in the morning paper but there's no mention of you.'

'Is it? Bring it in and let me see it.'

Andrea obliged and there it was on the front page of the Hull Daily Mail:

Goole Man Stabbed
Humberside police confirmed that a 24-year-old man from the Goole area was stabbed in what appears to have been a road-rage incident near a village outside of Goole. The man was taken to hospital in Goole where he remains in a critical condition. Police are appealing for witnesses who may have been near the village of Carlston on Tuesday evening around 6pm. It is believed that three vehicles were involved in an accident before the attack occurred.

So, it was now public knowledge that a man was stabbed but still little or no activity. Andy decided to try and concentrate on making some money to take his mind off the incident. He checked the sales figures to see where they were in relation to their targets and called the sales team in for a meeting. He delivered his usual cocktail of abuse and praise to motivate the staff into greater effort to hit their target which needed six more sales of new cars before the month ended. His best salesman, Peter Thomson, gave his usual explanation that he had three certainties on the go and they would definitely be in the bag before the weekend. Andy asked him if it was the same bag that the last three had escaped from last month. Thomson looked stung as the others sniggered, but the point had been made. Sales were required – not promises or leads. The team was dismissed to get on the phones and produce something, as his energy was turned to good use.

The day went by uneventfully and Peter Thomson even managed to close two of his deals; no doubt the sting of the barb earlier in the day had played a major part. Brilliant management, Andy told himself on his drive home. As he got out of his car, his mobile rang. It was an unrecognised number. Normally he wouldn't take the call but he pressed the green button.

'Could I speak to Mr Connolly, please?'

'Speaking.'

'Oh, hello Mr Connolly. It's PC Elliott here from North Yorkshire Police. I'd like to arrange an appointment to see you to take a statement about the incident the other night.'

'You don't need an appointment to see me – just call in at home or the garage.'

'We operate an appointment system here so that we can be sure to see you when we say. You know how it is – in the old days we might be called away in the middle of a statement or something but now you have a time slot and that's secure.'

'Okay, when do you want to see me?'

'I can do Wednesday next week between 3pm and 5pm or Thursday at any time in the morning.'

'Next week? Isn't this more urgent than that? What's being done to find this maniac? He's out there right now, I imagine.'

'I'm sorry sir, but that is the earliest day I can do. We are not the investigating force anyway; that's Humberside. We're just taking your statement and passing it on to them.'

Andy let it go but felt a surge of anger and resentment as he considered the delays, all of which seemed to be helping the black-shirted man evade capture. Surely they could see that the sooner they traced him the sooner they would have the evidence of the car. The thug was being given the time to repair the car and destroy the evidence. Maybe he did watch too much television.

Andy's mood for the night was set on low as he recounted the conversation to Rebecca, all the time imagining the BMW being re-sprayed after the bodywork had been repaired so that it looked as good as new, as opposed to how it looked when it disentangled itself from the back of his car. He felt frustrated and strangely vulnerable. In his imagination, there was a police station and blue uniformed officers pouring out of it to catch villains. Instead, he felt he was dealing with a call centre and very remote staff promising delivery of goods that may never come but there was no face to see or shop to visit.

The second story on News at Ten that night was about falling police numbers and budget cuts to reduce the country's deficit. Again, it took him back in time to his village and the resident police officer. He remembered going to football matches when the sheer presence of police officers was reassuring. He couldn't remember the last time he actually saw a policeman walking in uniform along a street. Feeling secure was so important and he hadn't noticed until now that a foundation of that security had been withdrawn ... the visible policeman. As he dwelled on this, his mood darkened further. Eventually he gave up trying to raise his spirits and, after Rebecca told him he had a face like a slapped arse, he went to bed.

In a small body-shop twenty miles away, a BMW in imperial blue was having replacement parts for the front section of the vehicle fitted. A silver BMW stood alongside it, its front section missing. The replacement parts would be re-sprayed to match and the damaged parts would be fitted to the silver car and sprayed silver to match its bodywork. In the hours of darkness, the stolen silver BMW would be driven on roads bereft of CCTV to a deserted spot and set alight. Only a shell would remain. There would be no history of ordered parts or repairs to the imperial blue BMW. All evidence of its involvement in the incident would be gone forever.

Chapter 5

Laura Peterson was sitting in front of her bedside mirror combing her shoulder-length dark brown hair. She was always so proud of the thickness of the hair but today it looked a little limp and lifeless. She leaned forward to take a closer look and caught sight of the faint tinge of dark circles forming under her hazel eyes. Added to the slight weight gain in the last few months, the image in the mirror caused her to sigh, avert her eyes and slump in her seat. What depleted energy she had this morning was draining away fast and she felt like climbing back into bed. The sound of the shower door opening in the en-suite bathroom sparked her into life as she sat up straight and continued the combing.

'What time did you say your brother and his floozy are coming over tonight?' Charles Peterson shouted from the bathroom.

'7.30. And don't call her that,' she shouted back.

'What was that you said?'

'I said, don't call her a floozy, her name is Rebecca.' Charles came into the bedroom, still towelling his body, which was remarkably toned for a man in his mid-forties. He stood behind his wife and looked at her reflection in the mirror.

'What is she again – a mechanic or something like that?' he asked smiling in a supercilious way.

'She's a salesperson, as well you know, and she seems a nice girl.'

'I don't think that was what attracted your brother to her,' he laughed as he wrapped the towel around himself whilst admiring his own reflection. Charles absent-mindedly kissed his wife's neck before returning to the bathroom.

He began to sing loudly and tunelessly as he shaved in the bathroom whilst Laura reflected on their lives together. He had been so charming when they met at a charity dinner ten years previously. She remembered she'd worn a bright pink dress that showed a little too much cleavage for her comfort but Charles was obviously taken by her daring look, especially when she stood up and the dress's discreet split showed her shapely legs subtly. She knew she was an attractive woman who was confident with male attention but the dress felt like a step too far for her.

She had been out with several men who were taken with her looks but had been less interested when she mentioned her daughter. Abigail was the result of a Bohemian phase she had gone through, experimenting with light recreational drugs and too much alcohol – the result of feeling she had been too restrained at university. The drug use was never more potent than smoking weed but it had made her careless with her birth control. When she discovered she was pregnant, she told the father who could hardly be described as a boyfriend and they both decided on an abortion. Well, she decided and the much-relieved boy went along with it. He was a couple of years younger than her and she struggled to remember how they met. She did recall his bad skin – the mottled face of his teenage acne leaving a moon-surface effect. She felt a sense of embarrassment that she had once found him attractive enough to have sex with in the first place as she reflected on those times.

Laura went as far as booking the clinic but, in the end, she cancelled, decided to have the child, and sent the father packing with a promise of no requests for financial support. It was then that her brother Andy had been so fantastic. Their parents tried to be modern but her father couldn't disguise his disappointment and the loss of his big dream to walk his beautiful daughter down the aisle to the perfect son-in-law. Her mother had cried a lot but promised total support in whatever decision she made. It was Andy though who saw her every weekend, took her out for dinner and attended all the pre-natal classes with her. He even agreed to say he was her boyfriend to avoid the explanations that went with telling people he was her brother. She would never forget the tears streaming down Andy's face as Abi was born and the love he showed to both of them when they needed it most. Abi was now 14 and Uncle Andy was someone who always made her feel special. When she was younger, he would tickle her to the point of wetting herself and chase her around their small apartment until she fell to the floor in peals of laughter and screams. He spoiled her terribly at Christmas and birthdays, and her face lit up when Uncle Andy entered the room. She often stayed with Andy and Hannah, and was like an older sister to her cousins, who didn't seem to resent the special relationship Abi had with their father. Laura smiled as she thought about them.

Laura remembered her first date with Charles; he had asked her out the night of the pink dress. On that first date they had gone to an Italian restaurant – a favourite of his – and she found herself very attracted to this intelligent, good-looking architect, who seemed just as smitten with her. She decided to declare her position early on in proceedings by telling him she had a daughter. Far from fleeing, he confirmed he already knew – he had asked around about Laura before approaching her at the charity dinner. She recalled feeling hugely flattered and asking him if he was some kind of stalker. His reply was that she was worth stalking.

Their relationship was very intense and physical in those early months. They could hardly keep their hands off each other when they met up and they met often. Charles told her that he had never felt this way about a woman before and, although he had been engaged twice, when it came to marriage, he had never taken the plunge. He fell short of a marriage proposal to Laura but instead proposed living together to make sure Abi was happy with him and the reality of sharing her mother. It was all so perfect; he seemed so sensitive and considerate. Abi took to the new arrangement, loved her new room in Charles's lavish house and seemed happy to swap exclusivity with her mother for a father coming into her life. She even started calling Charles 'Daddy' after a few months, and so the fairy tale was complete. Or so it seemed.

It was hard to say when things changed. It may have been Laura's failure to conceive when the decision was made to give Abi a little brother or sister. There were monthly disappointments when her periods arrived, then tests at the hospital to discover why pregnancy wasn't happening. The tests just seemed to confirm there was no reason for lack of success but simultaneously drained some of the physical enjoyment. Passion became more intermittent – more methodical than sensual. Ovulation replaced animal instinct as a reason to race to the bedroom and the couple's lack of success added to the disappointment.

There is a moment when you can see in someone's eyes that their feelings for you have changed. It is not something that is said, or the way words are spoken but rather a feeling that the eyes betray. You have to have been in love with someone to know when that love is not being returned or, at least, not in the way it once was. Laura was plagued by questions: was he seeing someone else? Did he regret the decision to take on the ready-made family? Whatever it was, they both felt it and truth to tell, Laura even thought of bailing out of the relationship. She probably would have done were it not for Abi and her connection with Charles. How could she tell her daughter that they were leaving the home they had made and the man she had adopted as her father? If Laura was brutally honest, she would admit the financial security Charles provided was a big factor in persistence with an ailing relationship. Whatever their reasons, they, along with a number of troubled couples, decided to try and rectify the problem by getting married. That was five years ago and it was a lavish affair with no expense spared in terms of recreating the fairy tale. Laura even had her tearful father achieve his ambition of walking down the aisle with his daughter, albeit in a five-star hotel, rather than a church. Marriage rarely fixes a fractured relationship and the euphoria of the day soon wore off as they returned to their normal lives.

How did she feel about Charles? She really wasn't sure. She willed herself to love him and was aware of the risk of another woman taking him from her, but did she actually love him? It was not a question she allowed to linger. She was married, as well as being a mother, and sometimes you just have to power through. As was often the case, Laura pushed away any negativity, replacing it with thoughts of some of her favourite things as Julie Andrews showed her every Christmas as she cycled through Austria with the Von Trapp children in her favourite film. Dangerous one that one as it reminded her of her own inability to add to her family and produce someone for Abi to cycle with. Abi was always a nice thought. Unconditional love transferred between them; at least for now until she grew up and turned into somebody else or fell under someone else's influence. A quick shake of the head to dispel that thought. The Spa day she had booked for next week with her best friend Hayley; now that really was something to look forward to. Girls again with no responsibility and time to giggle at anything and everything. How she loved Hayley and her easy-going personality that she had retained from school throughout everything that happened to her. She was infectious and made Laura smile at the sight of her anywhere they met or even her voice on the telephone. Yes, that would be something good to focus on for next week. The thought that produced the biggest smile and warmth coursing through her veins was dinner tonight with Andy who never had that look of disappointment in his eyes when he looked at her. His love was constant and unconditional and he was always on her side, no matter what.

Laura looked at herself again and had to admit that she felt older than her thirty-six years – even more so knowing her brother was bringing a fresh-looking twenty-something for dinner. She tried very hard not to resent Rebecca for her brother's sake, although she had never been close to his wife Hannah, who she found a little possessive, jealous even of her relationship with her brother. She would never have wished them to break up, but was open to her brother's new relationship. She had stayed in touch with Hannah, even crying with her at the break-up, as well as being Auntie Laura to her beloved nieces and nephew. Isabel was ten now, going on 25 and loved to take fashion tips from her trendy Auntie Laura. Ben was eight and would run away when she chased him for a cuddle, before they fell to the ground laughing, and little Phoebe just loved being cuddled full stop.

As she leaned forward again to check her make-up the marks on her neck caught her eye and she realised that she would have to wear her hair down tonight to hide them. She checked the tops of her arms and made the decision to wear something with sleeves; the bruises of two weeks ago were still visible.

Chapter 6

Saturday was gloomy and dark which always meant a poor trading day at the garage, especially in February. People tend not to want to look at potential new cars if it's cold and raining outside. Instead, it's a shopping centre or feet up by the fire at home for any would-be customers. The gloom of the day affected Andy on his drive in to work, and the absence of customers in the first couple of hours added to it. Bored and frustrated he decided to ring Kate. She answered on the second ring.

'Hi Kate, Andy here. I just thought I would give you a quick call and see how Gary's doing.'

'He is a little better today, thanks Andy. He is off some of the machines and they hope to move him into a ward in the next day or so.'

'That sounds very encouraging. Have the police been in touch again?'

'Yeah, there were two detectives here again yesterday and they took a statement from Gary.'

'Did you get their names by any chance?' Andy asked.

'One was DCI Cooper. I think he was the boss. Anyway, Gary said he did all the talking.'

'Do they have any idea who did this?'

'They didn't say but there's been a policeman here ever since they left.'

'Did they say why?'

'No. Do you think we should be worried, Andy?'

'No, I imagine it's just procedure. I just wondered why they've done it now and not before. I'm sure it's nothing to worry about. Tell Gary I'll pop in to see him when he goes on to the ward and that I'll take him out for a pint when he gets out.'

'Thanks, Andy, I will,' she said brightly but Andy could tell that tears had started again as the call ended. He also regretted questioning the fact there was a policeman posted there; he could tell he'd worried Kate.

Police guard. What did that mean? Must be that they have an idea who was responsible and that he's dangerous. Perhaps they would make an arrest soon but why has nobody been to see him? A key witness. Andy felt uncomfortable and realised the irony: he had been surprised there was no police presence at the beginning and now that there was, he was suspicious. Andy picked up the phone to ring Humberside Police to try and speak to DCI Cooper. After a couple of attempts at 101 and hash keys for different police forces, he gave up. He would wait until Thursday when the policeman came to see him.

His low mood caused him to leave his desk and walk into the showroom to vent his frustration on his staff. Or 'motivate them' as he preferred to put it. Peter Thomson had the day off so Andy saw Jimmy Gilbert as a new target for a managerial rocket.

'Jimmy! You seem quiet. I thought you would be taking advantage of Peter's absence to steal his leads and earn some bonuses.'

'I would boss but it is as dead as a three-day old corpse in here today,' Jimmy replied gloomily.

'Oh, are the phones not working or is the Internet

down? I better get on to BT.'

'I've been on the phone all morning but I can't get hold of people. I have a real hot one on the estate demo and I'm sure he'll be in today.'

'Yeah, I heard Santa Claus was bringing him in.'

'No. Honest boss, I will get him in.'

'Sure, you will Jimmy.' Andy changed tack: 'No footfall at all today?'

'No. Apart from those two mutes an hour ago.'

'Mutes?'

'Yeah, two guys wandering around the cars but the funny thing was they weren't looking at any in particular. I went over and made some crack about the weather, but they blanked me and sauntered out. Looked like wheel-kickers to me – not buyers.'

Andy returned to his office and switched on the CCTV to see the six cameras live pictures. Camera three was in the showroom. Andy pressed playback. After a bit of rewinding and forwarding, he saw the two men Jimmy had mentioned walking into the showroom. Neither looked directly at the camera and both were out of shot of the other cameras. He saw Jimmy approach them and then watched them walk away. It wasn't unusual for people to wander in and out of showrooms, and it may have been his heightened sense of caution that made him think there was something different about these two.

He checked camera six which picked up the car park and saw the men get out of a Mitsubishi Shogun, walk casually towards the showroom and then leave in no particular hurry. He did not know what to make of it or if indeed there was anything to be made of it at all. It must be nothing. He decided he was being paranoid and switched off the monitor.

* * *

After a largely uneventful day, Andy drove home to get ready for the dinner at his sister's house. Rebecca made an early gin and tonic, and they decided they would go by taxi as they both felt the need for a drink to break any tension that might be around over the meal. They were a little late as Andy found himself distracted by Rebecca's red-laced underwear as she was getting ready. So much so that he helped her out of it with a justification of 'what does it matter if we are a few minutes late?' That very pleasant interlude and the gin helped him relax in the short taxi ride. Laura was a very good cook and he would do his best to get along with Charles ... for tonight anyway.

As expected, the meal was superb and the wine was impeccable, as always. Charles liked to buy expensive wine and tell you all about it. Everything from its place of origin to its tasting notes. He would explain the delicate flavours, ever so subtle even to an expert like himself. Andy wanted to ask if he had any lager but resisted the temptation.

'So, Andy, any sign of an arrest in your little altercation the other night?'

'No, not so far, Charles.'

'So, this guy just stabbed the poor chap in front of you and buggered off. Is that right?'

'More or less,' Andy replied.

'What do you think made him do it then?'

'Hard to say, but he looked like a real thug. He just confronted the guy in front of me and seemed to be blaming him for the accident, which was weird as he was just stationary, waiting for a gap in the traffic. Anyway, by the time I got out of the car he had started a fight and when he seemed to be losing, he stabbed the poor guy.'

'And he hit you, too?' Charles persisted.

'Well he elbowed me in the stomach which winded me.'

'Did you hit him back?'

Laura looked at her husband and put her hand on his arm.

'Andy may not want to talk about it, darling. It was very unpleasant for him. He could have been hurt.'

'All right, all right! I was only asking,' Charles said sharply, pulling his arm away from his wife's hand.

'I don't mind talking about it really. It was surreal on the night and even now it is hard to believe that it happened at all. The guy who was stabbed is pulling through apparently and I imagine the police have an idea who did it. I realised on the night that he could have been killed. It just shows you that you never know what's going to happen; who you're going to meet. I think this guy must be a psychopath. There is a police guard at the hospital now.'

'Wow, real cops and robbers stuff then!' stated Charles.

'Yeah, I suppose so. But everything seems to be so slow. I'm not sure what I was expecting but nothing seems to be happening and they have a strong description of the guy and the car. Find the car with its damage and you have the guy. I have no idea if they are even looking for the car but you would imagine the wasted time is giving him the chance to get rid of the car or destroy the evidence.'

Charles took a large gulp of red wine, placed his glass in front of him.

'It's these bloody government cuts. Fewer policeman, demoralised officers and too many people getting away with too much crime. We need to get tougher and make sure the bastards are brought to book. It makes me sick that these animals are allowed to wander the streets.'

Andy sensed an anger rising in Charles and was confused by it. He didn't think Charles would be too concerned about the attack on him. He had never shown any warmth towards him and the feeling was mutual. Yet here he was, anger rising out of a conversation about the attack. Maybe Charles had been drinking too much of his expensive wine.

There was something about the expression on Laura's face when Charles pulled his arm away that troubled Andy. There was a tension or an exaggerated reflex to the movement that caused him to keep trying to catch her eye. She was also a little quieter after that, even when Charles raised the subject of the Garage again as he often did.

'Car sales going well, Andy?' Charles asked with another of his supercilious expressions.

'Very well, thank you.'

'Remind me Andy, when did you take over from your father?'

'Dad retired ten years ago. Since then I have changed the franchise and built the extension to the place.'

'And a grand job you made of it, too. Nice to have had the premises in the first place though. Must make life quite a bit easier for you. And cheaper.'

'Not really. Dad still owns half of it and I pay him rent. Laura was offered part of the business but said she didn't want to be involved as she was in full time work. That's right, isn't it, Sis? Hate to think your husband thinks I stole it from you.'

'You know I don't think that! And Charles is just being mischievous aren't you, darling?'

'Of course. Just a gentle bit of teasing that's all,' Charles answered, an irritating smile playing around his lips.

Andy was careful not to take the bait.

'Well believe me, there are some days I would give the whole bloody place to Laura or anyone who walked in off the street.'

An uncomfortable laugh ran around the table before Laura went to fetch dessert. Rebecca changed the subject to talk about property prices around the area and developments Charles was involved in. The rest of the night passed off uneventfully but, not for the first time, Andy found himself trying to tune in to some angst displayed by his sister and wishing she was married to somebody he liked and could play golf with, or share a drink with at the pub. Charles was never going to be that person.

On the way back in the taxi Andy whispered to Rebecca,

'Did you see that arse pull his arm away from Laura at the table?'

'Yes, but I don't think it meant anything.'

'Other than he's a complete prick, you mean?'

'He is all right really. I think he's a bit jealous of your relationship with Laura and maybe feels he needs to assert himself a bit.'

'You might be right, but he's such a nob,' he said, whilst remembering Hannah had also had a problem with the close relationship he had with his sister. Maybe that was the issue and nothing more. Still, he kept replaying that moment over dinner and the expression on Laura's face. It didn't seem like Laura at all; she was always so feisty and capable. It was almost a look of … something he was struggling to pinpoint. A look of … fear. Yes. That was what it was. What was she afraid of? Her husband? And if so, what had he done for her to feel that way?

Laura and Charles wordlessly cleared all the dishes and loaded the dishwasher. Charles was careful as ever to place everything in its correct compartment and pick out anything Laura may have carelessly placed in the wrong section. As Abi was staying at Hayley's house there was just the two of them. They headed upstairs and were having a light conversation about the evening as Laura undressed and went into the bathroom to put on her dressing gown. Charles asked her from the bedroom why she didn't want him to talk about Andy's incident and why she'd said nothing about the ownership of the garage. Gazing into the bathroom mirror, Laura removed her make up. She said they had talked about the garage before and there was no point doing so again. Besides, she thought Andy might want an evening to relax. Although calm, she felt an uneasy feeling developing in her stomach and a dryness starting in her mouth.

'Are you worried I might upset your big brother?' Charles snarled, causing her to pause and stare at her reflection.

'Of course not. It was no big deal,' she said, hoping to placate him.

'Really? Sounded like one when you told me to shut up.'

'I didn't tell you to shut up! I just wanted the conversation to move away from the assault.'

'And then stopping me talking about the garage?' Charles added raising the temperature.

'I didn't do that either, but you have raised it before and Andy isn't an idiot.'

'So, he's so fragile he needs you to protect him?'

'No, he doesn't need protection from me, but the conversation was in danger of becoming a little heavy.'

'Oh, God forbid we discuss anything important over dinner!'

'I don't want to argue Charles; can we just drop the subject?'

'Oh, so you decide when we can talk and what we talk about. Is that what happens now?'

'I'm not saying that, but can we drop it please? I'm tired and just want to go to bed?' Laura replied, aware of the danger. She knew that confrontation was not likely to play out well, but nor was capitulation. It was a balance she sought and as there had been silence for a minute or so she thought she had found it. She hoped Charles would be undressed and in bed trying to sleep. She deliberately took her time getting ready for bed herself.

Eventually, Laura walked into the bedroom but as she entered, she was grabbed by the collar of her dressing gown and pinned against the wall. Charles's face was inches away from hers and she could smell the whisky on his breath as his contorted face snarled at her:

'Don't you ever interrupt me again when I'm talking to

your brother – or anyone else for that matter – you bitch. And don't tell me when I can or can't raise a subject. DO YOU UNDERSTAND?'

Shouting the last three words, he moved his right hand up to her chin so that the back of her head hit the wall, stunning her.

'Did you fucking hear me, you fucking bitch?' he bellowed. Droplets of saliva landed on Laura's face.

Her emotions swirled with that now-familiar mix of fear and anger as she recovered from the blow to the back of the head.

'Get off me you pig!' she growled into his face, almost provoking a more extreme reaction; one that would solve this dilemma for her. An attack so bad, she couldn't forgive or overlook it. For which she wouldn't accept a grovelling apology the next day. One that would put her in hospital and then her dark, dirty secret would be exposed, but not by her. Instead, he threw her by the lapels on to the bed and stormed off into the guest room.

Laura curled up into a ball as the regular tears began to fall again. She was desperate, alone, and ashamed. Middle class domestic violence produces that reaction quite often as it is so unexpected by family and friends. The veneer of charm, money and position makes it an unlikely conclusion others will come to, even if they sense there's a problem. Once again Laura was confronted with her situation. She had to do something. Abigail was a big consideration as well as their lifestyles, but the most difficult part was the shame of how she – a bright, intelligent woman – had put up with it for so long.

When had the violence started? She almost struggled to remember. Maybe the first sign of it was before they were married when she was talking to a young waiter in the restaurant in Marbella that time on holiday. There was no violence as such, but a look that Charles gave her as they drove back to the hotel. That and the uncomfortable silence. Laura didn't challenge it at the time but politely asked if he was all right when they got back to their room. Although he said he was, he brushed past her into the bathroom, giving her the merest push, but no apology. In hindsight, there were the signs of a slightly altered man. She didn't know whether it was something or nothing at all. The next one however, left her in no doubt.

They were married and arguing about remodelling the kitchen. He snapped and grabbed her arms, pulled her close to his face and shouted an instruction never to challenge his area of expertise. His eyes were wild with fury and her polite, considerate husband looked like a criminal stealing her purse. Laura was so shocked she was rendered speechless. An hour later he apologised profusely, said he couldn't understand why he'd acted so badly and the matter was dropped.

The first slap came when their guests had left after a dinner party. Charles accused her of flirting with a neighbour and 'acting like a tart.' When insults were exchanged, Charles moved towards her and as she prepared for the grab of her arms, he slapped her left cheek with his open right hand. She felt a stinging red-hot pain on her face as she fell to the ground and, after gasping loudly, she started to weep. Charles had instantly dropped to his knees and apologised profusely again before sobbing himself. She had told him if he ever did that again, she would leave him. He had promised it would never be repeated – he couldn't live without her, he said. It had of course, happened again and she hadn't kept her promise to leave. With every new incident a small amount of self-esteem and determination seeped out of Laura, until she felt she had left it too late to go.

These memories made her heart beat rapidly; she saw so many lost opportunities to just leave and start again. She had slipped into becoming a victim and was in a state of denial about the frequency of violence, the emptiness of the apologies, and the promises of it never happening again. She knew in her heart of hearts that one incident was one too many. They were to be followed by many more, but none was great enough to make the decision to leave, to confide in someone that she was living with a wife beater. She had become an abused wife.

Chapter 7

PC 4863 Christopher Elliott had telephoned Andy and rearranged their appointment to the Tuesday night instead of Thursday as he'd had a cancellation of a statement on another case. It was 7.30pm when the fresh-faced young constable arrived in full uniform and sat in Andy's living room. His radio crackled incoherent messages as he pulled out his notepad and a cheap plastic ballpoint pen.

'So, I gather you were involved in a car accident in Humberside, where you were threatened by another driver. Is that correct, Mr Connolly?' he asked, as though Humberside were some far-flung place across the sea, rather than a county a few miles down the road.

'No, I was assaulted and another man was stabbed. The assailant hit the back of my car and pushed me into the other car.'

'The man who stabbed you, was he in the car that hit you?'

'He didn't stab me; he stabbed the guy in front. He elbowed me in the stomach.'

'Who did?'

'The same man who stabbed the other guy! Look, shall I just explain what happened from the beginning?' asked Andy, a little exasperated.

Having nodded his agreement, PC Elliot listened as Andy went through the whole incident and it became clear that all of this was coming as a major surprise to the young policeman, who had either not read the brief or had not been briefed at all. When Andy had finished, the officer started to meticulously write in his notebook. Andy could see this consisted of pre-printed blank witness statement sheets.

'Don't you guys do this on iPads yet?' he asked.

'No, we have to do it the old-fashioned way and you have to sign every page,' he answered without looking up. Andy could feel his exasperation rising but he patiently sat for the duration of a process that could have taken less than half of the time.

An hour later, PC Elliott had a twelve-page statement, signed on each page by his witness. A detailed description was given of the attacker, including his height, weight, skin colour, clothing, and hair. Andy double-checked that the full description was there on page four.

'So,' he asked, 'what happens now?'

'I'll pass the statement on to my colleagues at Humberside and either they or we will be in touch.'

'Any idea when?'

'I'm afraid not, but you have a crime number and can always enquire by phoning 101.'

'Yes, I've already had that pleasure thanks,' Andy said. The officer smiled uncomfortably.

At least it was done now and he could relax a bit. It was nothing like those police dramas on TV where everything is fast-paced and hectic activity is all around. On those programmes, villains are chased by cars with sirens, bad guys are caught and everyone sleeps safely in their beds. Reality seemed sedate, matter of fact or downright lethargic. There would be days in the not too distant future when Andy would think about that feeling and long for it again, but for now, he felt underwhelmed and disappointed.

The next few days were unremarkable and Andy found he was slipping back into his ordinary life. Rebecca had arranged a weekend away for them and to his surprise Hannah had agreed to the kids coming with them. Andy had been very careful on the subject of Rebecca being with his children. At first, he had explained to the children that Mum and Dad were going to live in separate houses, but that they both loved them very much and would never ask them to do anything they didn't want to. Consequently, Phoebe had asked if she could stop going to pre-school and then to big school; she didn't want to do that, she said. Andy had to explain the difference between things they had to do and things they could choose to do. Isabel was more probing and, for a while, very difficult with him, but she had thawed a little now and was curious about Rebecca. Ben just took it all in his stride, only enquiring if his pocket money would be affected. In fact, he asked if he would get it twice!

When they first met Rebecca it was awkward for all of them, but the girls were attracted to her clothes and her cheerful demeanour. Wisely, she let them make the moves and after a few visits they seemed to like her. This was going to be a whole weekend though and a real test. Maybe that explained why Andy's attention had shifted away from the attack. On the morning of their trip away – a Friday – Andrea buzzed him in the office to say that Humberside police were on the phone.

'Is that Andrew Connolly?'

'Yes, it is.'

'Ah hello, Mr Connolly. DCI Cooper, Humberside police. I was wondering if I could pop over and see you.'

'Is it about the stabbing?'

'Yes, it is. I'd like to have a chat and bring you up to date with our investigation. Are you free today?'

Andy hesitated. 'Well, I was hoping to get a flyer mid-afternoon but otherwise, yes.'

'We can come now, if it's convenient to you.'

'Yes, I suppose so,' Andy replied, somewhat taken aback by the sudden urgency.

'See you in about half an hour then.' The policeman ended the conversation.

Andy sat still for a couple of minutes, unsure how he felt. He was glad he was going to get an update but a strange tension came over him for reasons he couldn't understand. He was unfamiliar with dealings with the police – other than being caught speeding twice and being told off for shouting in the street when he was a child, he'd had no direct contact with them. He always found police presence at football matches, shopping centres and airports very reassuring but oddly, something unsettled him now.

DCI Cooper was led in by Andrea almost exactly thirty minutes later and he extended his right hand to introduce himself and Detective Sergeant Patrick Ames. Cooper looked about forty-five; he was around six feet tall and athletically built. He had greying-brown hair cut in a modern style and dressed a little better than the average policeman. Ames on the other hand was nearer fifty and looked like he'd slept in the park overnight. He was a little overweight and his mouth remained slightly open at all times, lending him a gormless look.

Whilst Cooper had a relaxed style about him, appearing comfortable in his own skin and confident in his ability to communicate, Ames looked every inch the archetypal policeman and Andy wondered if the DS realised he was staring at him as though he was a villain. Perhaps he did that with everyone. The garage had sold several cars to policemen and Andy was familiar with that stare. It was as if there was a second or two delay as information was processed to determine whether or not it was the truth being spoken. And to be fair, given that Andy was a car salesman, the truth was often stretched.

'Firstly, Andy … it is alright if I call you Andy?' Cooper asked, receiving a nod in response.

'Let me apologise that we haven't been in touch before now but we've been piecing together a number of statements and enquiries from other investigations'

'Other investigations? Has this guy done this before?'

'Well we're not sure who did this yet, but some of our colleagues are enquiring into other matters and they may be connected. I would just like to check the description you gave of the perpetrator in your statement if that's okay with you?'

'Yes of course.'

The detective pulled out from his file a copy of Andy's statement and read the description he had given the officer from North Yorkshire.

'Is there anything else you can remember about this man?'

'Not that I can think of.'

'We'd like you to have a look at some images at the station and see if you can recognise the man, Andy.'

'Do you want me to come now?'

'No, it's a different, independent arm that deals with that – they'll be in touch to set it up.'

'Do you think you know who it is then?'

'We have a good idea who it might be, but we're making a number of enquiries at the moment.'

'There was one thing I wanted to ask you: I saw there was a police guard at Gary Newcombe's bed when I popped in to see him the other day. Does that mean you think he is at some sort of risk?'

'I really can't discuss details, but that's just procedure and nothing to worry about.'

Cooper and Ames made a little more small-talk and then left. Even Ames seemed to be a little friendlier.

* * *

The weekend away was a success. The children were a little reserved when Andy collected them but maybe they sensed the uncomfortable atmosphere between their parents. Rebecca stayed in their car and Andy knocked on the door. Hannah wasn't unpleasant but couldn't disguise her discomfort at handing over the children. They drove to a cottage that Rebecca had booked in the Peak District. The kids thought it was brilliant, with its original beams and bunk beds. They went to local events as well as play parks and ate out most of the time. On the last evening at the cottage, Phoebe had climbed on Rebecca's knee and fallen asleep, causing Rebecca to look alarmed as she silently sought guidance from Andy. He just signalled for her to embrace the moment and the child, which she did. He even allowed himself to think that things might work out well between all of them.

* * *

The Monday after, Andy got a call from Humberside police and arranged an appointment for 6pm that night at Goole police station. He didn't know what to expect and it was on his mind for the rest of the day. Did six men line up? Did he walk past them and put his hand on the shoulder of the culprit, like he had seen in some movies? Or was it a two-way mirror and blank-faced, staring men?

The actual event was much more sterile: Andy was shown into a room containing a video camera so the entire process would be filmed. A civilian explained that on the screen in front of him he would be shown a number of images of men walking in, turning left and right and then looking straight ahead. Each short clip would bear a number and he could stop it at any time or replay any clip. He nodded his agreement to start and the film began. A mixture of men of differing heights, weights and ethnicity were shown but all were in the sort of age range he had given and broadly similar. As soon as clip number eleven started and the man on the film walked into the room, Andy asked them to freeze the picture. He knew it was the man but wanted to be doubly certain. He asked for the film to run and at the end of the clip, he held up his right hand.

'That's him.'

'Are you saying you can positively identify the man on number 11 as the man who attacked you and stabbed another man on the night of the 22nd of February this year?'

'I am, yes. That's definitely him.'

'Would you like to see any other clips – any that you have already seen, or some other images?'

'No, there's no point. That's definitely him.'

The civilian, who had introduced himself as Colin Blackwell of Mercury Support Services, then read out a statement for the benefit of the camera, confirming the procedure they had gone through, the time and date, and the positive identification of number 11, which was then witnessed by a female assistant.

'Who is he then?' Andy enquired.

'I'm sorry but we're not allowed to discuss details. I'm sure one of the police officers will be in touch,' Blackwell replied.

Five minutes later Andy was on his way home.

He didn't have to wait long; DCI Cooper popped in to see him the next day. Cooper was relaxed and friendly and as a sort of preamble, spoke about a couple of the cars in the showroom before getting down to business.

'So, Andy, thank you for a positive ID yesterday. That was very helpful.'

'Who is he then?'

'His name is Jamie Tasker and he is known to us.'

'Have you arrested him?'

'Yes, we arrested him first thing this morning and he's in custody as we speak.'

A surge of nervous excitement coursed through Andy's body,

'Has he admitted it?'

'I'm afraid I can't discuss the details with you but I will leave my card, so you can contact me if you need to and I will stay in touch. I'll keep you informed about how the investigation is going and when we charge anyone. It's important that we get people like him off the streets and keep people safe.'

'Okay. I'm glad you've got him. Have you told Gary? You know, the guy who was stabbed.'

'Yes, one of my officers is with him now, I think.'
Cooper shook Andy's hand and left after another theatrical look at one of the cars in the showroom.

Two minutes later Andy was on his iPad and googling Jamie Tasker. There were quite a number of references but he clicked the heading "Drug Case Collapses." The link was to the Hull Daily Mail, eighteen months previously.

The trial of Jamie Tasker ended today in Hull Crown Court when the prosecution failed to produce two witnesses who were to give evidence in the trial. Tasker had been charged with supplying Class A drugs and with assault causing grievous bodily harm. The trial had been ongoing for three days but the prosecution counsel, Mr Marcus Tavistock, told the judge that the prosecution was unable to call evidence from two principal witnesses. He did not explain why. Judge Angus Grey QC told the jury he had no option but to advise the jury to return a verdict of not guilty.

Andy was aware that his face was a little warmer and his heart rate a little faster as he re-read the article. What the hell had he got himself into?

Chapter 8

When Andy got home it was hard to concentrate on conversation or the TV as his head was too full of images of the type of person Jamie Tasker might be. He was not able to shake these thoughts for more than a couple of minutes at a time and although he found some reassurance in DCI Cooper's confidence, the sense of foreboding was stronger.

The next morning he phoned Kate to enquire about Gary.

'Hi Kate, Andy here. Any further news on Gary?'

'Oh, erm … hi Andy. Yes, he is getting better and they've moved him on to a general ward now, so that is a good sign, isn't it?'

'Yes, that's great news. That must mean he's out of danger. Has he had the police around again?'

'Yes.'

There was a tentative note in Kate's voice. It reminded him of a potential car purchaser who, when asked if they're looking at other cars, answers with hesitation as they try to arrange their thoughts. The buyer often can't disguise their discomfort at working out how much information they should give a salesman as they try to be measured in their dealings; it shows in the speed and tone of reply.

'Is everything alright, Kate?'

'Yes, yes … it's just been so difficult. I don't know what to think.'

'About what?'

'Oh everything. I just … I don't know if I can think straight anymore.'

'Has Gary seen DCI Cooper?'

'Yes, he has, but I don't like him. He's a bit of a bully. He keeps telling Gary what he said in his statement. I don't know if I should be saying any of this Andy ... I better go.'

'Don't upset yourself, Kate. Tell Gary I'll pop in to see him. Which ward is he on?'

'Ward 15 ... sorry Andy.' As the call ended, Andy was sure Kate had begun to cry again. He couldn't imagine anything he'd said had upset her but something was wrong.

He decided he wouldn't put off the visit to Gary and on finding out visiting hours he arrived at the hospital bang on 2pm.The hospital shop provided him with a bowl of fruit in cellophane as a prop and he confidently strolled into the ward. Gary was sitting up in bed and, although free from tubing, had a grey colour about him.

'Hello mate, how are you doing?' Andy asked popping the fruit on the bedside cabinet.

'Oh, not so bad,' Gary responded limply.

Andy chatted for a few minutes as he would to warm up any punter before he got to the real issue. He commented on the ward, the pretty nurse in the corner and the terrible weather outside that Gary was avoiding. Once he felt Gary was a little more relaxed, he moved up a gear.

'So, Kate tells me that you aren't keen on DCI Cooper.'

'He's alright I suppose but he gets a bit irritated with me.'

'Why's that then?'

'I told him I didn't really get a good look at the guy,' he answered looking away.

'I thought you said you remembered his clothing and hair – stuff like that.'

'No ... no ... not really. It all happened so fast, I can't be sure about who did it. I mean, you know ... to say who it was who did it ... even if I did see him again.'

Two spots of colour appeared on Gary's cheeks against the grey background of the rest of his face. His eyes wandered around the room.

'Have they asked you to do an ID parade or whatever they call it?'

'Yeah, and that's when he got a bit stroppy because I said I wasn't sure it would do any good. I mean, if you can't be sure, what's the point? That's all I said but he kept going on at me about what I said before and did I want somebody else to be attacked? I told him I didn't want any of this. I was just minding my own business and now look at me!'

Gary was getting very agitated and moving uncomfortably in his bed, just as Kate arrived. Andy stood up and kissed her on the cheek as he gave up his seat. She looked uncomfortable. The three of them chatted together for a few minutes but the atmosphere was different and, although he couldn't specify why, Andy felt he was unwelcome. He said his goodbyes, gave a friendly wave and left. Once he was out of earshot, Kate turned to Gary.

'Did you tell him anything?'

'No, of course not. I hardly know the bloke.'

'He seems so nice though – maybe he would understand.'

'Don't you say anything to him. Or anybody. Do you understand, Kate? Well do you?' he glared, leaning forward from the pillows.

'Yes, yes, calm down, Gary! People are looking.'

Andy started assimilating the information he'd gathered as he drove away from the hospital. Kate had told him on the phone that Gary had remembered Tasker's clothing and greasy hair; surely that meant he had a clear picture of him. Also, he had argued, then fought with the guy for a few minutes – they were face to face. He must have got a good look at him. Besides, you're hardly likely to forget the picture of a man who stabs you.

More answers seemed only to throw up more questions: why had the police put a guard at the hospital? Did they think Gary was at risk of another attack? Who were the guys who turned up at his garage? Were they connected to Tasker? If so, how would they know about him? His head was beginning to spin. Back at work he opened his laptop and googled Tasker again. He found the article he had read the day before but searched for more. There was a report of the first day of the trial.

Trial of local man begins

Jamie Tasker appeared at Hull Crown Court on the first day of a trial, which is expected to last two weeks. Tasker is charged with supplying Class A drugs and separate charges of grievous bodily harm. Counsel for the prosecution, Mr Marcus Tavistock told the jury that the prosecution would produce evidence that Tasker was part of a criminal group supplying cocaine and heroin over a wide area, thereby destroying the lives of many people. Evidence would also be presented that on the 26th July last year, he had viciously attacked Graham Todd in a public house in Goole, stabbing Mr Todd in the chest and right leg. Were it not for the swift response of the emergency services, Mr Todd's injuries could have been much more serious, indeed Tasker could well have been facing a murder charge.

The jury were told that evidence would show how the drugs were obtained and distributed, and how the attack upon Mr Todd was carried out. Due to a late start, the judge asked the prosecution to produce their first witness tomorrow morning. The trial continues.

The report of day two of the trial told of evidence of police officers who had searched Tasker's car and home at the time of his arrest, and ended with the standard comment that the trial continues. There was no mention of evidence from the victim Mr Todd. Did he not turn up or had he refused to give evidence? Andrea broke his concentration when she buzzed him to say his sister was on line two.

'Hi Laura, how you doing?'

'Fine thanks. Just wanted to apologise for Charles the other night.'

'Charles? Apologise for what?'

'Don't give me that. You might be able to fool your customers and even your lady friends but I'm your sister and I know you better than you know yourself.'

Andy laughed.

'No arguments there I suppose. But what particular thing are you apologising for?'

'The garage thing. Nothing to do with him really but there you are.'

'No problem sis, you know me; all water off a duck's back. Are we seeing Mum and Dad tomorrow for lunch?'

'No, that was the other reason for the call. I can't make it now so we will have to re-schedule for next week, if that's okay with you? I'll ring Mum and sort it out.'

'Yeah, that's okay with me, just text me the details.'

They chatted for a few minutes and both felt that easy

relaxation that deflected their attention from other aspects of their lives. In both of their cases they were prolonging the conversation as a means of distraction from their own problems and because of the mutual enjoyment of the banter that passed between them. It was probably true that either of them could say anything to one another without worry of causing offence and their sibling bond had been strengthened over the years. They were probably each other's best friend. Eventually, they reluctantly said goodbye to each other and faced up to the problems they needed to return to. Laura put her mobile down beside the huge bunch of flowers on the kitchen table. She picked up the card and read it again:

'To My True Love. I wish I deserved you more. Love for ever, Charles xx'

She wanted to throw it in the bin but that would only spawn another inquiry, so she placed it back in the bunch. Looking in the kitchen mirror, Laura applied a little more concealer to the marks on her neck. Andy may well have failed to notice them but there was no way her mother would have missed them, however much make up she put on. Next week would be safer.

Back at the garage, Andy resolved to focus on commercial details. He pulled out the figures for the current quarter and spent an hour checking the targets against performance and plotting a way forward to the bonuses the manufacturer would provide upon success. The need to succeed soon had him fully engaged and distracted from the issues surrounding him. He rediscovered his bouncy step and spoke to several members of staff about plans for tomorrow, the rest of the week and new targets. Maybe this was the way forward for him; to just let other matters take their course and to focus on things he could control – or at least influence. Yes, that was the best course of action.

His mobile rang, showing an unidentified number. He normally ignored them but he pressed accept.

'Is that you Andy?'

'Yes, it is. Who's calling?'

'A friend.'

'Oh yeah, which friend is that then?'

'You need to be very careful Andy,' the voice said, 'very careful indeed.'

The line went dead.

Chapter 9

Andy checked the call again to be sure that no number had been recorded and then asked Andrea if there was any check they could run on an unidentified number. He didn't tell her why and only nodded when she said there was nothing they could do that she knew of.

He thought about ringing the police but it seemed a relatively trivial thing. Subsequently, he decided against reporting it. He was lost in thought when his mobile rang again and the screen showed it was Abi.

'Hello! I think you must have the wrong number. I haven't had a call from this number for such a long time.'

'Very funny, Uncle Andy. I rang you last Tuesday, as you well know.'

'Oh, so you did ... is it money you're after? I only ask because I haven't got any.'

'No money, thanks, but can you pick me up from school on Friday and take me to my friend's birthday party? Mum can't do it but said you would because the party is in the next street to yours. Mum said she would leave my clothes at your house.'

'Only if I can come to the party as well,' Andy teased.

'It's not for old people, Uncle Andy!' she replied with a loud chuckle.

'Ouch! That one hurt ... you better get a taxi.'

'Please, Uncle Andy. Rebecca said she would help me with my make up.'

'Make up? What sort of party is this? So, you've been talking to Rebecca as well, have you?'

'Yes, but she said I had to speak to you.'

'Okay then, what time? Andy relented.

'Four o clock from school, then at the party for six. It finishes at eleven and I can stay at yours.'

'Oh, I have to pick you up and give you bed and breakfast?'

'You do ... I have to go, I'm late. Love you!'

'Love you too.'

Andy smiled as he always did when talking to Abi, already looking forward to being her chauffeur for the night. She had a way of taking his mind off other things. When the smile faded, his thoughts drifted briefly back to the previous call and the warning but, mercifully, calls from dealers and suppliers kept him busy.

Jimmy Gilbert was in and out on a difficult deal he was trying to pull off so they worked on the normal strategy: Jimmy would act as though he were pleading with Andy over the price of the trade in and, after much public head shaking, Andy would come out and bargain with the customer to make it look like they were very reluctantly giving in to the demand on the price. The customers always focused on the amount they were getting for their car, rather the price they were paying for the new one. There was nothing better than getting a good deal for the garage but letting the customer think he had won. The deal was eventually done and a further telephone deal changed the complexion of the day and put a spring in Andy's step.

It was well after five when Peter Thomson approached him: 'Got a customer looking at the hatchback in the showroom but says he wants to speak to you.'

'Do I know him?' Andy answered, trying to look in the corner where the car sat.

'You must do, I suppose. Said his name was Ken Smith.'

The name didn't ring a bell. Andy walked over to the well-built, tall man who looked to be in his fifties, He was wearing an expensive-looking grey suit.

'Mr Smith, how can I help you?' Andy said extending his right hand.

'I'm buying a car for my daughter and I was told you were the man to see,' was the reply, accompanied by a firm handshake.

'Oh, do we have a friend in common then?'

'We may do but he asked me not to mention his name.'

'Sounds intriguing … anyway what did you have in mind?

'Do you have anything for ten grand?'

'I'm sure we do but the one you're looking at is £14,950. We may have a nearly new one for the kind of money you are thinking about.'

'You have a lot of stock don't you, Andy? Cars all over the place. I couldn't park on the site so my friend just dropped me off. I said to him … look at all these cars for sale – we must be able to get something here.'

'Sorry you had a problem parking but the customer parking is over there to the right and there are normally a few spaces available.'

Smith didn't look to where Andy was pointing but continued to look straight at him whilst holding his fixed smile.

'Yes, my daughter wants a car and I've told her she has to feel safe in the vehicle – it's a dangerous place out there on the road. You worry about them, don't you? Kids, I mean. Even when they get a bit older.'

'Yes, I suppose so. Would you like me to get one of my sales people to show you some of the used stock?' he answered, not really knowing where the conversation was leading. He did know however that he was beginning to feel ill at ease.

'No, that's all right Andy. I think I've seen all I need to see,' the man responded, before adding, 'How about I give you the ten grand and you keep the car?'

'I don't understand,' Andy replied, looking perplexed.

'I think you do. My friend is being fitted up for something he didn't do and I'm trying to help him – that's all. You've had a nasty experience – probably got yourself properly shaken up by it all … totally understandable. Memory can play tricks on you when that happens.' The answer was coldly delivered.

All the saliva had disappeared from Andy's mouth and he tried to replace it to speak. His cheeks coloured as he tried to assimilate the information swirling around his head. He glanced around the garage for support but everyone was busy and nobody was looking in his direction. He could also feel a slight trembling beginning in his knees as he realised with a jolt that this was a dangerous situation. Acting on impulse, he said, 'I think you better leave Mr Smith, before I call the police.'

'Why would you do that, Andy? I've just offered you some money and haven't asked for a thing in return. What sort of crime is that?' The man's smile had turned into a mildly menacing grin.

'Anyway, you have a little think, my friend and I'll be in touch again to see if we can sort things out. Enjoy the rest of the day.'

Smith turned slowly, walked to the rear entrance of the showroom and was gone. Andy quickly followed but could see no sign of him. His heart was racing as he rushed back into his office to check the CCTV recording. Clammy hands struggled with the door handle before he got in, closed the door and sat down. He played footage from all of the cameras but there was nothing of Ken Smith. He realised the reason that Smith – or whatever his name was – had stayed where he was during the conversation was that it was an area the cameras did not cover. The rear car park was covered but only partly. The man who'd just left had managed to get in and out of the premises without being filmed. That was probably why he hadn't brought a car on to the premises. A cold chill descended on Andy. He picked up the phone, holding it for several seconds before replacing it. He needed to think about this. Maybe get some advice on how to handle the situation, but advice from whom? The man hadn't told him not to go to the police, but that was implied. He'd mentioned how many cars Andy had … was that a threat? What else did the man know about him?

Andy drove home carefully, vigilant to the traffic around him. At one point he braked sharply to avoid rear-ending the vehicle in front. He'd been too busy looking into his rear mirror at the car behind. It contained three men and he'd fumbled in his pocket to get out his phone to take a picture of the car and its occupants. By the time his unsteady fingers had opened the phone, the car had turned right and driven off in a different direction. Minutes later he spotted a dark BMW, which turned left when he did. He was just contemplating a change of route, when it stopped outside a greengrocer's and a middle-aged woman got out of the passenger side. He realised he was being paranoid and consequently had a more relaxed few miles home.

Once inside, he called Rebecca, poured two glasses of red wine and told her what had happened.

'Jesus, Andy! What are you going to do? I mean these guys sound dangerous. Did he say what would happen if you don't take the money?'

'What do you mean if I don't take the money? There is no question of me taking money to change my story. I'd go to prison.'

'But you said he didn't ask you to do anything?'

'Wake up Rebecca! What do you think the money is for? Once I take it, they have control over me. It was clear he was asking me to fail to identify the guy who attacked me and stabbed that other guy.'

Rebecca looked pale. 'I'm frightened Andy. We don't know anything about these people or what they might do. I mean, you see it on the TV, read about it in books but this is real. You have to tell that DCI Cooper.'

'Yes, probably.' Andy hesitated. 'I'll sleep on it.'

Although Andy had seen the car with three men in it and the BMW, which initially appeared to be following him, he'd failed to notice the white transit van in front of him. The one that was now parked a hundred yards from his front door.

Chapter 10

Andy had a poor night's sleep. He dozed and woke, with his mind unable to move down the gears to relaxation. He felt he was stuck in third or fourth gear, not sure whether to accelerate or brake. At 6am he gave up, slipped gently out of the bed so as not to disturb Rebecca and crept downstairs to make some tea. Why do we make tea when we can't sleep? What is it about a cup of tea that makes us think it will improve things? It didn't. Andy played and replayed all of the incidents over and over in his mind. There was always a background hum of regret that he had been in the car at that particular time. He tortured himself with thoughts of places he could have been, thus avoiding contact with the man who now loomed large in his life.

Rebecca joined him at just past eight o clock and he told her he had decided to ring the police to see what they could do to protect them. He realised, too late, that using the word 'protect' had alarmed Rebecca, so he hastily added that they probably didn't need protection.

Andy picked up DCI Cooper's card but saw for the first time that there was no direct number on it. It had his email address, stated he was a Detective Chief Inspector of Humberside Constabulary and gave the number 101 for non-emergency contacts. The email seemed a little impersonal, yet he hardly thought the offer of money was an emergency. He dialled 101 and heard the automated message saying that it was North Yorkshire police. If he required another force he had to press hash and say the name of the force he wanted. Already confused, he pressed hash and asked for Humberside. He was put through to a civilian controller who asked how he could help.

'Hi. I'm not sure which police force I need to speak to.'

'Can you confirm your name and address for me?'

Andy gave the details and after a couple of seconds, the controller asked, 'Do you wish to report a crime?'

'I'm not sure about that either. I was involved in an incident before that was reported and I–'

'Do you have a crime number?'

'Er... not to hand, no. But something else has happened and I need to speak to DCI Cooper.'

'Just let me check where he is today.' There was a pause of a few seconds. 'He's not back on duty until Saturday, I'm afraid. But if it's a new incident, you'll need to report it to your local police force.'

'Yes, I know, but DCI Cooper is dealing with the original crime.'

'Your local force will take the details and take whatever action they think is appropriate. Would you like me to transfer you?'

'I suppose so'

'Just a moment.'

There was a minute's delay before the line clicked again,

'Sorry about that. I'm afraid I can't transfer you at the moment, but ring 101 again and you will get through to them.'

Frustrated, Andy put the phone down. Two minutes later he tried again. When he was offered an appointment in two days' time with an officer he had never met, he declined and said he would think about it. Where was the old-fashioned police station when you needed it? You could go in and talk to a policeman, who would ask you to take a seat before a plain-clothed (usually) cynical detective came out, a cigarette hanging from his mouth, and took you into a room to tell your story. There was something strangely reassuring about all of that, although Andy acknowledged he had never actually experienced it; he had never been arrested or even reported a crime before – his images were from TV programmes and his imagination. Reality, it seemed, was colder and more distant. Finally, he decided to email DCI Cooper, sat at his computer and sent the following:

'Hello DCI Cooper, Andy Connolly here. I would welcome a chat with you as soon as possible about the case. I have been approached by somebody who might be involved. Regards, Andy Connolly.'

He kissed Rebecca goodbye and set off to the garage, again without noticing anything unusual in the street. As his car pulled out of view, the passenger door of the white van opened and a thickly set unshaven man in blue overalls walked towards the house. Checking for any cameras or security lights, he rang the bell. Rebecca, assuming it was Andy, opened the door wearing a friendly smile.

'Forgotten your key? Oh sorry! I thought you were my partner coming back.'

'Sorry to disturb you but we're in the area doing maintenance on central heating boilers installed in the last ten years. There is a defect on some of them which can give off poisonous gases and you might be eligible for a free check.'

The man held up a laminated plastic card which had his photograph on. Underneath was printed, 'Stephen Brown approved Corgi Engineer'

'Oh. I really don't know when it was done. You need to talk to my partner but you've just missed him. We haven't lived here very long so I don't know when the boiler was installed.'

'I can have a look if you want and should be able to tell you straight away,' the man offered.

Rebecca hesitated. 'It might be more convenient if you came back tonight.'

'Sorry – can't do that. We'll be finishing off this afternoon and we're in Luton tomorrow. You could get a local firm to check it, but I imagine they'll charge you.'

'So, you don't charge?'

'No. If the defect is there, we can get the local authority or your insurers to pay, but you really need to know if it's dangerous or not. It will literally only take a minute to check.'

There was a moment's delay. Rebecca's instinct was to say no but what if there was a risk and she did nothing? The guy had shown his ID and he wasn't pushy. Making a split-second decision, she took the line of least resistance, opened the door and asked that he be as quick as he could as she was going out. The man entered and closed the door firmly.

Andy arrived at the garage and before going into the showroom, walked around the site looking at the security cameras and the coverage they gave him. He wondered briefly why he'd not gone for more cameras when he placed the order with the alarm company, but he knew the answer:

it seemed low risk at the time and besides, the very existence of cameras had been enough to put off the local thieves and joyriders. But he could now see how someone who was determined and clever could get in and out without detection. Something else to worry about.

He said good morning to everybody then checked the post. He sat in his chair, swivelling from side to side. After a minute or two, he picked up his mobile and went to contacts rather than recent calls – it had been a while. He pressed the number and eventually his call was answered. It was often necessary to be patient.

'Hello, stranger. When the phone rang, I said to myself I bet it's those bloody PPI people again. I couldn't find my specs at first but then I saw it was you and I thought, yes I remember him.'

'Hello, Dad. How are you?'

'Oh, pretty good I suppose but your mum says I need another hobby. I told her I'm busy enough on the Internet, trying to find one of those dating websites for the not very fussy.'

'Very funny, Dad! You should ask Mum – she obviously used one.'

'Well that's a nice thing to say to the man who gave you life, isn't it? You cheeky bugger! What can I do for you?'

'How do you know I didn't just ring to say hello?'

'Forty years' experience son.'

'Ouch … okay, you win. I'd like a word about something but I don't want to worry Mum. Are you free anytime today?'

'I'm playing golf at eleven but I'll be finished by three.

Do you want me to pop over to the garage?'

'No. Let's meet for a coffee at Carlo's at, say ... four?'

'Sounds good to me. Do you not want me to mention to Mum that I am seeing you then?'

'Not for the moment. I'll explain when I see you.'

'Okay, son, see you then.'

'Thanks, Dad ... and sorry I haven't been in touch recently but ... well, you know.'

'I know ... see you at four.'

Andy felt immediately easier about his situation, just from hearing his dad's voice and knowing he was going to see him. He always seemed to know what to do or what to say and, at times, he resented him for that. It was so unfair – he knew that – but he often felt he was walking in his father's shoes, operating a business his dad had started and always feeling the need to prove himself, especially to his dad. Funnily enough, his father never acted as though he was watching him or comparing him unfavourably to himself, but Andy desperately wanted to show him that he could do better – or at least as well as he had done – with the business. One thing was for sure: he was glad his father was still around. He needed his calm input now as never before.

His dad had never criticised him for screwing up his marriage and he'd been friendly to Rebecca when they met. He was also in regular touch with Hannah. Andy smiled to himself when he remembered introducing Hannah to his dad all those years ago.

'Lovely to meet you, Hannah,' his father had said

warmly. 'And thank you for going out with my son. I know it must be difficult but give him time and you might grow to like him.'

They'd all laughed. That was Paul Connolly, always likely to make you laugh or squirm, yet always there for you.

At lunchtime Andy telephoned Rebecca to tell her he would be seeing his dad but there was no reply. He left a message.

'Hi babe. Just to let you know I'm having a coffee with Dad this afternoon so I may be a little later than usual tonight.'

He thought no more about it until 3.45pm, when he was about to set off for the cafe. Andy checked his phone and saw there had been no response from Rebecca. He phoned again but it went to voicemail.

Chapter 11

Finding a parking space was harder than he expected, making him ten minutes late getting to the cafe and a little flustered. He hated being late, especially for his father. He had rushed to Carlo's and was out of breath when he arrived. He saw his father sitting in the window seat, spectacles perched on the end of his nose, checking emails on his phone and looking like he hadn't a care in the world.

Andy's earliest recollections were when he was a young child. His dad opened the door at the end of a working day and Andy would run into his arms to be flung in the air or twirled around in a dizzying circle. He couldn't recall an occasion when his dad seemed to be in a bad mood or worried, when he came home from work. He associated his dad with fun and laughter; he was the leader of the pack as far as Andy was concerned.

In later years, he remembered being driven to school in what seemed to be a different car every day, and chatting endlessly about sport, cars and TV. He trusted his dad, told him everything and asked him anything – he knew his father would have the answer; all he had to do was follow his advice.

When had that stopped? When did he start filtering information from the man who had always been the same and was always on his side? His dad hadn't changed, so it must be him. No, his dad was level, consistent. Even when telling his son two years ago that although they had found a small tumour on the back of his leg and he was going into hospital to have it removed, there was nothing to worry about; they hoped to avoid chemotherapy. Andy's eyes pricked with tears as he remembered that day and the moment his father had looked away, just in case his eyes betrayed his real fear. How he had followed suit as the panic of the moment struck him. Life without this rock beside him had never before occurred to him until that moment and it struck him like an arrow. One more deep breath, a clearing of the head and in he went.

'Sorry, Dad! Couldn't get parked; it's all those cars you used to sell!'
Paul stood, smiled and embraced his son.

'God, there must be a lot of old cars parked out there!' he retorted.

They exchanged a few pleasantries and family updates before Andy turned the conversation to recent events.,

'You know that accident I had a few weeks ago?'

'Yes. Is that other guy out of hospital yet?'

'No, not yet, but he is on the mend at least. Anyway, the police have been to see me and identified the guy who did it, or rather, I've confirmed who it was from a line up.'

'Well that's good. At least they can get him off the streets.'

'You'd think so. But let me tell you what's happened since.'
Andy proceeded to tell the story of the problems with two different police forces and the frustrations that accompanied this. His father nodded, listening carefully. Then Andy told him of the phone call warning him, and about the man at the garage offering him money.

'So, some complete stranger offered you ten grand?'

'Yes.'

'And what did you say?'

'I told him to leave or I'd call the police.'

'And did you?'

'Did I what?'

'Call the police?'

'Well I did, but it was that bloody 101 number so I tried to contact the DCI but I don't have his number so I sent him an email.'

'Has he got back to you?'

'No. He's on leave for a couple of days.'

Paul looked at his son whilst collecting his thoughts and Andy waited for the guidance that would inevitably follow. He felt like he used to as a kid, sitting in the back of the car, looking at the back of his dad's head as he drove. He could read his comic, eat his sweets, or just go to sleep until they arrived at wherever they were going. How safe that seemed now, with no responsibility and an able captain steering the ship.

After a few seconds the captain spoke. 'Okay Andy, I think you have to be very careful here. There are a number of possibilities and none of them are good. This could be a proper villain you have accidentally come across or it might just be some yob. If the offer was genuine, I suspect he's likely to be a villain. The offer might be an attempt to compromise you and weaken any evidence you give … who knows? Do you think they might've made the same offer to the guy who was stabbed?'

'I don't know. Oh … hang on a minute. He was

different when I last saw him at the hospital. So was his fiancée … yes. I bet that's why all of a sudden, he was saying he wasn't sure about the identity of the attacker. He said something about not getting a good look at him, despite the fact they were face to face. He must have been nobbled and the policeman in charge must know too because Gary reckoned he was impatient with him.'

'All right,' his father said calmly. 'So, we have money being offered to alter evidence. I can check with Tony Sanderson but I am pretty sure that would be conspiracy to pervert the course of justice, which is pretty serious and an immediate go-to-jail card.'

'Who for?'

'Anyone involved. You weren't thinking of taking the money, were you?'

'Of course not! But I don't know what I'm getting myself into. Should I just back out? Tell the police I'm not pressing charges and don't want to be a witness.'

'Let me talk to Tony and maybe get him to ring you. He'll know what you can and can't do. But I'm not keen on this twat getting away with it.'

'Hope you don't speak like that in front of Mum!' Andy replied with a mock-startled expression. His father ignored the light-hearted remark. He had real fire in his eyes.

'These people are scum and need to be brought into line, otherwise they'll take over. I think you have to talk to that DCI and tell him everything that has happened, but you need some legal advice from Tony as well. We'll tackle this as a family and work out the right thing to do.'

'Thanks, Dad … I always feel better after I've talked things through with you. Have you ever been wrong about anything?' Andy asked earnestly.

'Yes, I think I made a mistake back in … what year were you born?'
They both laughed and any tension was dispelled. They talked some more about sport, films and the kids before hugging and going their separate ways. Paul asked his son to say nothing of this to his mother for now.

Once back in his car, Andy checked for messages. There were three but none from Rebecca. He tried her again and once more was connected to her answerphone. He drove home, puzzled.

Andy arrived back home just before 7pm and saw the house was in darkness. Unlocking the front door, he called out for Rebecca but there was no reply and her car keys were gone. He checked the kitchen table and fridge for notes – their normal places for messages but there was nothing. His concern was low level but growing steadily. Where did she say she would be today? Did she say and he wasn't listening? Where was she likely be at this time? It dawned on him that he didn't have a clue. With Hannah, he'd known all of her friends, her family, her tastes and, of course, her life revolved around their children anyway. Rebecca was more of a free spirit. She had no particular ties but the truth was, even though they lived together, he didn't know that much about her.. He didn't even know who to call. Her father had died some years ago and her mother lived in Spain.

She had a sister, who lived in Dorset but they'd never met. She had friends but Andy didn't have their numbers, even if he wanted to. He rang Laura.

'Don't suppose you've heard from Rebecca today?'

'No, was I supposed to?'

'Not really, but she isn't answering her phone and she isn't at home.'

'Hope she hasn't done a runner,' Laura said and instantly regretted it, especially as there was a brief silence.

'Sorry, Andy, that was tasteless. Are you worried?'

'Not really, but I don't know if I should be … it's the phone really – she's never far from it.'

'Does she have a diary?'

'I'm not sure,' he responded, again revealing how little he knew about the woman he was living with.

'You could see if she puts her appointments on the calendar on her iPhone – if so, they'll also show on the laptop.'

'Yes, I suppose so,' Andy replied vaguely.

'You don't know her password, do you?'

'Yes, I do!'

'Liar.'

'Okay, I don't. Anyway, I don't think she uses the Calendar app.'

'Give it half an hour and ring me back if you haven't heard anything. I'm sure there's a perfectly innocent explanation.'

When Paul arrived home, he rang Tony Sanderson of Parker Lewis – his lawyers for as long as he could remember. Tony was now in his fifties and senior partner of the firm but had been a trainee when he first met Paul. When they played golf together, Paul would often ask him if his training was still underway, especially if he missed a short putt. Tony would reply that he would realise just how long he'd been qualified when he got his next bill.

'Is that my brief I'm speaking to?'

'It certainly is. Hang on – just let me set the costs clock ticking.'

'I thought you guys did that the minute the phone rang.'

'Insulting your lawyer can be a very expensive business, I should warn you. Unless you're going to make my day by telling me you have been arrested, that is. What can I do for you Paul?'

Paul repeated the conversation with his son in as much detail as he could and listened very carefully to his lawyer's response. Despite the banter, he had the utmost respect for Tony, who was never afraid of a fight and upon whose judgement he was happy to rely. After listening to the details, Tony agreed to ring Andy there and then, which he duly did.

'Hi Andy, Tony Sanderson here. Your dad has instructed me to ring you immediately and talk to you about the Kray twins or whoever you have got tangled up with.'

'That's great, Tony,' Andy laughed mirthlessly. 'Has he told you the whole story?'

'Yes, he has. So first off, we don't press charges in this country and we can't withdraw them either. A complaint is made and it doesn't have to be the victim who makes it. Once made, the police investigate it and then the Crown Prosecution Service decide whether or not there should be a prosecution. They prosecute if there are reasonable prospects of a conviction and if it's in the public interest.'

'So, the guy who got stabbed can't tell them to drop it?'

'No, he can't, but he can say he's not prepared to assist them. He may then be ordered to attend court and be cross-examined. He could even be prosecuted for wasting police time. In practice, the police work with a witness – particularly a victim – and offer protection if they feel he or she is being intimidated.'

'What about the guy who approached me and offered me money, will they charge Tasker with that?'

'I doubt it. There's no evidence connecting him to the man who offered you money, and no evidence of this offer, other than your claim. I imagine the police will encourage you to get some evidence of the attempted bribe, by setting up a meeting they can listen into.'

'Can't I just back out of everything?'

'Not really. You're in the same position as the man who was stabbed. You run the risk of impeding an enquiry and facing the consequences. Plus, it goes without saying that taking the money may well be a serious offence: perverting the course of justice.'

'What do you suggest I do?'

'Cooperate with the police. I'll make some enquiries about this Tasker character and the policeman in charge with one of my criminal partners – try and get a little background. You have my mobile number, so ring me if you have any concerns. What's the name of the DCI you dealt with?'

'Cooper. That's great Tony, you're a star.'

'That's what your dad said when I beat him at golf on Saturday … well, he didn't use those exact words. Take care Andy.' Tony hung up.

Andy felt better knowing what he could or, more to the point, couldn't do. He glanced at the clock. It was now after 7.30. Where the hell was Rebecca?

Chapter 12

Andy tried Rebecca's number again but with the same response: answerphone. He was on the verge of ringing staff from the garage at home when he heard a key in the front door and the door opening. He rushed to see Rebecca putting her shopping down.

'Where the hell have you been?' he said not knowing whether to be angry or relieved. He was both.

'Sorry Andy – I've lost my phone. I had to go out and get some food as we had nothing in and I only realised when I was rushing out that I couldn't find it.'

'I've been worried sick here. Why didn't you get somebody to ring me on the landline?'

'I didn't think you'd be worried ... my God, you never have been before!' she said raising the temperature.

'What's that supposed to mean?' Temperature maintained.

'Well, just that you never seem that interested in what I'm doing or where I'm going. How was I to know you might be looking for me?'

There was a slight lull in the argument as they regrouped and began to calm down. Andy's voice took on a softer tone: 'So where do you think you lost your phone?'

'Somewhere in the house I think, because I had it last night, didn't I? And I'm pretty sure I had it this morning. Didn't you see me with it last night?'

'I don't know... I suppose you had it. Let me ring it again.'

Andy took out his phone and pressed Rebecca's name. He heard the ringtone on his phone, and they walked around the house listening for her phone ringing. There was nothing.

'Okay, when did you last see it?'

'I'm not sure but I thought it was in the kitchen when the heating guy was here.'

'Heating guy?'

'Yes, some engineer called and needed to check the boiler.'

'Check the boiler? Who was that?' Andy said, a note of anxiety creeping back in.

'A guy called in – he said boilers in the area were being checked for leaks or something and if we had one it would be fixed for free or something like that.'

'And you let him in?'

'Yes, I did but he had a card or a badge or something so he was who he said he was.'

'You let a man into our house because he had a badge?'

'It was an official-looking badge.'

'Official-looking? Oh well that's all right then. What the hell were you thinking?'

The row really began in earnest; voices were raised, insults exchanged and after a few minutes, Rebecca stormed off in tears telling Andy to go and fuck himself.

He sat in the kitchen flitting between emotions. On the one hand he was furious with Rebecca for letting a stranger into their house. On the other, he had been aggressive and instead of being relieved at her return, he had upset her. He reminded himself that she was much younger than him, but resisted dwelling on the thought that Hannah would never have let some random guy in. Who was he? What was he doing in their house? Could he have taken the phone? If indeed, the phone had been taken at all. If it had, maybe the guy was just some opportunist thief. If not, was there something more sinister?

Andy rang Laura to tell her of Rebecca's return and his concern about the engineer. She told him he sounded paranoid and he had to agree he did. He told Laura about the row – what he had said, which prompted much tutting and sighing. She urged him to apologise to Rebecca and he did as his sister told him. The apology led initially to an angry response, followed by tears and then furious fumbling as they tugged at each other's clothing before having noisy and enthusiastic sex.

Two days later, Rebecca told him that she had found her phone in the boot of her car. She couldn't understand it, she said. She had checked the car thoroughly and anyway, she was sure she had used the phone in the house. Andy reminded her that they had once found her phone in the fridge. That same day, just as Andy was in sight of the garage, his phone rang. It was an unrecognised number but he pressed the button on his steering wheel to accept the call.

'Hello, is that Andy Connolly?'

'Who's calling?'

'It's David Cooper from Humberside Police.'

'Oh hello, yes, this is Andy.'

'Is it a good time to talk?'

'Yes, of course.'

'I got your email and, rather than discuss it on the

phone, I thought I'd pop in and see you – today if possible.'

'I'm just about to pull into work. When did you have in mind?'

'I could be with you in, say, twenty minutes if that's any good to you.'

'Sure, that would be fine. See you then.'

Andy was not sure how to feel as he parked up. He had to think how to play this, to decide how much he could say and how to best present it. He was reassured that Cooper had called and noticed that he gave his first name. Did that mean he was relaxed about how things were going in the criminal case, or was he being played? Andy knew all about the strategy of use of first names to breed co-operation and play for advantage. This was something he now did as a matter of course, after picking it up from Tony Blair in the 1990s. The Blair approach – using reporters' first names and referring to himself as Tony – did disarm people and, for a while at least, made him seem very approachable – a regular guy. Politicians all now referred to reporters by name; it was a sharp contrast to the formal and stiff Thatcher years. Once inside, Andy told Andrea that Cooper was coming in and told her to be discreet. She gave him a scowl that told him she always was and the warning was unnecessary. Almost exactly twenty minutes after their conversation, Cooper tapped on Andy's door. He entered with his usual jaunty air of authority.

'Thanks for seeing me, Andy. I got your email. Tell me what's happened.'

Andy felt the strong handshake, sat down and whatever plans he'd had or was considering melted away as he told

Cooper everything, including the offer of ten grand and Rebecca's missing phone. Perhaps Cooper was playing him. If he was, he was very good at it. The DCI listened carefully, nodded at regular intervals, smiled occasionally and looked in control and relaxed.

'Well, that is quite some story, Andy! And a lot of stress for you to carry. What I'm going to do is give you my private mobile number. Feel free to ring me any time – day or night if anything happens, or if you have concerns. Our first objective is to keep everyone safe and protected from any intimidation. Believe me, that is exactly what this. You're being tested to see if they can manipulate you, and you've done exactly the right thing by contacting me. We need to keep a close eye on these people and we will do. Just report everything directly to me when anything happens. You don't need to involve your local police anymore.'

'That's really reassuring. I don't mind telling you that contacting the police on this bloody 101 system is an absolute nightmare.'

'Yes, we know it can be awkward, which is why I'm bypassing it. I'll be your point of contact from now on.' Cooper paused, sat back in his seat and crossed his legs. His arms were open and resting on the chair arms.

'One thing I have to tell you, Andy, is that Tasker's lawyers applied for bail yesterday. I'm afraid that, although we opposed it, it was granted.'

Andy let this news hang in the air for a second. 'What does that mean?'

'It means he's out and about. However, he has a 6pm curfew and there are other conditions – one of which is avoiding all witnesses. He has to check into a police station daily. He has to be at his approved address by six o'clock every evening and is not allowed to leave it until 9am the following day. If he does break the curfew, an electronic signal alerts us and we would arrest him straight away.'

'Is he dangerous? Well, obviously I know he is but I mean, is he a danger to me?'

'No, he might be dangerous but he isn't stupid. We will be keeping an eye on him and he will know that. Also, if he breaks any of the bail conditions, he'll go straight back to prison and will stay there until the trial. I just wanted you to know.'

'When is the trial likely to be?'

'I don't really know but I would guess somewhere between 3 and 6 months.'

'Shit! I didn't think it would take that long.'

'I'm afraid so. He'll appear in a Magistrates Court and then be transferred to a Crown Court, where he'll be tried before a jury, if he pleads not guilty. If he pleads guilty, there will be no jury, you won't have to go and it will be over quickly.'

'Will he?'

'Will he what?'

'Plead guilty.'

'Well, he never has yet I'm afraid but he gets a discount on his sentence if he does, so who knows? It might be that in this case he has little option but to accept it and that is what we'll be working towards.'

They chatted for a while on procedures and, to lessen tension, Cooper occasionally changed the subject to talk about his kids, Andy's own family, sport and of course cars. Although Andy knew what Cooper was doing, he found it worked and he actually did feel slightly more at ease.

'So, Andy, if you were contacted again would you be prepared to arrange a meeting and let us listen in?'

'You mean … wear a wire?'

Cooper laughed. 'That's a little out of date now. You wouldn't need to wear anything. We would just need to know where the meeting was going to be and have a listening device nearby. Or we can put something on your phone in case you're stopped in the street.'

'So, if I did, would you arrest anyone who talks to me?'

'Almost certainly not. Unless you were in danger, of course. We'd just be compiling evidence for the case. We may arrest other people near the trial date, depending on what was said.'

'But eventually they'd know that I'd lured them into a trap and because of me they went to prison.'

'Well, you could put it that way but it is their occupational hazard. Remember, having contacted you, they're likely to do it again.'

'I need to think about it, David. I have a young family and a business to think about.'

'I totally understand, but we can offer you protection and your family and mine will be a lot safer with scum like Tasker off the streets.'

The two men shook hands warmly as Cooper got up to leave. On the way out, he stopped to look at one of the cars in the showroom, opened the door, sat in the driver's seat, made a thumbs-up sign to Andy and left. Andy grinned and thought to himself, 'That guy is so full of shit … he has no intention of buying that car – he must think I was born last Tuesday.'

Andrea popped her head into his office a few hours later to remind Andy he had a lunch meeting at the Peacock Inn just outside of town with two other motor dealers. He was looking forward to talking cars, targets, customers and generally whinging about the motor trade. He had several calls to make first, as Andrea also reminded him, and some sales figures printed off for his discussion.

Shortly before he left, he pulled the various papers together and walked out into a cold crisp day. He hesitated and considered going back for his coat but decided just to park as close as he could to the pub. Climbing into his car, he glanced down and saw a brown envelope on the passenger seat. He knew he hadn't left it there and wondered how it could possibly have got there; his car had been locked. He looked at the envelope for a second or two then glanced around for signs of anyone lurking nearby, but there was nobody there. The envelope was fat with its contents and he eased open the top flap to reveal a stack of £20 notes. Flicking through them they totalled £500. Andy went cold.

Chapter 13

'Can I get you a drink, Madam?' the young waiter asked Laura at the small seating area in Mario's restaurant near her home.

'No, thank you. Not at the moment. I'm just waiting for my friend and I imagine we'll order at the table. She should be here any minute.'

Almost as soon as she had said that, Hayley rushed in, apologised for being late and took off her expensive-looking coat. They were shown to their table and ordered a bottle of sauvignon blanc.

'Why not? We can always get a taxi back,' Hayley said and they both laughed.

'Oh, Laura you should have seen the tosspot I was out with last night! He's a friend of a friend and I was told he was charming and well heeled. I didn't get a look at his heels as he was in danger of boring the pants off me ... mind you it would have been the only way he would have got my pants off.'

They both roared with laughter, causing the middle-aged, rather stiff-looking couple on the next table to turn around and glare. Oh, how good it was to see Hayley! She was always infectiously cheerful and just what Laura needed at the moment. They spoke of the old days, holidays planned and the need to arrange a shopping trip to Leeds, as Harvey Nichols hadn't been poured over for months. Laura was trouble-free again, younger, happier and more hopeful ... perhaps the wine was helping. Whatever it was, a huge weight was temporarily lifted and that now-unusual feeling of being relaxed and tension free was washing over her.

Hayley had been married twice and divorced twice without seeming to bat an eyelid. She spent a fortune on facials, nails and hair and always looked attractive. Men came and went in her life but always on her terms. How Laura envied her.

The dessert they both said they wouldn't order had been delivered and devoured and Hayley sat back in her chair to take a long look at her friend.

'It's been great seeing you again, Laura. It seems like months since we did this.'

'Yeah,' Laura agreed, 'we should do it more often. I can't remember when I last laughed so much.'

'So, what's the problem, Laura?'

'Problem? What problem?' she replied with a staged laugh.

'Come on … I've been your friend forever. I know you better than anybody. I can see it in your eyes and your gestures … your whole body language tells me something's wrong, so what is it?' Hayley said, her smile morphing into a concerned frown.

'I don't know what you're talking about. I thought we were having a good time.'

'We are! But I'm not the problem – I'm pretty sure of that. I've noticed it for a while now and wondered if it was the baby thing or maybe that you were worried about Abi. Or, God forbid, that you were ill. Anyway, whatever it is, I want you to tell me, even if I have to get you pissed first.' Hayley extended her right hand and placed it over both of Laura's hands. Laura laughed at the remark and perhaps it was the laugh that sent the protective wall crumbling. Maybe it was Hayley staring in such a fixed, determined way. Maybe it was the affectionate touch – whatever it was, the laugh was fading, replaced with a burning sensation in her throat and a panic that started to wash over her. The first tear was brushed away, but it was soon followed by a few more, then an uncontrollable stream. Her head fell forward and her tears hit the table.

'Oh my God, Laura! what is it?'

Laura couldn't speak. When she tried, her throat was constricted by emotion and words wouldn't come. Hayley realised this wasn't the place to have this conversation. She went to the bar and paid the bill, allowing Laura to go the Ladies, pull herself together and touch up her make up. Minutes later, Hayley followed Laura into the toilets, put her arm around her and told her they would go and sit in the car for privacy.

Sitting in the car Hayley turned to Laura. 'Now come on. We're not going anywhere until I know what's going on. Is Abi okay? Is it your health?'

'No, nothing like that'

'Then it's Charles, isn't it?'

The sobbing really started then and Laura's head slumped on to her friend's shoulder. Hayley held her for a while to let out all the pent-up emotion. She spoke softly to her friend.

'Been in the wars, have you?'

Laura sat up and blew her nose. What did she mean?

'I only ask because I see some old bruises on your neck. I noticed some on your arms the last time we met. If that bastard has been hitting you, I'll break his fucking neck.'

'Oh, Hayley, I just don't know what to do. He doesn't

hit me exactly and he's always sorry for anything he has done because he didn't mean to do it. I just … I think I … maybe I provoke him.'

'Don't give me that shit! Provoke him? Come on Laura – listen to yourself. If you heard somebody else say that you'd say what a silly bitch she was and how she needed to dump the guy. Wake up! How often does he hit you?'

'He doesn't hit me … I told you that.'

'Okay, well how often does he grab you, push you or whatever the bastard does to make bruises on you?'

'I don't know.'

'So, too often to count?'

'I didn't say that.'

'Okay, how often are you afraid of him?'

Laura swallowed. 'All of the time.'

And with that, an avalanche of tears was released.

Hayley felt a rage erupting inside of her at the genuine fear she saw in her oldest friend. She also felt confusion bordering on anger. How had someone as bright and self-assured as Laura allowed herself to sink so low and to stay with a man who evoked fear in her? The only man who'd dared to threaten her during an argument a few years ago had quickly regretted it. Her right knee had quickly made contact with his groin and he was left breathless on the pavement.

Laura couldn't explain how it had all happened; how she'd arrived at where she was. She spoke of the shame of being a battered wife or whatever the phrase was and how she couldn't understand why she had allowed it. She spoke of her concern for Abi seeing the dark side of a man she now saw as her father. Abi loved her life now; how could she hope to replicate that lifestyle without a husband, who had no responsibility for her daughter? She admitted she felt a failure and, as kind as her parents would be, they would be disappointed with her.

'Oh, what bullshit, Laura! Your dad would probably go round and beat the shit out of that smarmy bastard. Plus all of your family and friends would be on your side. Abi is just a child; she'll adapt to any changes you make but she won't want her mum to be unhappy. Does Andy know about this?'

'Absolutely not. And you must never tell him, Hayley … promise me you'll never tell him.'

'Why haven't you told him?'

'Andy would go apeshit and God knows what would happen. Promise me now, Hayley. Promise me,' Laura said, grabbing Hayley's arm and gripping it tightly.

'Yes, yes, okay. I promise.'

They talked for another hour before Hayley drove her friend home, forgetting all about getting a taxi. She hugged her deeply and cried herself when she told Laura she would always be there for her and would never let anything happen to her or Abi. Hayley also promised again (on her life) not to mention it to Andy or Charles or indeed anybody, and eventually drove away not knowing what to do.

Laura felt drained as she showered and tried to contain the tears that kept coming. Instead of feeling relief that her dirty secret was out, she felt exposed and vulnerable. The outpouring of emotion had been a shock to her; above all it had made her feel weaker and less in control. She had told Hayley how she felt and what was happening but that had made it all real; not just a thought. Even then, she had denied Charles had hit her. Somehow underplaying the description of the assaults seemed the appropriate thing to do. More than ever, Laura felt like a cork bobbing about in the ocean with no real direction of travel. She would normally discuss serious stuff with Andy but not this time. She knew he would never forgive Charles; he might even confront or attack him. She knew she should leave Charles, but the slow eroding of self-worth had left her almost incapable of finding the strength to go. It was almost as though each attack, each blow, each threat had chipped away at her confidence and strength. She was losing respect for herself and was intelligent enough to realise that Charles was in a spiral of increasing violence. She was exhausted and diminished.

★ ★ ★

Andy was listening to Bill Turnbull and Paul Anderson talk of their plans for the upcoming changes in car funding and how it would affect them. Bill had the local Seat franchise and Paul had the Audi dealership. Andy had been looking forward to the meeting to discuss pooling resources on advertising and used-car funding and always enjoyed the banter. Paul would tease Bill about not selling the prestige end of the new car market and Bill would retaliate by asking Paul how long he felt he could hang on to Audi, when the company was rumoured to be looking for a change. All of this was going on but all Andy could think of was the envelope stuffed with cash in his car. And, more importantly, who had put it there. An uncomfortable thought had crossed his mind about the culprit: could it have been David Cooper as some sort of test? Cooper had acted strangely when he thought about it. He was friendlier than last time and more familiar, as though he was trying to manipulate their relationship. Was he testing him to see if he would take money? Perhaps he already knew of the offer, even suspected Gary Newcombe had accepted a cash bribe?

The logical thing to do was to contact Cooper and hand the money over. On the other hand, that would add to the pressure to set something up with the police – to trap Tasker and his associates in the act of attempted bribery. Maybe that was why Cooper had done it … if it was him. Surely if Andy did play any role in a setup, those involved would want some form of revenge against him. Another dark thought occurred to him: what if Cooper had planted the money because he worked for Tasker, or someone higher up the criminal food chain. Tasker got off the last charges against him, so he was getting help from somewhere. What if Cooper was corrupt and Andy was totally exposed with nowhere to turn?

'Come on, Connolly! Have you got any suggestions, or are you even listening? You seem miles away today.' Bill shook his empty glass.

'Sorry, guys. I promise I'll start to listen … once either of you says anything interesting, that is,' he replied to laughter.

'Same again?' Andy said, picking up the glasses.

As he headed for the bar, he was plagued by one thought: is DCI Cooper bent?

Chapter 14

Back at the garage that afternoon Andy thought he would do a little more research before deciding what to do about the cash. Using Google, he looked up the Tasker failed trial again. He searched for several minutes and encountered many James or Jamie Taskers living here and in the USA. There were several actors and musicians with that name; one in particular came up a great deal as he had been a character actor in one of the soaps on TV. The contrast was chilling when he came up with the Jamie Tasker he was looking for. There were several mentions of him connected to crimes but the one he was interested in was the stabbing of Graham Todd. He found several reports of the trial but also a more detailed report of day two when the police officers gave their evidence:

Evidence was given by Detective Chief Inspector Cooper of Humberside Police. DCI Cooper told the Court that he had arrested Tasker after the police had received a tip off concerning the delivery of drugs at a local address. The officer said that although no drugs were found at that address, a search of separate premises lead to the discovery of large quantities of amphetamines.

What did that mean? Was Cooper helpful to Tasker? Did Cooper intimidate the witnesses or allow Tasker to? Why did he even think that was a possibility? There was just something about Cooper that made him uneasy but he couldn't put his finger on it. There was no doubt that Gary Newcombe was afraid of him but that might be because he had received the cash offer and taken it.

There was no press report of the assault charges relating to Graham Todd other than the earlier mention of him being stabbed in a pub near Goole. What happened in the assault and where was Todd now? Cooper was involved in that case and could maybe answer some questions. The research had made Andy even more uneasy but nonetheless he picked up his mobile. He realised his dad was right – he had no option.

'Hello, Andy, what can I do for you?'

'Hi David, I need to see you. Some kind bloke left five hundred quid in my car.'

'When was this?'

'Earlier today, just after you left.'

'What? It was just there when you got into the car?'

'Yes, it was on the passenger seat in a brown envelope.'

'Okay. Have you touched the cash?'

'Yes, only to count it. But I just opened the envelope and then brought it to my office in the garage.'

'Just keep it there. I'll have forensics take a look at it. I'm not going to be able to get to you until late tomorrow if that's okay, so just lock it up in your desk or something. Don't let anybody else touch it and, in fact, don't mention it to anybody else.'

'Okay. What time tomorrow?'

'Probably around five, if that suits you.'

'Fine, see you then.'

Andy then rang the family lawyer Tony Sanderson,

'Hello Andy. You must be psychic!' said the ever-cheerful Tony Sanderson.

'How's that then?'

'Well your Dad was on to me the other day asking if

we'd found anything on Tasker or that DCI and I must be honest, I had forgotten to raise it with my criminal department. Anyway, I did make the call and have some information for you.'

'Sounds intriguing Tony, what have you got?'

'I'd rather not discuss it over the phone but my last client is at five today, so we can have a chat around six if you want to pop into the office.'

'That would be great, Tony. See you then.'

Soon after five o'clock, Andy drove to the out-of-town offices of Parker Lewis. They had been in the centre of Goole and had a main office in Hull as well as two smaller branch offices elsewhere. A few years ago, they had taken over another firm and relocated to the Hollingsgate Business Park, to the west of Goole, where they had the most prestigious building with CCTV, private and client parking, as well as a reception area that wouldn't have looked out of place in a small hotel. It was still a bit early to meet Tony and Andy knew of a very nice coffee shop on the estate and so decided he'd grab a coffee before the meeting.

He arrived at the Artisan coffee and bake-shop shortly before 5.30pm, and ordered a cappuccino and a biscotti before taking a seat near the window. A young girl made his coffee and brought it over to his table with a manufactured smile before returning to her work-station. A young couple sat at the other end of the cafe, both on their mobiles frantically texting, whilst ignoring each other. He reckoned they were in their early twenties and he always found the lack of engagement in younger couples amazing when he watched them eat and drink in restaurants without saying a word to one another, preferring to play with their phones. Maybe he was getting old. Maybe it was the distraction of the mute couple that caused him to miss someone else walking into the café. Instead of going to the counter to order, the man, dressed in jeans and with a dark hoodie pulled over his head, walked over to where Andy was sitting.

'Got a call for you,' said the stocky, unshaven man who looked about forty.

Andy looked up in surprise. 'Sorry?' he replied, genuinely confused.

'This call is for you. You are Andy, aren't you?' said the man in a monotone. His accent was local and without waiting for a response, he placed the phone to Andy's ear. Andy pulled away instinctively, before taking the phone.

'Hello, Andy. I believe you got a little deposit today.'

'Who is this?'

'Just a friend, trying to look out for you that's all.'

'Do you have a name?'

'What I need to know is, do we have a deal and can I arrange to drop the rest of the cash in to you? I appreciate you've had some problems and stress. You need some compensation, so you can put all of this behind you and get on with your life. I'm sure Rebecca would want that, and your family.'

'What do you know about Rebecca or my family?'

'Oh, the people I work for know all kinds of things about all kinds of people, believe me. What you need to do is get back to that very pretty girl you live with and just relax. Does that sound so bad?'

'What makes you think I'm not relaxed?'

'Well I wouldn't be if I was under pressure from a copper who didn't care whether I lived or died and had a track record of causing trouble for innocent people.'

'Are you threatening me?'

'I'm offering you money, that's all. I'm trying to help you.'

'Sounds like a threat,' Andy said, somewhat timidly, whilst looking at the unblinking eyes of the hooded well-built man in front of him.

'I haven't threatened you and nor has the man in front of you, but I need to know if we can rely on you and make sure that a big mistake isn't made in court. This is a world you don't understand, my friend. I'm offering you a way back to your own world, where you'll be much more comfortable.'

The voice was fairly cultured and Andy wondered if it was the man who had called himself Smith at the garage. He could feel his heart rate rising.

'I don't think there has been any mistake,' Andy said feeling a rage building up in him; an instinct to fight back. A confusing cocktail of emotions swam around his system.

'Okay, Andy, have it your way. So, do we have a deal or not?'

'I can't take your money. You know that and I haven't done anything other than watch somebody get stabbed. I can't take money, then lie to the police and commit perjury in court, can I?'

'All you have to do is be a bit hazy with your description – a little unsure about what you saw. Is that so hard? After all, it was dark and you can't be certain who you saw.

Nobody is going to blame you for that, are they?'

'But I gave a description at the time. I didn't know who it was but I can't just pretend I didn't see the guy.'

'You can say that you've seen a few people since that could have been the man. That you're not sure about the ID you gave – the person you identified. It happens all the time.'

'How do you know who I identified?' Andy asked, wondering if Cooper had passed the information on.

'Never mind that. We know an awful lot of things. Are you going to take the money or not?'

'I can't. I just can't.'

'That's unfortunate Andy ... really it is. I've tried to be nice and to help you but if you won't be helped then the matter is out of my hands. Give the phone back to my colleague, please.'

Andy's hands were shaking and his mouth was as dry as sand as he handed back the phone, now clammy with sweat from his hand. He tried to prepare himself for an assault by looking around for support or for a weapon on the table. The only items available were a teaspoon and a now lukewarm coffee. In any event he was no match for the man in front of him, who looked like a former boxer or a nightclub doorman. His heart was pounding as the man took instructions of some sort on the phone whilst looking hard down at Andy. The man never blinked during the call and Andy could hear his own breathing and feel his thumping heart. He wanted to get up and leave – or even run – but he knew he would be too easily stopped, so he was temporarily frozen to the spot awaiting his fate. Surely, he wouldn't do anything to him here – in a public place in broad daylight. Maybe that was the point: to show him their lack of fear by attacking him publicly. The hooded man finally spoke to the caller:

'Yeah, okay.' He turned and left without a word or a glance in Andy's direction. The young girl at the counter continued to clean the coffee machine; the iPhone couple continuing to stare at their devices. So far as he knew, none of the three of them had even noticed the man who had come in and left. His hands were shaking as he got up and walked the short distance to Parker Lewis. Whatever doubts he had before about any danger he was in, he had none now.

Chapter 15

Sitting in the palatial waiting area, Andy tried to compose himself. He had started shaking in the cafe and it had now developed into an alarming trembling from head to foot. He moved into the gents' toilets and looked hard at himself in the mirror. His pupils were slightly dilated and he had lost some colour from his face. He splashed cold water on to his grey cheeks and the cooling effect on his hands and face was instant. He tidied his hair, dried himself and stood up to his full height to take in several deep breaths. Although his temples were still throbbing, he felt a little stronger as he walked back to the waiting area.

Tony Sanderson walked down the stairs to greet Andy with a friendly smile and handshake before escorting him to conference room six on the second floor. The room was a picture of light oak with its large table, twelve chairs and two matching cupboards, on which stood water bottles, tea and coffee equipment and biscuits.

'Can I get you something, Andy?'

'Yeah, coffee would be nice. I left my last one at the cafe around the corner.'

Andy proceeded to tell the open-mouthed lawyer the whole incident and about his meeting with DCI Cooper and the cash in the car.

'Gosh Andy! That must have been a little scary to say the least. Look I did have some news but in the light of your experience, let me go and see if my colleague Malcolm Chalmers is still in the building. He's the head of our criminal department and the chap I was talking to. It might be better if he speaks to you directly.'

Sanderson rushed out of the room, giving Andy more time to control his nerves. He already felt better, simply by being on the premises, as well as being able to tell someone about what had just happened. He got up and poured himself a glass of sparkling water, which he almost drank in one gulp. He was feeling something in addition to fear and he was struggling to place it. After pouring a second glass it came to him: he felt tarnished by his contact with the world of professional criminals. The fact that they knew him, knew of his family and business and that they were in contact with him made him feel ... contaminated in some way. As well as terrified. Theirs was a dark, murky world and he hated it.

The door opened and a breathless Sanderson breezed in with a much larger man in his early forties close behind.

'Andy, let me introduce Malcolm Chalmers, our expert in all things criminal.'

Chalmers wouldn't have been out of place as a bouncer in a nightclub himself with his tall heavy build and full beard,

'I'm not sure I like that description but I concede I am a criminal lawyer,' he delivered in a cultured voice that was at odds with his appearance.

'Tell me the whole story from the beginning, Andy, just to make sure I have the full background.'

Andy did just that and in the telling of it, he became clearer himself as to the distance he had travelled from what he thought was a troubled life to one that had genuine danger attached to it. How he longed for that former life and how clearly he saw the risk he was in. How small his previous difficulties appeared by comparison.

'All right, that was more or less what I'd heard, so let me give you some background. It has to be on the basis however, that this is confidential and not for discussion outside of this building. Is that acceptable to you?'

'Yes, of course.'

'Okay. Well, let's start with Tasker. This firm has never represented him but a pal of mine does represent him and his cronies. I was in court a few years ago with a group of them on a three hander.'

'Three hander?'

'Sorry – three defendants on a joint charge, one of which was my client. Tasker was one of the other defendants and he was represented by my friend.'

'What were they charged with?'

'Affray, amongst other things, but it was effectively a fight in a pub. My chap was said to have thrown a beer glass at Tasker. This had led to a scuffle and other people were injured in the melee. Anyway, as a result of that case I did learn a little about Jamie Tasker.'

'Were they convicted?'

'No, the trial collapsed on the third day, when one of the witnesses changed their story about what had happened and it became unsafe to continue. The Crown Prosecution withdrew on the recommendation of the judge.'

'What was the change of evidence?'

'The witness made a statement that Tasker had been brandishing a knife in the pub but changed their story to say he never saw a knife and that the police had asked him to say he had seen one.'

'What happened to the witness?'

'Nothing really. There was a lot of huffing and puffing

and threats of perjury charges but, as far as I know, nothing was done about it. Anyway, the point is that the officer in charge was the then-Inspector David Cooper.'

'Shit.'

'Exactly.'

The three of them discussed what might have happened and why, but could draw no firm conclusion. There was certainly no hard evidence one way or the other about who was responsible for the witness's change of heart. Andy tried to assimilate the information and turned to Chalmers.

'But if Cooper is bent, why did the case go to court in the first place? Why not cover things up at the investigation stage? And he's been promoted since that case, hasn't he?'

'I'm not saying he's bent and you're right about the promotion. There are several potential theories; one at the time was that Tasker was one of Cooper's informants and a reason why Cooper's successful arrest record is so good.'

'You mean Tasker serves up criminals and in return Cooper makes sure any cases against him fail?'

'Possibly.'

'What are the other theories then?'

'Well, another one I've heard concerns the Baldwin Brothers.'

'Who are they?'

'A couple of real grade A criminals. They deal in the supply of drugs on an industrial scale apparently, but so far there are no convictions against them. They're more sophisticated than Tasker but no less dangerous. They operate primarily out of Manchester but they moved into Yorkshire a couple of years ago and there was a trade war with the main suppliers of cocaine and heroin in this area and Leeds.'

'I take it they won.'

'Well the war is still ongoing, but I am told they're on top.'

'Is Tasker one of the ones fighting them?'

'He's more a second or third division player and not directly involved. He's probably supplied by both sides and works the streets.'

'So, what was the theory you heard about the Baldwins?'

'I heard that the Baldwins' unblemished criminal record is due to police protection, in that they get information from a police source as to where surveillance may be taking place so they can avoid it. Also, I was told that lesser criminals are served up by the brothers in exchange for a get-out-of jail card.'

'I don't understand.'

'Well, if they're dealing in say the supply of cocaine and lesser drugs, a blind eye is turned to capture the more lethal variants of heroin or trendy cheap alternatives. Maybe information is fed to the police source to help them hit arrest targets and show that the war on drugs is being won or, at least, not being lost ... even though it is.'

'And you think Cooper is that source?'

'I'm not saying that, only that some might think he is, assuming there is any truth to the rumour.'

'So where does this leave me?'

'Hard to say. But you have to be very careful, Andy. You're caught between a rock and a hard place in that you cannot refuse to cooperate with the police or you may render yourself liable to charges – particularly if you withhold evidence. On the other hand, there is no denying that Tasker is dangerous and may have some level of protection from someone.'

'What am I supposed to do then?' Andy said, realising that heat was returning to his face and the turmoil was causing his head to spin.

'I think you have to disclose everything to Cooper and, to some extent, trust him. We have no evidence that he's dishonest and he may just be flying by the seat of his pants. If he's dishonest, he may present a risk, but the greater risk is to make an assumption and be wrong. Tony and I feel we should write a formal letter to the police to say we represent you and have genuine concerns for your safety and ask what action they are going to take to protect you. That way, he knows you have legal protection and either way he will have to be very careful.'

'Either way?'

'Yes. If he's honest, he knows that if he cocks up with you, there will be legal consequences. If he's dishonest, it's unlikely he'll do anything detrimental to you as he'd know we would chase him.'

'Very reassuring. You'd chase him after I disappear and end up in the foundations of a new supermarket,' Andy said sarcastically.

'We're not saying that. Besides, your risk might be low, despite today's incident. Frankly until something happens, there's nothing either we or the police can do. You can't get a restraining order unless you can tie an incident to a specific person. Nothing you have does that. I know it isn't much, but the letter is the best we can do. Other than that, I would suggest you increase your security at home and at work.'

There was a moment's silence before Sanderson spoke.

'We have a very good client who might help you on the security front. He's a former police officer who set up his business a few years ago. Toby Billings is his name; his company is Trent Securities. Shall I get him to call you?'

'Yes please,' Andy replied gloomily. 'So, there's no way I can just back out of this Tasker case?'

'No,' both lawyers said in unison.

Andy walked back to his car more anxious than ever.

Chapter 16

Charles Peterson was in a bad mood as he drove home. He had endured a bad day at the office, which had started poorly enough with a cancelled appointment on a project that was already giving problems. The flat conversion development in town was supposed to be a straightforward affair, for which his fees would be around £40,000, but the planners had started being difficult and the optimism he had shared with the client was eroding. The cost of the project was rising fast and the client was asking why these expenses hadn't been foreseen. Charles had reassured the client with heavy use of his privately educated charm, delivered with the supreme confidence he knew was a mask to his own self-doubt. The meeting was to be with a planner he believed he could manipulate but she had cancelled at the last minute.

One of his partners added to the misery and tension of the day by telling him another client had spoken to him about a previous commercial development; he believed Charles had overcharged him and was thinking of going elsewhere. Charles was told that although the client had been persuaded to stay, someone else would handle the next piece of business.

The current planning problem bubbling away would no doubt raise some eyebrows at the next partners' meeting. And the cherry on the cake was when he returned to his car and found a parking ticket on the windscreen. He had parked in the street, rather than the car park as he was expecting to drive to the planning department and thought the two-hour free parking was better than manoeuvring in and out of the firm's restricted car park at the office. He had forgotten about the parking , his meeting was cancelled and a rage flared up within him as he saw the ticket. It was one of those days where nothing went well and the harder he tried to find something positive, the less there seemed to be any chance of it. His normal confident exterior was becoming harder to maintain as the day dragged on.

His head was thumping as he drove home and the pressure he was under appeared to be mounting. He felt as though he were surrounded by swordsmen all trying to run him through; he was keeping them at bay, but only just. As he arrived home and opened the front door, he dropped the frown and wrinkled brow and replaced them with his false confident mask once again.

Abi was watching TV in the living room and didn't look up when he said hello.

'Did you hear me, Abi?' he said in a firm voice.

'Yes, Daddy ... sorry. Hello,' she replied without turning away from the screen, but lifting a hand to wave.

'Well you could at least look at me,' was his reply, a slight increase in firmness evident.

'Oh, I thought I did!' Abi said turning and smiling. The gesture removed the inclination in Charles for conflict.

'That's better. Where's your mother?'

'Upstairs I think' Abi said returning to the screen.

Charles illogically felt irritated that Laura was not downstairs to meet him, even though she could not have known when he would be home; the pent-up frustrations of the day were simmering like a pressure cooker. He was subconsciously looking for a release of his anger as he entered the bedroom and saw steam coming from the en suite bathroom. The steam seemed to encapsulate the pressure that had been building inside him all day. Laura emerged wearing a bathrobe with her hair in a towel.

'Oh, hello, Charles! I didn't hear you come in.'

'Obviously not,' he replied, looking away and taking off his suit jacket.

She ignored the comment as her now finely tuned sense of danger and mood had picked up the negative atmosphere.

'What time of day is this to be showering and washing your hair?' Charles barked as he pulled a clothes hanger from his wardrobe.

'Quite normal, I would have thought. I wanted to freshen up before dinner.'

'Freshen up from what?' he persisted.

'Nothing in particular. I've been in town and met Hayley for lunch.'

'Oh, that ball breaker. Who's she screwing at the moment?' he said with an upward head flick to demonstrate disappointment.

'Charles! Why are you talking like that about her? She's never done anything to you,' Laura replied; annoyance had trumped her anxiety.

'I don't care for her. She thinks a little too much of herself for my liking.'

'Had a bad day, have you?'

'No, I haven't as a matter of fact. I was having a good day until I got in and found you both slouching about the place whilst I go out and provide this lifestyle for us all. It would be nice to come home and feel some appreciation for the benefits you both enjoy.'

The signs were there and that familiar churning of the stomach returned for Laura. She wanted to challenge this unreasonable outburst but she knew where it would lead and Abi was downstairs. It was clear Charles wouldn't need much provoking and another night of nervous misery lay ahead. She decided instead to stay quiet and get dressed. She felt strangely vulnerable doing so in front of her husband, so she picked up her clothes and dressed in the bathroom before emerging to dry her hair. The mood was set.

Dinner was ready an hour or so later and Charles, Laura and Abi sat at the large kitchen table. Charles told Abi to switch off her mobile and other than her tutting response, the three of them were silent for a few minutes. Charles then asked Abi about her day at school in a very formal way, like a lawyer taking instructions from a client. Laura joined in the conversation, but only asking other questions of her daughter in a lighter-hearted and affectionate exchange. From time to time Charles and Laura looked at each other, but only when the other was looking away. Abi seemed unaware of the tension at the table and was more concerned about her lifeless mobile.

'Don't think I want any dessert. Is it okay if I go to my room?' she asked switching gaze from each parent, looking for support.

'No, Abi, you can wait until we've all finished,' Charles answered tartly. Laura was tempted to intercede and suggest she may as well leave the table but she thought better of it. Instead, the tension was maintained for another ten minutes before Abi was allowed to make her escape, unaware of the ticking bomb she was leaving behind.

'I've got quite a lot of homework tonight so I'll pop down to say goodnight later. I will have to do some research on the Internet for some of it'

'Oh, what research is that?' Laura enquired.

'We have to do a paper on the Roman Empire and compare its values with today's political scene.'

'Okay, but don't stay up too long.'

'I won't, Mum' the teenager replied, grabbing her phone and rushing upstairs.

When they were alone and clearing the table, Charles asked, 'So, what did you and Hayley talk about over lunch then?'

'Just the usual girlie stuff.'

'And what might that be?'

'She told me about a holiday she'd just been on and we talked about holidays we'd shared together. Why do you ask?'

'Just curious what you talk about, that's all.'

'Nothing to worry about,' Laura replied and straight away regretted it. This was the constant danger of walking on eggshells.

'Why should I be worried?' was Charles' eerily calm response. It was delivered in the sort of tone Laura imagined an assassin might use whilst setting up a hit.

'I didn't say you should be worried,' she replied as she continued to tidy up and avoid eye contact.

'It was implied … you said "nothing to worry about," which suggests there may have been something to worry about that you didn't discuss.'

'No, it doesn't and anyway, I'm not going to argue with you.'

'So, you decide what we are going to do or not do. Is that it?'

'Charles, you're raising the temperature for no reason at all,' Laura said in an attempt at a calming voice. Instead, it came out as condescending.

'I'm not aware of a rise in temperature unless ... there's something you're not telling me,' Charles replied with a menacing control.

'Like what?'

'Like what you really talk about with your little friend. Do you talk about us?'

'No! Why would I?'

'Exaggerating problems maybe, for sympathy.'

Laura was conflicted. She knew the danger signs well enough and her strong instinct was to avoid it but the suggestion of their problems being in her mind rather than real made her angry.

'How would you categorise our problems then?' she answered defiantly as she turned from the dishwasher.

He was calm for the moment as he put down the dishes he had been holding and replied smoothly,

'I would say you don't appreciate how hard I work for this family and how little I ask for in return. And I would add that you are a little on the cold side.'

'Really? Well it's difficult to feel warmth for someone who is argumentative and, when things aren't going their way, resorts to violence.'

'Oh, here we go again! I have apologised for that and anyway, you provoke me – you really do. No reasonable man could put up with it without ever snapping. You can be a very difficult woman and I'm only human.'

'My father never hit my mother and no other woman I know has been hit either,' Laura added, her courage growing.

'I don't hit you and anyway, what do you know about what happens behind closed doors?' Charles said seeming to be on the back foot.

'I know my family well enough and I know I'm not going to live in fear anymore ... I KNOW THAT!' Laura shouted the last part to her utter surprise, but this sudden shift moved Charles to the front foot: he lunged at her unexpectedly, grabbed her shoulders and in so doing knocked the plate she was holding in a splintered crash to the floor. Charles's eyes were wide and ablaze with rage.

'What do you mean you're not going to live in fear?'

'Look at you now ... mad with rage and threat!'

'There you go again PUSHING ME ... making me act like ... like ... '

'Like the bully you are.'

Charles pulled his right arm back and clenched his fist to strike as his face contorted with anger.

'Go on! Punch me! Give me the reason to walk out you bastard and let everyone know what you're really like. Go on, do it ... DO IT!'

Charles was caught by the ferocity of Laura's response and unclenched his fist, but the fury was still present as he pulled Laura so close she had to tilt her head backwards to move away from his face.

'Don't you dare threaten me! And don't think I would

ever let you leave me. THAT WILL NEVER HAPPEN. You belong to me and you always will. I will never let you go and you will never embarrass me with my friends or family. I will never let you be with anyone else. NEVER under any circumstances. ANY circumstances at all … IS THAT CLEAR?'

Again, Laura felt the desire for Charles to hit her so hard that the pretence could be over. Images flashed through her head in milliseconds; images of her in a hospital bed with tubes and machines around her, friends and family crying at the bedside in total shock and support; images of Charles in police custody or even dead from self-inflicted wounds caused by shame; Abi vowing unconditional support and a monster uncovered. The spell was broken when Abi shouted from upstairs.

'Is everything all right? I thought I heard a crash.'

'Everything's fine, Abi… Mum just dropped a plate,' Charles replied. He let go of Laura and walked off into the living room. Laura glared at him; the threat that he would never let her go was ringing in her ears. She really was frightened now and believed him capable of more violence, maybe extreme violence. A feeling of being trapped enveloped her. She could see that he would stalk – or even kill her – if she left, rather than see her happy on her own and away from him. She had a feeling of clarity: she hated him and was terrified for herself and Abi.

Abi thought little of the explanation as she moved back into her room. She was more concerned with her iPad and the conversation she was having as well as wanting to keep it well away from her parents. She clicked back on to Snapchat and the conversation she was having with Harvey from San Francisco.

'Sorry, Harvey. That noise was a plate smashing, they tell me. As if. Must think I'm blind, deaf and dumb.'

'My parents are the same – always fighting and then pretending they weren't when I walk in. Then that shitty stuff about how important family is – how important I am. Stop fighting then if I am so freakin important!'

'Same here all the time. I told you Charles isn't my real dad. Sometimes he freaks me out.'

'Is he a paedo?'

'No, I don't think so but he did come into the bathroom a couple of weeks ago when I was having a shower. I screamed and he ran.'

'Sounds like a paedo to me.'

'Who knows? But I always make sure the door is locked now.'

'My dad is a weirdo and a perv.'

'Ouch!'

'Yeah. He likes to watch porn when he thinks we're all asleep. Weird stuff ... makes me sick.'

'Kiddie porn?'

'No just weird stuff with whips and crazy shit. He doesn't know how to hide the history on his laptop or that I have his password, so I get to see what the pervy bastard has been baking his eyeballs with.'

'Does your mum know?'

'No, she lives in La La land and would freak big style if she found out.'

'You make me laugh, Harvey! Don't know what I

would do if we couldn't talk every night.'

'Me too, Abi. I wish I could see you in person. I hate it here. My school stinks and I hate it at home. My brother left for college and that's all my folks talk about.'

'Why can't we Face Time?'

'I told you, I'm shy. I can't do that camera thing but I feel I can say anything to you like this and it's cool. You're like my only true friend and you make me feel normal.'

'What if we did meet?'

'That would be different we would just be hanging out which would be cool too.'

'Pity you're so far away.'

'Yeah but the folks are still talking about coming to London.'

'If they did, do you think you could get away for a bit?'

'Yeah, no problem. I looked at the train schedules and I could come spend the day with you, which would be cool as.'

'So, when are they coming?'

'Maybe a month or so. Maybe even sooner as Mum's sister is real bad, they say, and they want to get over to see her. She lives in Chelsea like the soccer team and we'd be staying in her place which is humungous, they tell me.'

'Maybe I could come and meet them as well?'

'Sure, but don't say anything to your folks yet coz mine would freak if they knew I had a friend in England.'

'Okay, Harvey. I would love to meet you for real.'

'Me too. Never felt so good with anybody like I feel with you. You look real pretty on the photo too.'

'You don't look too bad yourself, you smooth talker!' Abi smiled as the blush formed on her cheek and she looked at the image of Harvey on the picture she had printed from the account. Blond hair, slightly upturned nose and maybe a little young looking for fifteen but he looked good to her.

'You're the only person who gets me, Abi. I know it's only been a couple of weeks but I feel like we've known each other like, forever.'

'Me too, Harvey. Better go now, before Mum comes up and asks me what I'm doing. Talk to you tomorrow at the same time?'

'Sure, Abi. It's the only thing I look forward to all day xx.'

'Same here xx.'

Abi closed the page, picked up the photo of Harvey and kissed it. 'Good night, my love.'

Harvey closed the page and the heavily tattooed arm of a forty six year old balding man closed the laptop and winked at his associate.

Chapter 17

'Hello, David, Andy Connolly here. I need to see you again.'

'Oh, hi Andy. Has something else come up?'

'Yes, but I don't want to talk about it on the phone. Can I come into the station and see you and your sergeant?'

'Well I'm out of the office today and Patrick's not in town. Is there some reason you need Patrick there?'

'Not really, but three heads are better than two,' Andy winced, realising how ridiculous it sounded.

'Look, I can be over to see you in an hour or so. How does that sound?'

'Yeah that's fine. See you then.'

Andy put his phone on the desk and shook his head at how badly he had played that and how easily he was controlled in the conversation. The idea that he had started with was the extra insurance of another policeman there but how did he know if he needed it and how did he know that if Cooper was corrupt that his sergeant Patrick Ames was not as well? He felt like his hands were nowhere near the steering wheel of his life.

His next call was to his ex-wife Hannah. There was a moment's delay as he composed himself to think about the tone he should adopt and how he would open the conversation. He spoke to her often but only about arrangements for the children and money. She was not difficult as such but an awkwardness lay between them now, even on the phone. They both knew they had to move on but both felt a sense of sadness in their dealings with one another; a sense of lost opportunity, wasted investment … a sense of bereavement. Yes, that was it; the end of their relationship was like a death – a death for which Andy felt entirely responsible.

As he looked at his phone and Hannah's name staring back at him, he thought of times spent together, when they were happy and she was a woman not just a mother. Times when they laughed and played and were lost in each other's lives, which were so intertwined with each other's. They would speak every day on the phone, even when they lived together, and share every piece of news – good or bad – like excited children. Andy shook himself from his reflective mood and pressed the green button.

'Hello, Hannah, I'm not disturbing you, am I?' he surprised himself with the politeness of the words and tone.

'No, I was just starting to … No, you aren't disturbing me,' she replied with an inquisitive intonation.

'I wondered if I could meet you for coffee later today, if you're free.'

'It's not about the house again, is it?' she replied with a touch of agitation.

'No, it's not. I just want to have a chat about something … no big deal but not over the phone and not in front of the kids so I was thinking about two if that suits you.'

'I suppose so. Do you mean here at the house?'

'If that's okay?'

'Well, half of it is still yours.'

'Can we meet in that half then?' he added and they both laughed a truncated laugh.

'Okay, see you at two, Hannah. Thanks.'

'See you then.' Hannah immediately ran down a list of possibilities for the discussion. The one that sprang to mind was Andy telling her he was going to marry Rebecca and therefore needed to turn their separation into divorce. They had agreed all of the terms of the separation and had lawyers draw up a formal document but had decided they would divorce later, when the children were used to things and wouldn't be upset as much. Had he decided now was the time and he wanted to re-marry? She wasn't ready for that. She knew their relationship was over but she wasn't ready for him to be married to anyone else, or for the children to see anyone else as a stepmother. Hannah's pulse quickened and an unpleasant feeling settled in her stomach.

Andy had a short discussion with the sales team, then instructed Andrea to send in the police officer when he arrived. Otherwise, he said, he didn't want to take any calls. He closed the door to his office. He reckoned he had half an hour or so to plan for his meeting with Cooper. Whenever he was planning, he always did it on paper, rather than electronic equipment. There was something real and connecting about holding a pen and writing on a blank piece of paper. It made him feel in control of his thoughts and, more importantly, his reasoning. Taking the time to write forced him to think at a controlled rate and it calmed him down, even in difficult times.

When he separated from Hannah, he had done it several times when he felt an intense sense of loss caused by his own carelessness. One list reminded him what he could retain in his life, including the love and support of his parents and his sister, as well as always being a father to his children. The list on finances had been more troubling but it proved helpful in terms of driving him on to earn more from his core business, as well as looking for other business opportunities.

One thing he knew was that he was the world expert on Andy Connolly. He knew what made him tick; he was aware of his weaknesses and not overly modest about his strengths – but nor did he overestimate them. He knew how to motivate himself, to calculate what needed to be done in most situations and was not afraid of failure, however painful it might be. This latest list was to try and calculate the danger he was in and how he might reduce that risk.

The first point he wrote down was DCI Cooper; could he trust him? The list of pros and cons about Cooper made him feel uncomfortable, as there were no firm facts to enable him to reach a conclusion. On balance, his instinct was to cooperate with Cooper, largely because he had little alternative. He thought back to the phone conversation at the cafe and wondered again if Cooper had told Tasker or the man on the phone about the ID parade and other conversations they'd had. He decided to talk to Cooper, assuming everything he said was being reported to Tasker; that way he would be covering all eventualities.

The next list included those at risk of action from Tasker and his associates. Andy himself was top of the list, then Rebecca but naming his children on paper sent a chill down his spine. He added his sister and his parents as possibilities. Places in jeopardy included his garage and home, along with the house Hannah shared with their children. Just as Andrea buzzed to say DCI Cooper had arrived, Andy decided he was being paranoid and overreacting. Cooper walked in with his palpable air of control that Andy found so reassuring.

'Hello, David.' He met Cooper with a warm handshake and asked Andrea to bring them some coffee and to make sure they weren't disturbed.

'So, I gather something else has happened Andy. Why don't you bring me up to speed?' Cooper's relaxed approach was evident in his body language; he sat, legs crossed with his fingers tapping gently on the arms of the chair.

Andy told him the whole story of how he'd been approached in the café, but made a point of saying he had involved his solicitors; how they knew everything and were there to protect him.

'So, as you can see, David, I'm obviously at risk and need to know what levels of protection you can offer to my family and me.'

'Okay, Andy. I'm sorry this has happened. It must have been frightening, but I can assure you we will look after you and take whatever steps necessary to ensure your safety.'

'What steps are we talking about?'

'Well, firstly I don't think Tasker or anyone else intends to harm you. I think that Tasker – if indeed this guy is associated with him – might try to intimidate you, but you don't look like the kind of guy who is easily intimidated.'

'Don't be fooled by appearances. I'm really worried about what they'll do next. I said no to the cash but I have a family to think about. The truth is, I'm shitting myself.'

Cooper paused and let this sink in, before responding.

'Well, what we could do is set up a meeting in which you agree to take the money and we nab them there and then – charge them with attempting to pervert the course of justice, which is a serious offence. If Tasker is connected, that would add to his list of charges and extend his holiday inside.'

Andy hesitated.

'Yes, but we talked about this before. That course of action really makes me a target for revenge by his family or business partners.'

'As soon as he's nailed, he'll be toast in his world – trust me. He has a small network but they're small-time. They'll melt away once he's inside.'

'What about the Baldwin brothers?' Andy persisted. The usually unflappable Cooper failed to hide his surprise at the mention of their names.

'What about them?'

'How are they likely to react to all of this?'

'So … how do you know of them?'

'I've made my own enquiries.'

'I wouldn't do that, Andy. You don't necessarily know what you are getting into. This is our job. The Baldwin brothers are known to us, but I doubt they're involved in this case. We need to concentrate on this particular case and getting a result.'

There was a moment's hesitation as Andy thought of raising the stakes, of asking who exactly the result was for or how well Cooper knew the Baldwins. He decided against it.

'I'm not keen to do the set-up thing and get more

involved – I just want to know how I can be protected.'

'What I can do is give you a phone – a direct link to me and a specialist team so that if, for any reason, you can't use your own phone, you just press the call button and we'll trace where you are and be with you within minutes. The phone would be on a permanent trace so you'd have to always keep it with you. We can have the uniforms keep a check on your house and place of work, as well as making sure CCTV cameras in the area are trained towards them.'

'What about my kids?'

'I think you have to be careful not to get carried away here. There's no reason to assume your kids are at risk and there's nothing to suggest they will be, but if that does happen, we will of course act very quickly. I don't see it happening though.'

'Okay, David, thanks for that. When do I get the phone?'

'I'll get it to you later today.'

At 1.50pm Andy pulled up a hundred yards or so away from his former home and looked at it. The garden wasn't as tidy as when he'd lived there. Some shrubs were overgrown and needed pruning and weeds were beginning to show on the driveway that he had always kept so immaculate. Bleakly, Andy thought the house was showing signs of the love that had been lost. He composed himself, ordered his thoughts and drove the short distance on to the drive. Even though he had a key, he rang the bell and waited.

Hannah answered almost immediately. He could see she had made an effort: her slightly curled shoulder-length brown hair was recently washed and her lipstick was his favourite light red and freshly applied. She had never struggled with her weight, but she looked especially trim in her jeans and loose-fitting top, which revealed one shoulder and a glimpse of her shapely chest.

'Hello, Andy, nice of you to ring the bell,' she said with genuine feeling rather than sarcasm. They hesitated for a second or two, both wondering whether or not to greet the other with a kiss but after a couple of seconds, eventually they just walked into the living room. Hannah asked if he wanted a coffee and when he declined, they sat opposite each other on the matching sofas. Hannah was nervously steeling herself for the news of a wedding and was determined not to cry or become angry.

Andy spoke first.

'Feels strange to be sitting here as a guest. Surreal almost.'

'Yeah, I know what you mean,' she replied.

'So, Hannah, you know that accident I had a few weeks ago.'

'Accident? I thought you saw somebody get attacked. That's what I was told.'

'Well yes, I did see that, but the attacker ran into the back of my car, then stabbed the guy in the car in front.'

'Stabbed? I didn't know that. I thought there was a scuffle or something – some random road-rage thing. But stabbed? How is he?'

'Oh, he pulled through.'

'Pulled through? You mean he might have died?' she asked, wide eyed.

'He might have. In fact, at the scene he thought he was

going to, but they told me on the phone what to look for – you know, colour of blood and stuff – and to keep him comfortable.'

'You were there on your own with him?'

'I was for a while. Then the ambulance and police came and he was taken to hospital and into intensive care.'

'Oh, Andy! I really didn't know it was that serious,' Hannah said, wiping away a single tear. She tried to make the movement casually, whilst trying to hide it from her former husband.

'It all happened so quickly and I was winded when he attacked me.'

'Attacked you? Nobody told me anything about that. Did he stab you?'

'No, no, he stabbed the other guy after he hit me.'

'So, he could have stabbed you?' With that, the single tear was replaced by a trembling chin, then a stream of tears as Hannah's hands covered her face. The fear of hearing news of her husband remarrying was swept away, replaced with a greater emotion: the thought of losing him altogether. Her defences crumbled.

'Come on, Han. It's all right now. I'm all right,' Andy said, not knowing whether to move and comfort her.

'Oh my God, Andy! I don't know what to say or think. You could have been killed. The children … what would I have said? How would I have told them?' The sobbing continued in earnest.

Andy did move over this time and put his arm around Hannah's trembling shoulders but although the tears continued, she froze at his touch. He handed her a tissue and she slowly composed herself, allowing him to return to his seat.

'The thing is, Hannah, the police want me to give evidence against this guy. I was able to identify him so he's been charged.'

'That's good, I suppose. Will he go to prison then?' she replied, wiping her eyes and doing her best to compose herself.

'Probably, yes.'

'Probably? He stabbed somebody and they could have died.'

'Yes, but there has to be a trial and he may plead not guilty.'

'How can he do that if you saw him do it and the man who was stabbed can say it was him?'

Andy was losing confidence in telling Hannah everything. Her reaction to his part in the incident had thrown him and he doubted she was strong enough to hear about the possible dangers. On the other hand, he felt he needed to warn her to be careful, to take greater care of the children, but he didn't know how much to say.

'The guy is out on bail. So we should just be a little more cautious, that's all.'

'What? He got bail? And what do you mean we have to be cautious? Is he going to come after you? Or the children?' A look of rising panic flashed in Hannah's eyes. This was not going well.

'No, we don't think so but just to be absolutely safe, there are a couple of things we can do.'

'Like what?'

'I can arrange for somebody to take the kids to school

and collect them every day if I can't do it. And maybe for a while, we just keep a closer eye on them.'

'Oh my God, Andy! You're really scaring me. You think somebody might snatch the kids?'

'No, I don't … of course not, but why take any risks?'

Andy decided against telling Hannah about the money he'd been offered, or the threat he'd received, or his doubts about DCI Cooper. Instead, he did his best to reassure her and made a joke about his paranoia but regardless, she was properly spooked. They talked about a few other domestic matters before he got up to leave. At the door he spontaneously held her shoulders, leaned forward and kissed her forehead. As he did, she put her arms around him and hugged him tightly as tears came once again.

'It will be all right Hannah. Try not to worry. I just needed you to know everything,' Andy said, realising guiltily that he wasn't, in fact, telling her everything. She let go and looked a little embarrassed as he pulled away and walked to his car. Andy waved as he reversed out of the driveway and Hannah slowly closed the front door. He felt confused and raw. Which was why he failed to notice the black Mitsubishi Shogun parked opposite the house start up and follow him.

Chapter 18

Rebecca was sitting in the reception area at the garage awaiting her ten o'clock appointment. Somebody had called and asked for her by name, wanting a test drive of the new sports coupe. Mr and Mrs Drysdale was the couple's name. It was now 10.10am and they hadn't arrived. Rebecca had asked Andrea to call them, but she said the contact number they had left was unobtainable. Minutes later, a breathless good-looking man in his late thirties hurried into the showroom, spoke to Andrea and was pointed in Rebecca's direction.

'I'm so sorry I'm late! My wife got a call from her mother and had to dash to take her to the doctor. Sorry ... I'm Michael Drysdale,' said the man extending his right hand.

Rebecca stood, shook his hand, introduced herself and asked if he wanted to re-schedule the appointment. He was here now, he said, and might as well have the test drive and come back another time with his wife. Rebecca nodded, collected the keys and told Andrea she was going.

When they reached the car, Mr Drysdale asked, 'Do you mind if I drive, Rebecca? I get nothing from being a passenger.'

'No of course not ... please, help yourself. I will sit in the passenger seat.'

The car was parked on the forecourt and the confident Mr Drysdale pulled out carefully on to the main road and turned right.

'There's a turning on the left, Mr Drysdale, which will take you out on to the dual carriageway. It's a good place to test the acceleration and handling of this model.'

'Call me Peter, please Rebecca.'

'Okay, Peter it is. It's this left coming up.'

They drove past the turning.

'If it's all right with you, I'd like to go this way – drive on roads I travel on every day. It's perhaps a mile or two more but I already like the road holding and the feel of the car.'

'Yes, that's absolutely fine, Peter,' Rebecca responded. They drove for several minutes and Drysdale entertained Rebecca with his cheerful, slightly flirty chat as he asked about her job, whether she had targets to reach and if being a woman made it easier to sell. Rebecca answered his questions whilst thinking this was a very real potential sale. She was already planning her approach about finance and trade-in options when she realised they were getting close to where she lived.

'Oh, I live not far from here,' she said and instantly regretted it.

'Do you? We must be near neighbours then,' Drysdale replied as he indicated left, turning into Rebecca's street.

'Where do you live, Peter?'

'We've just rented a property about a mile from here in Franklin Street or Frederick Street … something like that.'

'Franklin Drive?'

'Yes, that's it,' he answered, slowing outside Rebecca's house.

Rebecca stopped herself confirming this was her home. She was beginning to feel uncomfortable.

'Why are we stopping here?' she asked nervously.

'Really nice area this. Maybe we'll look to buy in this

street. Any idea how much these properties go for?'

'No, not a clue.' Rebecca tried to control her nerves.

'Is this a safe neighbourhood? You know, is there much crime around here? Is it a safe place for a woman to wander around at night?'

'How would I know?' she replied with a slightly aggressive tone.

'I thought you said you lived here.'

'No, I said we were on our way to where I live.'

'Oh, so it isn't here then?' came his reply, alarming Rebecca further.

'I thought you were testing the car, Peter,' she replied, ramping up the aggression.

'Sorry, Rebecca, I seem to have offended you. I didn't mean to – I was just chatting.'

'No, I apologise, Peter. I shouldn't have snapped. I'm a bit tetchy at the moment.'

'No problem,' he answered, with a dismissive wave of the hand. 'Shall we go back?'

'Yes please.'

They drove back to the garage, but Rebecca still had a sense of unease and, despite Drysdale's apology, he looked very calm – not uncomfortable at all. Wouldn't a man who felt the need to apologise feel a little embarrassed? And why had he slowed down outside of her house? They chatted lightly but she was relieved to see the garage forecourt ahead and even more so when the car pulled on to it.

'So, what do you think, Peter?'

'Very impressed. With everything.'

'Do you want to come in and discuss details?'

'Not today. I need to talk to my wife but rest assured, I won't deal with anyone but you. I hope we'll see each other soon.'

Rebecca was used to flirty men and, as an attractive woman, compliments and flirting were nothing new to her. This however, seemed different. He held her gaze for a second or two and she was disquieted by the fact she couldn't tell if his looks were flirting or … vaguely menacing.

'If I'm not in, you can always deal with one of my colleagues.'

'Oh, I would never do that, Rebecca! Not now we're neighbours,' he replied with a wink, before turning and walking off the site.

It was only after he had gone that Rebecca wondered where he had gone. Had he driven to the garage? If so, where had he parked? Did somebody drop him off and were they waiting to pick him up? She hurried out to the back of the building to see if she could see him but there was no sign. Perspiring a little, she dashed back into reception and asked Andrea if she had noticed anything about the last customer.

'Which one?'

'Peter Drysdale.'

'Who's he?'

'That's what I am asking you,' she snapped.

'Do you mean the test drive you just did?'

'Yes.'

Andrea flicked through her notepad feeling a little under pressure and irritated at Rebecca's tone.

'Yes, here it is: Mr and Mrs Drysdale interested in the diesel 220 XL asked for test drive with Rebecca.'

'Contact details?'

'Mobile number 07718 922435.'

'Ring it, please.'

Andrea did so but received the number unobtainable bleep. Rebecca heard its constant hum.

'What does that mean?'

'It means the number is not in use.'

'Did you make the booking?'

'I think so.'

'So, did you take down the wrong number?'

'It's possible, but unlikely. I never normally do as I always repeat the number to the customer. What are you trying to say?' Andrea replied, going on the offensive. Rebecca might be Andy's current girlfriend but Andrea had known him a lot longer than she had and was not about to be bullied.

'Sorry, Andrea. I'm not saying anything. It was just that he was … I don't know … he acted strangely. A little creepy.'

'How do you mean?' Andrea replied, softening her tone.

'Not sure really, but it didn't feel right. Is Andy in?'

'Yes, he's in a meeting with the manufacturer's rep but shouldn't be too long.'

'Thanks, Andrea … and sorry if I barked.'

'No problem. I'll watch out for the creep. Probably just fancied himself … and you!' she laughed.

Andy's meeting went on for almost another hour and as he walked his guest to the door, Rebecca slid into his office to wait. He came back in, still smiling from his banter with the rep.

'Hello! Were you missing me?' he remarked lightly, still feeling a buzz from the meeting. Rebecca ignored the remark and told the tale of her meeting with Drysdale, the drive to their house, the awkward pause outside and the conversation. Andy listened intently.

'So, this guy took a test drive and drove twelve miles to our house?'

'Yes.'

'Did you try and stop him?'

'How would I stop him? He was driving!'

'You could have asked him to turn around or why he was going so far.'

'So, it was my fault?'

'No, I'm not saying that, I am just trying to get a hold on what happened.'

'He stopped outside of our house, that's what happened,' Rebecca added sharply.

'He actually stopped outside our home?'

'Well, he slowed down and almost stopped but it was weird. More than weird.'

'Did he threaten you?'

'No, not exactly but it wasn't normal and he was … he sort of … he kind of hinted that he knew about me and knew where I lived.'

'Hinted?'

'Oh, for God's sake, Andy! You sound like the police. I was fucking scared, all right?'

'Sorry. I think we're both a bit on edge. Do you want me to ring the police?'

'And tell them what? A man was flirty on a test drive and may or may not know where I live and took a circuitous route. They'd think I was crazy – like you obviously do.'

Andy moved over to her and rubbed her shoulders but she was rigid and tense.

'It may be nothing, Rebecca, but we'll take extra care. I think we ought to start coming into work together for a while. I don't know if something's going on or not, or if it's connected in any way to this stabbing thing. I met with DCI Cooper again and they're going to step up security, though he reckons they wouldn't dare try anything with us.'

'How can he know that?'

'I suppose he can't, but the point is, we'll get whatever protection we need.'

Rebecca turned and kissed him. She managed to stop a tear that was threatening to fall, before saying she would get on with some work.

As soon as she was outside, she dabbed the corners of her eyes with a tissue. She was worried, very worried.

After she left, Andy thought about ringing Cooper but decided there was nothing substantial to tell him. He felt like an open target with no real idea of which direction to take for cover. He wanted to talk to his dad or his sister, or even Rebecca but he didn't want to worry them. He knew he'd upset Hannah with the little he had told her and so decided to carry the burden alone. At least for now.

DCI Cooper pulled up outside his sergeant's house and Patrick Ames, who was waiting for him, opened the door and jumped in.

'So, what do you want to do about our friend Newcombe, boss?'

'What did he say to you yesterday?'

'The same old shit – he wasn't sure now about the ID. Thought maybe he was in shock.'

'Did you lean on him?'

'No. I thought I'd talk to you first and we could decide on a game plan.'

'Was his girlfriend there? What's her name?'

'Kate,' Ames replied.

'Yes, that's her. Frightened little rabbit, isn't she? Let's get them both together and turn up the heat.'

'At the station or their place?'

'Their place. Let's relax them first and then move in.'

'Okay, boss. I'll tell them we'll call on them tonight about six so they're nice and hungry when we talk to them.'

'You are a bastard, Paddy.'

'Learned it all from you, boss!'

They both laughed but Cooper looked out of the window, wondering whether or not Newcombe's evidence was going to be what he hoped for. It was a complicated game he was playing.

Chapter 19

Later that same day, Cooper provided Andy with his new phone and a quick lesson on how to use it. He reminded him that he should keep it with him at all times so that they knew where he was, and was familiar with the emergency system that would have them running to his aid. He also repeated that he thought it unnecessary, and that police cars would be patrolling the areas of Andy's home and work. Even so, Andy was glad to have it and even made Cooper laugh when he asked if things became really bad, could he arrange for 'Scotty' to beam him up to the Starship Enterprise. Cooper told him he hadn't taken him for a Star Trek fan but would see what he could do. As for Rebecca, she had relaxed a little and was beginning to think she'd imagined some of her fears about Drysdale, particularly as he hadn't been back in touch. Hannah, in stark contrast, was in a heightened state of agitation when walking the children to Andy's car and she was at the school a full thirty minutes before the end of each school day to collect them. She noticed every car, parent, relative, nanny and teacher.

Andy's phone buzzed as he was doing a stock check. He took it out of his pocket, smiled and accepted the call.

'Hi Dad, how's it going?'

'Fine for me, but I'm not in trouble with the police. Are you still on the run?'

'Very funny. Still one step ahead of the mob.'

'How did things go with Tony Sanderson?'

'He was great, Dad – he put my mind at rest.'

'Cheeky bastard wouldn't tell me anything because of

all this client confidentiality stuff, even when I reminded him how much I've paid them over the years.'

Andy proceeded to tell his father the whole story, omitting the quasi threat in the cafe and Rebecca's experience. He didn't want his father to worry too much; he wanted to sort it out himself. His dad asked some questions about the legal proceedings and what the police were doing, but Andy realised he knew little about it himself. He was relieved when the conversation switched to football and Hull City's latest struggles.

'Were you at the last home game, Dad?'

'Was I there? I should have been playing! I'm still faster than either of our wide midfielders and your mum is a better tackler than our new centre back. We lost two nil and we were lucky to get nil.'

'Glad you're still enjoying it so much,' Andy chuckled and they chatted for a few more minutes.

After he'd hung up, Andy leaned back in his chair and thought of a customer who had ordered a car a couple of months ago. He was about the same age as his dad. In fact, he reminded him a lot of his dad in some of his mannerisms and, in particular, the way he held a gaze. It made you think he could see into your mind ... or maybe smell the bullshit. Anyway, Andy had warmed to the man. Two weeks before the car was to be collected, the man's son came into the showroom. He said his father had collapsed and, after being rushed to hospital, had died. He offered to forfeit the deposit if Andy would cancel the order; the car would be too big for his mum to drive comfortably. Without hesitation, Andy had cancelled the order and returned the deposit. He found out the details of the funeral and went to the church on the day, standing discreetly at the back. The distress of the man's widow and the son as they walked in behind the coffin had instantly touched him and he found himself unable to control his emotions. That could have been his mother walking behind the coffin of her life's love. That son could have been him comforting his mother, whilst feeling totally lost himself. As he watched, he felt for his handkerchief.

Ever since that day he had meant to spend a little more time with his dad but hadn't managed to get round to it – life had a habit of getting in the way. Now they were talking a little more often, Andy tried to stave off the picture of one day being without that voice on the end of a telephone, that encyclopaedia of information and wisdom that was his father.

★ ★ ★

David Cooper and Patrick Ames stood outside Newcombe's flat and rang the doorbell for the second time. They heard two locks being disconnected and then the door opened on a security chain as Kate Brown peered out through the gap the chain allowed.

'Hello, Kate. Can we come in and have a word with you and Gary please?'

'Oh yes, of course!' she replied as she tried to open the door with the chain still in place, establishing that this was a new security addition. After some fumbling she managed to open the door and they walked through into the living room before she left to make some tea. Gary was watching daytime television and turned towards them as they crowded into the tiny room.

'Hello, Gary, still on with the gameshows then?' Cooper said playfully.

'Oh, er … I … I don't like them really, but there isn't much else to do until I get back to work.'

'Do you know when that might be?'

'The doctor says it might be in the next six weeks or so but they're still doing blood tests and stuff.'

'Do you get out much?'

'No. We stay in most nights but we had a little drive out the other day to the shopping centre.'

'Are you not supposed to go out?'

'No, it's not that. It's just that Kate is a bit nervous now, you know about going out and, well, just being out really.'

'That's a shame. Is everything all right?' Cooper asked.

'How do you mean?' Gary answered as Ames sat silently, staring intently at him – that look that some police officers have of unnerving people; a look of waiting to pounce, of unspoken disbelief in what they are hearing.

'You seem a little bit nervous to me, even just chatting,' Cooper probed.

'No, no, I'm just stressed with it all, you know … being off work and the tablets and tests and then all the questions,' Gary stumbled and looked away.

'What questions are you worried about, Gary?' Cooper pressed.

'I don't know … I just worry that … I mean I can't really say things that I don't remember. I just get confused when

I think about it all,' Gary added whilst looking round the room for something to look at, some support or distraction as his face coloured.

At that moment Kate came in carrying a tray of tea and biscuits and the tension was released a little.

'I couldn't remember who takes sugar so I brought the bowl in and you can help yourselves. I think everyone takes milk, don't they?' she said whilst looking uncomfortable and placing the tray on the coffee table with very unsteady hands.

'Looks perfect, Kate. Biscuits too! We'll get fat, won't we, Sarge'?' Cooper said to Ames with a grin. The smile wasn't returned as Ames stood, leaned over and tipped two full teaspoons of sugar in his cup.

'How long have you two been in this flat then?' Cooper asked, as though passing the time of day.

'About a year now isn't it, Gary? We're just renting but we have been saving for a deposit on our own place. They're building some lovely flats just outside of town and you can get a nice two bed for a reasonable price if you're a first-time buyer.'

'They do those affordable homes, don't they?' Cooper replied. 'Reduced prices or help with the costs or something. It was in the paper the other day.'

'Yes, we looked at a few options but we couldn't afford some of them until we saved up the deposit. We didn't like the shared ownership thing. My dad says we should own it all or just keep renting,' Kate rambled on as Gary squirmed.

'My mate has a son buying one of those flats, I think. They're about 120 grand or so, aren't they?'

'Well, the Dunmore flats are 129 but the Hinchcliffe flats are ten grand less.'

'So, what is the best mortgage you can get then?'

'We went into the building society a few weeks ago and they told us we can borrow 90% on the Hinchcliffe with our salaries.'

'You better be quick. My mate told me they were selling like hot cakes and he thought his son might miss out,' Cooper said whilst spreading the web.

'We've paid the reservation fee so we should be okay.'

'Ah well that should be secure then,' Cooper concluded having the information he needed. 'So, Gary, we wanted to go through your statement again. The one you made when you spoke to the officer after the attack,' Cooper said as he pulled the handwritten sheets from his briefcase, causing Gary to shift anxiously in his seat.

'Let me see now. Yes, here we are on page three. "The man walked up to me and was obviously very aggressive. He called me a 'wanker' and asked why I had stopped. I told him he had crashed into the car behind and the accident was his fault. The other man got out of his car and as he approached us the first man headbutted me causing me to fall back on to my car." You describe the fight and the other man being attacked and go on to say, "the man who attacked me was over six feet tall and I would say was heavily built. He was wearing a black shirt, black trousers and had fairly long, dark, greasy hair that was combed back behind his ears. He was a white male but I would describe his skin colour as swarthy or suntanned. I think he was wearing a Rolex-type watch on his left arm and had a signet ring on his ring finger on his right hand." Do you remember saying that, Gary?'

'Well I must have, but I was in shock and I'd just been stabbed. I think the policeman maybe told me something or came up with part of the description.'

'How could that be, Gary? The police officer hadn't seen the man and had no idea who attacked you. How could he have come up with a description?'

'Maybe he got it from the other guy who was there.'

'That officer didn't interview the other witness. He was interviewed later by another police force. Now let me read you what you told my sergeant last time he spoke to you: "I cannot say for sure how tall my assailant was or be sure of the colour of his hair. It all happened so fast I don't think I would be able to identify the man who attacked me" Is that more or less what you said?'

At this point Kate was beginning to tremble and her face was changing from a healthy pink to a very pale white. Gary was beginning to perspire and had adopted a wide-eyed expression; a mixture of anxious and furious.

'Look, I don't know what you want from me. I didn't ask to be attacked and you're treating me like a criminal. I mean, do I need to have a lawyer or something?'

'Why would you need a lawyer, Gary? Have you done something that you don't want us to know about? Something you're not sure about perhaps?' Cooper answered in a cool, controlled manner.

This was too much for Kate who burst into tears and dropped her cup and saucer on to the carpet splashing tea on to the chair where Cooper was sitting.

'Now look what you have done!' Gary shouted as he got up to comfort his girlfriend. Cooper stood up too, checked for tea stains on his trousers and signalled to Ames it was time to go.

He turned to the distressed couple. 'I'm sorry you're upset, Kate but I'm not satisfied about things here, and so we'll have to come back in a couple of days. Have a little think about your evidence, Gary, but we will be talking some more about this.'

The warm smile had gone from Cooper's face; it had been replaced by a determined expression.

Patrick Ames closed the driver's door and turned to Cooper, who was gazing straight ahead.

'So, what do you make of that then boss?'

'He's lying through his teeth, isn't he?'

'So, what do you think has happened?'

'I think he's been paid off, maybe threatened. What I want you to do Paddy is check the bank details of our couple here and see what funds they had the day before the knifing. They need twelve grand for a deposit, as well as legal fees, plus they've paid the reservation fee. If they weren't close to having the deposit before the night of the attack, then their finances have had a big boost at some point since. Something has given them the confidence to reserve that property. I think they've been nobbled and you're going to get me the proof.'

'Yes, boss.'

Two hours later Damien Baldwin's phone rang at Silks restaurant at Chepstow race track. He put up his right hand, signalling to his brother Alfie that he was taking the call.

'Yeah?'

'Can you talk?'

'Yeah.'

'The first rider has been nobbled we think and is looking to miss the race.'

'And the second?'

'Not sure.'

'Keep me informed.'

'Will do.'

As he put the phone back in the top pocket of his Savile Row suit, he turned to his brother without altering his expression.

'Looks like we may need to ramp things up.'

Chapter 20

It's all too easy to watch a clear blue sky and think what a beautiful day it is, without being aware of the storm that is relentlessly approaching. Not being able to see a dark cloud doesn't mean it won't be with you soon.

Andy was laughing with Peter Thomson as he heard how one sale had led to two more. Thomson had used his closing pitch to get the telephone details of the customer's next-door neighbour and then his brother, both of which had produced the business. It was a double dose of pleasure for Andy to hear of three new sales towards this month's target, plus the anecdote from his best salesman was so good he knew he would be telling it sometime soon in a pub or a restaurant.

It had been a few days since anything significant had happened and he had somehow begun to believe that the police phone in his pocket was some kind of lucky charm or force field protecting him. He was beginning to remember how things were before his preoccupation with the accident. He looked through the sales office window and watched Rebecca walk past wearing a tight red dress that showed off her trim sexy body. The dress was three or four inches short of her knees and when she sat at her desk the tight material climbed up her tanned legs and reminded him of how much he was still physically attracted to her. She seemed to sense his attention and smiled a knowing smile. Yes, things were definitely looking up.

Sergeant Ames gave a quiet knock on Cooper's door and entered, closing the door behind him.

'Got that info for you on the Newcombe purchase, boss.'

'Ah, good man, Paddy, what have you found out?'

'Well, they have a joint account with the Nationwide which they opened thirteen months ago with £280. They've been paying £150 a month into it since, although they missed a payment in December – probably to buy Christmas presents. So, as of last night, they had a balance of … just let me find it here, yes here it is £1,942 and a few pence.'

'So, their deposit was twelve grand or so wasn't it?'

'Yes. And they paid a reservation fee of £500 but that didn't come out of this Nationwide account either. They have separate current accounts with Santander and the £500 was paid with Gary's credit card, which has a debit balance of just under two grand. He's never been more overdrawn than that.'

'What's his limit on the card?'

'Five grand.'

'And Kate's?'

'Two grand, but she's never overdrawn.'

'When is the full deposit due?'

'In five weeks' time.'

'So, they have to find ten grand or so in that time?'

'Yes, boss … unless somebody has dropped them a few quid.'

'What about parents?'

'Gary only has a mother who lives in a rented house and works at Morrison's. Kate's parents live in a former council property in Birmingham, which they bought at a big discount and has a small mortgage. Her dad works at B&Q in the stores department and her mum doesn't work. Can't see any money coming from parents.'

'No other accounts then?'

'No. If they have been paid, it must be in cash and my guess is it's at home. Do you want a warrant to search the place?'

'No. Not yet anyway. I think we'll pay them another visit.'

'What about the motor dealer, boss?'

'What about him?'

'Do you want me to check his accounts?'

'Nah, what's the point? He has large sums coming and going on a regular basis so he could hide it pretty easily. Anyway, I don't think he is doing that because he's told us about approaches, hasn't he? I'll stay in touch with him though – keep an eye on him. What's the score on Tasker? Is Johnny Mulville's team keeping up with him?'

'Pretty much. He's out and about and keeping up his profile so he doesn't lose his supply chain or his place on the greasy pole. Johnny said he could have nicked him at the weekend – they had enough on him for a supply charge but you said no.'

'Yeah, I stopped that one because it would have been a distraction. If we're going to get him on supply it has to be a bigger shipment and a lead to his suppliers. He's just a dangerous thug – we want a bigger prize than just him. We need to keep watching him.'

'Okay, boss, anything you say.'

Laura Peterson pulled into the health club car park and checked her handbag for her ticket. There it was in gold lettering: 'All-day spa. Access all areas.' She smiled to herself at the prospect of a pampering treatment and a bottle of Prosecco with Hayley. She was a little early and so texted Hayley to say she would meet her in the pool area. She had good reason to be changing on her own.

Having checked in, she went into the ladies changing area and saw that a cubicle was free so she opened the door and locked it behind her. She was not normally overly modest but wanted to be careful today. She had chosen her dark blue one-piece swimming costume as it was a little on the big side and covered more flesh than her pink one. A bikini was out of the question. She took off her silk shirt and pulled off her skinny jeans before turning to the full-length mirror to look at herself in her underwear. Angry bruises bloomed at the very top of her thighs and she moved closer to the mirror to inspect them. She had thought they were smaller when she checked them this morning but now she worried she wouldn't be able to conceal them. She removed her bra and looked at the bruise on her left breast, then the red marks on her right breast. She was less concerned with those as the costume fully concealed them. The older bruises around her neck had almost vanished and the scratch on her scalp was completely covered by her hair. She took off her underwear and pulled on the swimming costume. To her utter dismay, it not only failed to hide the bruising below her pelvic area, but almost highlighted the bruises. She flushed with embarrassment and concern and wondered why she hadn't thought to cancel. She knew why: she needed this day, this time with her friend and the thought of missing it was too hard to contemplate. Anyway, they had arranged this two weeks ago; Hayley would have been too suspicious if she had cancelled yesterday.

Two days ago, Laura had come home, prepared the meal and helped Abi with her history homework. They both loved history and enjoyed chatting about it before Abi completed her essay. The meal had been a quiet affair and, maybe because Abi looked so content with her night's work, Laura had felt a little more relaxed. Even Charles seemed to be in a good mood, opening a bottle of red wine to have with the meal and asking Abi if she would like a little taste. She said she would but promptly frowned, telling Charles it was gross.

Once Abi had gone to bed, the couple even had a nightcap. Laura had gone upstairs as usual at around eleven and had read for a few minutes before putting her light off and drifting off to sleep. It was about an hour later that she felt Charles get into bed beside her and move his cold legs into the back of her bed warm legs. She was startled by the change of temperature which woke her and was about to object when she felt his firm hand on her shoulder pulling her over towards him. Before she had a chance to react, Charles had covered her mouth with his and kissed her roughly. He forced his tongue into her mouth at the same time as pushing her legs apart with his knee. So sudden was this movement that she didn't have time to react.

They had not had sex in several weeks; Charles had shown no inclination and she had no desire. The evening had gone well and maybe this was his clumsy attempt to restart an intimate relationship. Maybe she should assist the process but things were moving very quickly and Charles had never before been rough in their lovemaking. He had pulled her nightdress over her head and thrown it to the floor whilst pushing her legs wide apart. Initially Laura felt some passion at his surprising interest in her and the rawness of the sexual encounter, but this was soon replaced with alarm as he bit her right breast sharply, causing her to gasp in pain. His hands moved roughly all over her body as he pulled and pushed her, wordlessly moving her from position to position as he entered and re-entered her body, all the time groaning loudly. Her feelings were no longer confused as adrenaline pulsed around her system and shock set in. She tried to gain some control over what was happening but found she had none. He grabbed or held her firmly throughout the episode until his climax led to him collapsing across her as her heart pounded.

Laura lay there wide-eyed, breathless and in shock. The adrenaline subsided but her heart rate stayed high. She had not been raped as she had more or less consented or at least tried to join in. It was not lovemaking however; it was a sexual encounter – a violent sexual encounter – and she was not sure if it was his passion or just abuse.

When she saw bruising slightly below her groin the next day, and the marks on her breasts, she realised with horror that it was abuse. It was a new level of shame in an already difficult relationship and it was accentuated by the fact that neither of them mentioned the incident either at the time or the following morning. Was it further evidence of how far she was falling and how lost she was becoming?

Two days later and liberal use of concealer did the trick initially. Once the bruising was hidden, she left the cubicle to grab her dressing gown. Laura walked to the poolside, picked up a magazine and reclined in comfort to wait for Hayley.

★ ★ ★

Gary Newcombe told Kate that DCI Cooper wanted to come back and see them tomorrow and would not be put off.

'Oh, Gary what's he going to ask us? I can't take any more of this. Just tell him I had to go and see my mum.'

'No, he said he wants to talk to both of us.'

Kate burst into uncontrollable tears before falling to her knees.

'I knew we shouldn't have taken the money, Gary! They know; they must know.' she howled.

Chapter 21

Laura was so relaxed sitting by the side of the pool that the warmth of the spa and the sound of gently moving water caused her to drift off into a light sleep. She didn't hear Hayley approach, but heard her quietly inquire if this was where the older ladies sat to have a snooze. They both laughed and then ordered cappuccinos. Hayley said she had decided to have the seaweed wrap as her treatment but Laura knew that she couldn't as it would raise too many eyebrows when she removed her clothing. She told Hayley she was going to have a facial instead. She expected some sort of inquisition but her friend seemed to accept the choice without cross-examination.

The coffee arrived and the caffeine kick added to Laura's feeling of wellbeing as Hayley told her about her date last night with a wealthy but boring businessman she had been introduced to.

'So, did you fancy him?'

'Oh God no! He was a little chubby and he wore a suit … I mean who wears a suit on a first date? Also, he ate with his mouth open. I nearly told him that I could see the food on his plate – I didn't need to see it again as he was mashing it up in his mouth.'

'Hayley, you are terrible!' Laura said, laughing.

'And he spent the night telling me about his divorce and how evil his ex is. She left him for the odd-job man who used to work for them. This bloke was totally pissed off because he didn't have any money and he was now supporting both of them.'

'So, I take it you won't be seeing him again.'

'Well, I'm not sure about that. He invited me to a box at York races and I haven't been there for ages.'

'So, he likes you then?'

'Of course, darling! Even when he was churning his food like a threshing machine, he couldn't take his eyes off my tits,' she replied as they both rocked with laughter.

They were called for their treatments and went into separate treatment rooms. Afterwards, they had a glass of Prosecco and then lunch was ready. They moved into the palatial bistro, where its dressing-gown-clad customers seemed incongruous, mingling with the well-dressed guests from outside.

The day was flying by, despite Laura wanting it to go on indefinitely. She couldn't remember when she had laughed so much and Hayley had not probed her about her marriage which she had been expecting. She had even prepared a series of lies to suggest that things were improving and maybe their chat last time just happened on a particularly bad day. Thoughts of all of this were banished as they finished their sparkling wine and went into the jacuzzi in mid-story of a mutual friend who'd been robbed whilst holidaying in the Caribbean. It may have been the distraction of the story or the just the sense of wellbeing that cleared Laura's head of caution.

A few minutes later, she and Hayley stepped out of the whirlpool, showered, then sat in the steam room, where three other ladies were talking about last night's TV documentary on obesity. Hayley winked at Laura through the steam as the lady talking looked as though she could have taken part. Laura stifled a giggle. After a couple of minutes, the other women left but as they did so they hesitated at the door, allowing most of the steam to escape. Hayley tutted rather loudly and in the now fairly clear room, Laura turned to admonish her for being impatient. She saw that Hayley was looking at her in horror. When she looked down, she realised the combination of the jacuzzi and the steam room had washed away all the concealer and the ugly bruises at the very tops of her legs were now visible. She turned away in a vain attempt to hide them.

'Laura, how did you get those bruises?' Hayley asked, the mood shifting entirely.

'Oh, that was me. I tripped and fell into some furniture at home.'

'You tripped and hit something with your groin?' came the withering response.

'Well, I fell awkwardly and had bruises all over.'

'So where are they now then?' Hayley quizzed her.

'They've cleared up, more or less,' Laura replied unconvincingly as she sat and crossed her legs.

'Show me those bruises at the top of your thighs,' demanded Hayley.

'What – are you a doctor now?'

'Show me those bruises Laura, or I'll ask someone here to have a look at them.'

'What are you talking about Hayley? This is a health club, not a hospital, and why are you being so difficult? We're supposed to be having a nice day out.'

'I mean it, Laura. I want to see those bruises now.'

Laura recognised the determination in her friend and

followed the line of least resistance as she uncrossed her legs. Hayley got up and came to have a closer look, gently moving Laura's knees apart so she could clearly see the damage.

'That bastard did that to you, didn't he?'

'No! I told you, I …'

'Don't give me that. Those bruises are finger marks, where he's either pulled your legs open or held them open.'

'I bruise easily,' Laura added weakly.

'Not that easily. What else has he done?'

'Oh, Hayley please …' Laura replied helplessly as her resistance crumbled.

The rumbling of the steam generator kicked in and steam gushed from under the benches to fill the room. Hayley sat beside her friend and put her arm around her, the vapour disguising the tears which now fell from both of them.

★ ★ ★

Cooper and Ames arrived at Gary and Kate's property bang on the appointed time, but this time, there was no preamble of pleasantries. Both policemen refused tea and Cooper allowed the tension to build before he opened.

'So, Gary, you told us you've paid a reservation fee on a property and you need a ten per cent deposit – about twelve thousand pounds. Is that correct?'

'I'm not sure.'

'Not sure about what? Not sure you've paid a reservation fee or if that's what you need for a deposit?'

'No, we have paid the reservation fee but I don't know what the deposit is.'

'So ... you've committed yourselves to buying a property but don't know how much money you actually need to buy it?'

'Well, not exactly. That's all I'm saying.' Gary's face flushed.

'Your mortgage application form says you have the ten per cent deposit already and it isn't a loan.' This last detail was a bluff but it was worth a try.

'Yes, well you have to say that don't you.'

'You have to lie to the building society you mean? I think that's fraud, isn't it, Sergeant Ames?' Cooper said, theatrically turning to his colleague.

'It was the last time I checked, sir' replied an unblinking Ames.

'No ... I didn't mean that – we do have it.'

'Oh, that's good isn't it, sergeant? So, where is it?' Cooper responded coolly, fixing his glare on the hapless and sweating Newcombe.

'We've been saving up like, haven't we, Kate?' he desperately said, looking at his partner who appeared close to fainting.

'Where have you been saving that then?'

'In our savings account,' Gary replied.

The fly had stepped firmly into the spider's web.

'Is that with the Nationwide?'

'Yes,' Gary said weakly, sticking to the web he now recognised too late but couldn't avoid.

'Looks like you have a lot of saving to do then, Gary! You're ten grand short in that account. Do you want to have a look at the statement we have?'

There was a moment's pause when nothing was said. Gary

and Kate both looked at the carpet, as if the answer lay there. They looked childlike; neither had an answer but in staring at the floor, their body language shouted that they yearned for this torture will stop. Predictably, Kate burst into tears but was ignored, even by Gary. Cooper maintained his glare and the pressure.

'You see, Gary, I think you were saving and thought you had a couple of years to wait for your own place but then somebody came along and solved the problem for you. They said they would give you ten grand if you developed a bad memory and bingo! You had your deposit and everybody was happy. That's what happened isn't it?'

'No, I don't know what you are talking about,' Gary insisted stubbornly. 'I'm going to get a lawyer. You can't come around here threatening us. I'm the victim here.'

'Okay, Sergeant Ames,' Cooper sighed. 'Pop round to Judge Collinson's house and get the search warrant. Looks like we're going to be here all day.'

Kate stood up still crying and shouted, 'It's in the loft! All of it! Let them take it away, Gary. For God's sake let them have it! I knew we should never have taken it.'

* * *

Andy had driven home after a very successful day. He told Rebecca they were going out for dinner as they hadn't been out in ages and she should keep that red dress on for the restaurant. She replied that she'd had it on all day but Andy assured her she wouldn't keep it on long when they got back from their meal. Rebecca told him he was a big talker and they laughed; it was good to laugh. She freshened up her make-up and Andy booked the taxi and the restaurant. A perfect day was continuing.

Shortly after the main course was cleared away, Andy's phone vibrated on silent in his pocket. He thought about leaving it but curiosity got the better of him and, mid-conversation, he took it out and saw it was Paul Bevan the service manager.

'Hi Paul how are you doing?'

'The security firm have been on to me, Andy. Somebody's nicked the 4x4 demonstrator off the site.'

'What, tonight?'

'Yes, about an hour ago.'

'Shit!'

'Yes. The police have traced it to the Barmpton Industrial estate.'

'Well, that's good news then.'

'Not really … it's on fire.

Chapter 22

Andy told Rebecca about the theft and then left the restaurant to call DCI Cooper, who did not pick up, causing a bout of cursing. Just as he was thinking who to call next, his phone rang and he saw it was Cooper.

'Hello, Andy, sorry I didn't pick up. I had to excuse myself to talk in private. How can I help?'

Andy proceeded to tell him about the car; how this clearly represented an escalation of pressure and how Rebecca was freaking out in the restaurant. Cooper said he would investigate it straight away, but that Andy shouldn't jump to conclusions. There had been a spate of car thefts in the area recently and it might be unconnected. He didn't have an answer when Andy asked him how many of those cars were torched within a couple of hours.

Cooper was at home having dinner with the next-door neighbours, whom he did not particularly like. His wife did however and their kids got along well. Here was his chance to escape the coffee and chat, which inevitably got around to police work... 'is it really like they portray it on TV?' and what was he 'working on now?' He rang Patrick Ames.

'Paddy. Pick me up at mine in half an hour. A car stolen from Connolly's site's been torched.'

'I've got the night off, boss. Remember? The wife and I have just rented a film from Sky – we were just settling down.'

'Watch it tomorrow night, Paddy. Half an hour.'

Laura had pulled herself together and, after Abi had phoned and said she was sleeping over at a friend's house, Hayley had insisted Laura come home with her. Having checked Abi's plans were okay with the friend's parents, Laura left a voicemail for Charles to say that she'd be back late and there was a lasagne in the fridge. Also Abi wasn't coming home tonight.

Partly relieved not to be going home, she was apprehensive about the consequences of staying out. They drove back to Hayley's house and the host poured two glasses of wine, telling Laura she could either leave her car and take a taxi home or, better still, stay the night. Laura thought that was a step too far but was sorely tempted.

'Laura, we're not going to be disturbed and you're going to tell me everything, or I swear I will go and see that bastard and get it out of him.'

'Don't even joke about that, Hayley.'

'I'm not joking. I'm deadly serious.'

She felt remarkably relaxed and, although a little tearful, it wasn't like last time, when she was overwhelmed by emotion. She told Hayley the whole story and this time left little out. She told of the escalating violence, Charles' threat of never letting her leave and the recent episode of violent sex. Hayley called Charles a variety of unflattering names and eventually Laura concluded.

'You see, Hayley, it's complicated and I know you are going to tell me to leave him but I'd have to tell Abi everything that's gone on. She'll lose the only father she has ever had and he's always been good to her. Not only that, but she'll lose his financial support and we'll both have to fend for ourselves. If it goes to court, Charles will get his best friend to represent him and they say he never loses. He's called Gilbert Lassman from James and Robinson in Leeds and I just know it would be a nightmare.'

'I doubt that some lawyer can do much to defend a wife-beating monster or somehow turn that around against you. As for Abi, isn't it better she sees him for what he is?'

'Maybe, but she's so young. I think she would be devastated if we split up and she's at a very impressionable age.'

'Listen, Laura, your first duty is to yourself and you can't look after Abi if you're in a terrible state. This will get worse. You know that, don't you? He might end up hurting you badly or even killing you. Where would Abi be then?'

'Well, where would I go?'

'You could come here. Anytime. Both you and Abi. And if that bastard comes around here, I will happily deal with him.'

'I need to think about it, Hayley. In fact, I do little else but think about it, but I'm not ready to leave yet. Maybe we need counselling or something.'

'Counselling? He needs a fucking bullet!' Hayley spat out and they both laughed.

Oh, how good it felt to laugh again; to feel safe and relaxed; to not have pounding temples and nerves on red alert.

* * *

On the way to the police station, Cooper checked the information on the stolen car and discovered the car had been parked on the garage forecourt and appeared to have been stolen just before 6pm. The service and parts department was closed but the security gates were open as the sales department was still active. The car was parked outside of the range of the cameras but had been picked up on CCTV leaving the premises at 5.58pm. The camera image was not clear as to who was driving but it looked as though the theft was timed for when there would have been very few staff on site.

The car itself was reported as being on fire at 7.45pm by one of the security firms covering units on Barmpton Industrial Estate. The security guard had taken down the number plate and phoned the police, who traced it to Connolly's garage. A squad car in the vicinity called in on site and reported the details. Once the owner was established, the police rang the security firm operating Andy's garage and they in turn rang Paul Bevan.

The car was a shell so there would be no possibility of any fingerprints or DNA. CCTV cameras in the area were being checked for any sightings of the car en route. Paddy and Cooper took in the damage.

'Looks like Tasker's team, doesn't it, boss?'

'Can see why you became a detective, Paddy.'

'Very funny.'

'Don't think Connolly will find it funny. We could pick up Tasker but I'll bet you a tenner he has ten witnesses who were with him all night and cameras that prove it.'

'Well, at least you've turned Newcombe.'

'Not sure of that either. Sure, we've threatened him

with attempting to pervert the course of justice, but they can threaten him with losing his kneecaps or being inside the next slab of concrete on a motorway flyover.'

'What do you reckon will the CPS say?'

'They don't like temperamental witnesses, even when they're victims. It'll look to them like we've forced the pace and Newcombe might collapse in court. All it takes is a smart-arse brief to say he was coerced by the police and it looks like a frame. These days, judges won't take a chance with that and, if the evidence looks unsafe, they just throw it out.'

'Do you think Newcombe will go for the set up on the bribe?'

'Don't know.'

'Why didn't you get them to fetch the cash down and arrest them so it was in the system?'

'For just that reason: I didn't want it in the system. We need to keep our options open on this one or another one will slip through the net.'

'Fair enough,' answered Ames but he didn't agree. He couldn't understand why his boss hadn't arrested Newcombe for attempting to pervert the course of justice. They could have taken him to the station, applied maximum pressure and built a stronger case. He knew from experience, however, not to press his boss too hard.

Late into the evening, Hayley thought she'd made some progress with her friend and again tried to persuade her to stay the night but Laura was adamant she needed to go back and asked her friend to ring for a taxi.

'What are you going to do next, Laura?'

'What do you mean?'

'I mean, are you going to get out and move in with me, or move somewhere safe?'

'No … I need to think things through and then have a plan. A real plan.'

'Are you not frightened of him?'

'Yes, a little, but I think I can handle him better now. I need to be sure about what I'm doing.'

'Why not talk to Andy?'

'God, you must be joking! He'd be round there taking a hammer to Charles!'

'Not necessarily. Maybe he would deal with it all calmly.'

'You must be thinking of another brother I don't have.'

Hayley persisted. 'I'm worried about you Laura … really worried. You seem to think you're caught in some net or a trap, but you're making it harder than it is. There is no excuse for a man hitting a woman and you know that. All that charm or smarm just disguises a dangerous man. Charles is pretending to be somebody he isn't, but you get to see the real person. He's never going to stop hitting you or frightening you and you're losing a bit of strength each time he does it. Wake up girl!'

'Oh, Hayley I know you're right, but let me try and sort it out as peacefully as I can. I'll be all right, I promise.'

The taxi arrived and the two friends hugged each other, then Laura was on her way home to an uncertain fate. Hayley was too alarmed and alert to go to bed. Instead she quickly wrote down the names she had teased out of Laura in a seemingly casual enquiry about Charles's past:

Samantha Lewis, Dawn Taylor and Glynis Marborne were names of former long-term girlfriends and she fired up her laptop, determined to try and find them.

Cooper and Ames went through the details on the stolen car back at the police station. There was no direct information that helped them with the culprit. CCTV footage showed the car being driven off and there seemed to be only one occupant, but it was hard to tell. One of the team was checking camera footage around the industrial estate but, typically, the place where it was set on fire was out of range.

'Looks like they knew about the cameras, boss.'

'Yeah, it does.'

'Reckon that rules out joyriders. Still, we have a good idea who did this, don't we?'

'We might think we do, Paddy but the CPS will say we have no evidence.'

'What will you say to Connolly?'

'I'll think of something.'

Cooper was already two steps ahead but realised he was on thinning ice.

Chapter 23

Hayley had been online for more than an hour and was tiring after a long day. She had googled all the names she had obtained from Laura and found lots of women with those names, but none that looked likely to be the people she was trying to find. She'd moved on to social media and, as she expected, there were many women with the same names and, of course, some might now be married and have different names. There was a Samantha Lewis who lived in Manchester and might be a possible ex-girlfriend, but there was nothing for Dawn Taylor or rather, too many to make a shortlist. Glynis was a less common name, and there was a Glennis Archibald who caught her eye on Facebook because she had a striking resemblance to Laura. She searched her Facebook page and saw no clue to any association with Charles, but she appeared to be married to Colin Archibald. When she went through her list of friends, she saw she had more than 800. She flicked through them all until a picture emerged of a friend, Thomas Marborne, who could be a relative. Almost at the end, a Marjorie Marborne appeared and looked like she might be her mother. Hayley pinged a friend request to Glennis Archibald and awaited a reply. She also sent a message on Messenger:

'Hello, Glennis. I presume you were Glennis Marborne and believe we have a mutual friend. I would love to have a chat with you if possible. Kind Regards, Hayley.'

The following day she got out of bed to check for a response but there was nothing on either Facebook or

Messenger. Checking again she saw that the 'About' section on Glennis Archibald's Facebook page said she worked for Marigold Art and Design in The Calls in Leeds and she thought about ringing, but thought that might seem strange or needy. Instead, she decided on the spur of the moment to drive to Leeds, despite that seeming even more desperate but she was now on a mission. Having quickly showered and dressed, rushed to her car and nervously entered the full address into her satnav. She took a deep breath and was off.

During the drive she rehearsed several things she could say to this complete stranger, and dismissed them all for making her sound like a lunatic. One or two made her laugh out loud as she realised the difficulty of this approach. She decided to fall back on her usual position of trusting herself to be spontaneous and convincing. Hayley had never been one to shy away from risk. At 10.45am she pulled up outside 68 The Calls in Leeds and parked on double yellow lines outside the trendy warehouse-style shop front of Marigold Art and Design. Through the large window, she could see a young attractive receptionist talking to a client. Behind her there were several design desks in the open-plan space. She pulled up Glennis's Facebook page on her iPhone and looked at the several pictures of her. She couldn't recognise her as any of the people visible, so she decided to wait. After half an hour or so a traffic warden tapped on her window and told her she couldn't park on the road and directed her to a car park. Hayley had hoped to sit under cover in her car, like she'd seen in the movies and not be spotted. This was real life however, so she drove off and parked.

There was a Costa coffee shop nearby and the lack of breakfast was now affecting her, so she went in and ordered two croissants with her coffee and tried to watch the shop front of her target, which was now at a slight angle. Clients came and went but there was no sign of Glennis.

She stayed as long as she could, then at around 12.30pm walked up and down the street in the hope that Glennis would go out for lunch. Why did she assume she was working today? Or not on holiday? Or off on sick leave? She began to feel a little foolish. Shortly after one o'clock and just when her usual confidence was waning, an attractive thirty something with dark brown hair walked out of the design shop and away from her. Hayley quickened her step and tried to get a better look, but she was on the other side of the road and she couldn't be sure. The traffic was heavy and she was struggling to find a gap in it, so finally she shouted – a little too loudly for comfort – at the woman across the road,

'GLENNIS!' It was so loud that five other people turned, including two men and a taxi driver who looked from his open window. In any event, the dark-haired woman also stopped and looked across as Hayley waved and then weaved her way through the moving traffic and cacophony of horns, before appearing before the startled brunette.

'Sorry about that but I thought I would never get across the road! It is Glennis isn't it? Glennis Archibald?'

'Yes … I'm sorry but do I know you?'

'No. Well, not yet, but I wondered if I could talk to you?'

'I'm sorry, I am just heading out for lunch but I can

arrange a time to see you if it's about work. Have you been recommended to us?'

'No, it's not that. I know this is going to sound strange but I wondered if you ever went out with a Charles Peterson … you know … some years ago.'

'Sorry … you are?'

'My name is Hayley Anderson and I am trying to find out some information. Well not information exactly but some background.'

'Why?' Glennis said, her warm smile disappearing and being replaced with concerned bemusement.

'I just need to know what sort of a man he is … or was.'

'Are you seeing him?'

'No, it's not me.'

'Look, I'm sorry but I'm going to be late. I don't think I can help you. I don't wish to sound rude, but you're a complete stranger. I'm hardly likely to talk to you about my life or previous life or people I may or may not have known. I don't wish to offend you, but you could be anybody. Sorry – I must dash.'

As she turned and walked away Hayley could understand her reticence and realised she would have reacted in the same way. It didn't stop her however spontaneously calling after her.

'Please talk to me! I think he's physically hurting my closest friend. I think he's very dangerous and may hurt her really badly.'

She realised the dangerous step she had just taken. After all, this was a stranger who might still be on good terms with Charles and may tell him. She may have just inadvertently worsened Laura's position. Charles was a powerful man with powerful friends who may decide to take action against her, including legal action. She had said it now; the step was taken.

Glennis stopped in her tracks but did not turn immediately. There were a tense few seconds as she appeared frozen to the spot before she slowly turned. Hayley saw she had hit a nerve with the last remark, or had appealed to her better nature. Either way the woman appeared more receptive now.

'Please, Glennis,' Hayley continued. 'Come and have a coffee with me. I'll buy you lunch.'

Glennis nodded in assent and walked back with her to the coffee shop. They sat at a table at the back, well away from anyone else so that they could speak privately. Hayley ordered and then started to tell Glennis about her friend Laura and her marriage to Charles. She left out the actual detail of the violence and the sexual attack but painted a broad picture.

'I started to notice a change in Laura more than a year ago. Some of the sparkle was missing from her eyes – some life force was ebbing away. I thought I noticed a bruise or two, but to be honest I thought self-harm was more likely than wife beating – Charles is so stiff and respectable it was the last thing I would have guessed.'

'So, what makes you think he's harming her now?'

'I finally got it out of her. My worry is how bad it might get and she's afraid of leaving him. I'm really worried about her.'

There was a delay as Glennis assimilated all the

information. She seemed to be calculating to what degree she should get involved, but she had listened intently to her story.

'Listen, Hayley, I did go out with Charles for about a year but I'm married now and I really wouldn't want my husband to get involved in all of this or to have to explain things to him. My husband is a lovely guy and we have a small child. I just don't want to bring what was a dark chapter into our settled lives.'

'Dark chapter?'

'I mean my past – not that I have anything to be ashamed of.'

'But you said dark chapter. I promise you Glennis, I am not here to make problems for you. I won't be talking to your husband or turning up at your house. I didn't ask for you at your place of work as I know how important it is to be discreet. I'm just really worried for my friend. It's me who's taking the risk here.'

There was a further moment's silence and then Glennis spoke: 'You seem like the kind of friend everyone should have, Hayley. Yes, Charles can be violent.'

'Did he ever hit you?'

'Only towards the end and nothing really bad. In the first few months he was brilliant as a boyfriend; charming, good looking, sophisticated and caring. I worked up and down the country then, so we didn't see all that much of each other and although he was keen for us to live together, I wasn't sure. Anyway, one night we'd both had a bit too much to drink and he tried to get me to stay the whole night at his flat. I mean, we were sleeping together, but normally I would go home or he would if we were at my place. When I wouldn't stay, his mood changed and he grabbed me. He didn't really hurt me but it was the look in his eyes. In that moment, he morphed into some sort of … well, monster. Later he apologised – said he'd been stressed and seemed so ashamed that I accepted his apology. A few weeks later we were at a party and an old boyfriend was there, and he came over and had a short conversation. I could tell Charles was jealous and when he drove me home; he drove like a lunatic. I was really scared. I told him he couldn't come into my flat but he pushed his way in and grabbed me around the throat. He made so much noise that my neighbour knocked on the door and asked if I was all right. I told him to ring the police and Charles ran out. Obviously, I broke it off with him then.'

'Did he leave you alone?'

Again, there was a moment's hesitation.

'Not at first. There were texts and emails, all pleading with me to give him another chance and telling me I was the one he was looking for in life. Then flowers. Then the messages became a little more menacing. Nothing too dramatic but certainly not friendly.'

'How do you mean?'

'Sort of hinting that he wasn't going to give up; that I would never be free of him … in so many words. Almost like a stalker but he was clever about it.'

'But he stopped?'

'He did, but only after I met Dawn Taylor.'

'I've heard of her but I couldn't find any trace of her on the internet.'

'You won't. She changed her name, both names in fact. She came to me and warned me about him. I went to solicitors and got a restraining order against him. Dawn had been engaged to Charles, but she said he had an uncontrollable temper. I'm not sure what he did to her – she didn't give me the details – but it must have been bad. She did tell me that he had become rough with her in a sexual way which really scared her the most. She finished with him and had the same story of messages and flowers and all that stuff. Anyway, he wouldn't accept the rejection when she broke it off and he started to stalk her, but I mean really stalk her. She was terrified. He would hang around places she went to and she received more and more of the texts and emails. She felt he was watching her all the time. She got a restraining order but he still continued and, in the end, she had him arrested.'

'What happened then?'

'I think he may have been arrested twice, I'm not sure, but Dawn thought he would never leave her alone. He did once tell her that she was his and he would never let anyone else have her because she belonged to him. She was really spooked; she changed her name and moved out of the area. She was very kind to me and helped me which is why I stopped to speak to you … a kind of payback to Dawn.'

Hayley sat and took it all in. Eventually she spoke.

'Gosh that's terrible, Glennis. Has he bothered you since?'

'No. My lawyers wrote and told him they had taken a statement from Dawn Taylor and would press for a prison sentence if he bothered me again. That seemed to do the trick. Remember I was just a girlfriend though – your friend is his wife and there's a child involved.'

'Yes, but the child isn't his.'

'I doubt he'll see it that way. They need to escape him. One day he'll lose it completely. Looking back, I think I was lucky. I think men who hit women don't ever change. The violence often gets worse as the respect drains away with every attack. Most men would never hit a woman, but those who do are dangerous. Very dangerous. Nobody would guess it about Charles but I think he's a monster. There's something about him that you only see when that veneer slips, but when it does, you can see ... something very dark and scary. Get your friend out of there, Hayley ... seriously, get her out.'

Chapter 24

The first call Andy received the next morning was from DCI Cooper.

'Hi Andy. David Cooper here, just checking in on what we have so far on your stolen car.'

'Hello, David. So, what have you got?'

'Not a lot I'm afraid. We're checking as many cameras as we can, but so far there is no ID on a driver and no forensic evidence on the car.'

'We know who did it though, don't we?'

'Not really. I know what you're thinking but, as I told you, there have been a spate of these recently, though I agree, it might well be our man.'

'So much for the protection then,' Andy replied despondently.

'Can we revisit the idea of the recorded meeting – give us a chance to nail him on that? You can even ask him about the burned car and if he admits it, we can put him away for that. You could insist you meet Tasker himself.'

'You know how I feel about that.'

'I do, but you might like to think again.'

'Leave it with me, David.'

'Okay. I'll give you a call in a couple of days. Still got your phone with you?'

'Yes, I have.'

'Good. Talk soon Andy.'

Andy placed his phone on his desk and felt for the police mobile in his jacket pocket for a little security. Security? That was beginning to feel like a thing of the past. His own phone rang again.

'Hello young fella. Do you fancy a game of golf with a relative?'

'Hi Dad ... golf? Isn't that an old man's game that retired people play?'

'Possibly, but I felt like humiliating you again and last time I looked at you, you looked like you needed some fresh air.'

'Humiliated? Didn't I win the last one?'

'I think you cheated on a day I wasn't very well and scraped through ... in fact I let you win because your mum said you needed a confidence boost.'

'Yeah right! You let me win? You didn't even let me win games when I was a child. In fact, the idea of you letting anyone win anything is something my poor brain can't compute.'

'Nothing new there then.'

'Ha ha, very funny. No, I would love to play, Dad, but I really haven't got the time this week.'

'I checked with Andrea and you have nothing on tomorrow so the tee is booked for 9.30. Don't be late or I'll put the rent up.'

'Okay, Dad. You win ... see you tomorrow.'

* * *

Cooper had moved on from his chat with Andy, which he regarded as a holding call to give him some time to reconsider. Sergeant Ames had been in touch with the team watching Tasker and he and Cooper were outside his flat in Potter's Bank, a large council estate two miles from

Goole. Cooper was always amazed at the contrast between how much money these moderate-grade dealers made and where they lived. The higher-level dealer tended to go the other way and live in palatial houses with security gates, but Tasker and his type stayed close to their roots and either lived in rented flats or low value properties. The irony was that they often had expensive cars sitting outside. Sure enough, as they approached the cold concrete blocks that housed the poorer end of society, there were two sports cars sitting side by side in the communal car park. A hooded youth sat on a wall nearby as either a lookout or car minder. As the unmarked police car pulled up, the youth immediately pressed his mobile to his ear to warn of their presence. The two police officers climbed the graffiti-scarred staircase and encountered two youths who were just about to assert themselves but then recognised the walk and attitude of policemen, so they dropped their gaze and walked wordlessly past.

On the eighth floor they stood outside flat 835 and hammered on the door. It was the third flurry of banging that produced a slow opening as Kimberly Aitchison glared at them from the dim light inside the flat.

'Hello, Kimberly, is your boyfriend home?'

'Partner,' she growled as her white vest struggled to contain her large breasts, which were held up by a straining red bra. A heart tattoo was visible on the left breast and the birthdates of her two children were fully on display on her right arm, which was holding open the front door.

'Is that business partner or domestic?' Cooper asked with a patronising smile.

'Smartarse aren't ya?' Kimberley answered as she pushed straggly blonde hair from her eyes. Ames took the lead and walked in, followed by Cooper, who smiled again at the thirty-year-old woman who was attractive, two stones ago, but now looked like she'd given up.

As they moved into the living room their attention was drawn to the state-of-the-art 65-inch Sony TV with full sound bar and extra speakers dominating the small space. A man lay on the settee.

'Bet your neighbours love you, Jamie,' quipped Cooper. Tasker got up from his prone position and stood to his full height, whilst pulling up his jogging bottoms over a developing paunch, only partly hidden by a large short sleeved shirt.

'Well, if it isn't Holmes and Watson, out solving another case.'

'So, Jamie, where were you last night?' Cooper enquired.

'I was in all night. Just ask the missus.'

'Know anything about a car being nicked and torched, do you?'

'Not a thing, mate. Don't get out much these days.'

'Did think about getting a warrant to find the phone you used to organise it, but of course you don't keep it here do you? You did have plenty of visitors yesterday though, didn't you?'

'Family and friends have been very good to us since you tried to fit me up.'

'Yeah, I bet they have. Some have got phones and some have got petrol, haven't they?'

'Don't know what you're talking about, mate.'

'I'm not your mate, Jamie and pretty soon I'll prove that to you. I'm here to warn you that we are on to you; we're watching what you do. You might well get another pull soon, then we can put you up for a while, until your trial and conviction. The charges are piling up for you ... mate.'

'Are you threatening me?'

'You're fucking right I am,' Cooper snarled as he moved close to Tasker's face. Cooper could take care of himself and, like most police officers, he had no fear of violence. He had scanned Tasker's clothing and there was no sign of a knife on him. If Tasker was provoked enough to strike out, he and Ames would be more than a match for him, dangerous as he was. Tasker however, did not rise to the bait, partly because he was expecting them, but also because he sensed the danger.

As the two police officers left, Ames again wondered about his boss's tactics. Why had he told Tasker he was under surveillance? What was the point of surveillance if you told the mark he was being watched? He decided not to challenge it in the car.

'Think it's worth getting a warrant, anyway boss, just to see what he's got in there?'

'No, not really. He isn't that stupid. He will have gear for his own use in there but not enough for anything other than possession and he won't have arranged anything on any device that's there. We'll keep an eye out and hope our garage man agrees to a set-up meet.'

'Do you think he will?'

'Might do now they've nicked one of his cars.'

'What's the score with Newcombe?'

'Keeping him on ice. All about timing on that one. Nearer to trial we'll make sure he'd rather take the risk of giving evidence against Tasker than share a cell with him.'

'Don't you need to tell the CPS?'

'Tell them what? Our victim is taking money and our only other witness is running scared. Are you fucking mad, Paddy?'

'Just asking, boss.'

* * *

Andy was clearing up for the day and had reported the stolen car to the insurers, and ordered a replacement from the manufacturers. He worried about next year's premium, especially if there was another incident. He looked again at the security camera configuration and thought he might add two more cameras to take out the blind spots. He quite liked the idea of concealed cameras, so that anyone coming on to site wouldn't realise they were there. The normal job of a camera was to warn off potential thieves but he had the others for that. If Tasker and his men thought they were safe they might give themselves away on a concealed camera, and that would be less aggressive than setting Tasker up, as Cooper wanted. He imagined criminals would take a different view of that; perhaps be less likely to seek revenge. Yes, that seemed a good plan and he always liked to leave work on a positive note. The idea seemed like that bit of positivity he was seeking.

As a last job before going home, he checked his emails

on his phone. It was the usual combination of junk mail that had snuck through and inane messages on nothing in particular. He scanned down his inbox and here was nothing of interest, until he saw an email from Facebook that read 'Rebecca Gates has updated her profile picture'. Curiosity caused him to go on to Facebook and look at the updated picture, which popped up on his phone: it was a full-length picture of Rebecca in a revealing bikini. She was pushing her hair away from her face with her right hand. He felt a jolt of surprise on seeing the image chosen by Rebecca as her new profile picture. His girlfriend was rightly proud of her body, but was not the sort of person to flaunt it, especially on Facebook. She looked great in the photo – of that there was no doubt – but it was so out of character for Rebecca to post it. In fact, he couldn't remember her posting much recently. There were already 22 Likes and 5 comments including 'stunning' and 'what a fantastic picture!' As he stared at the page, his phone rang and Rebecca came up as the caller. He clicked the accept button.

'Hi babe, are you okay?'

'Jesus, Andy! Have you seen Facebook? Somebody must have hacked my account and posted a picture of me in a swimsuit. What the hell is going on?'

'I'm on my way home.'

Chapter 25

When he arrived back home, Andy was met at the door by a frantic Rebecca, iPhone in hand.

'Look at this picture, Andy! Who the hell has done this and why? I mean, what's the point? And where did they get hold of the photo? What the fuck is happening, Andy?'

'Okay calm down and let me in.'

'Calm down? It's them, isn't it?' she exclaimed with eyes wide open, fear spilling from them. Andy took off his jacket and sat in the kitchen to examine the new profile picture. He was trying desperately to act, look and feel calm.

'Do you recognise the picture?'

'Not really, but it's me and my bikini ... the red one.'

'What's in the background?' he asked, looking at what appeared to be a hotel room or at least not a room in their house. The background was a little dark so he highlighted the picture and enlarged it on the screen.

'Isn't that our room in Ibiza?'

'I don't know, I didn't look at the background. I can't even remember the picture.'

'Yes, it is. Remember, I took this picture on your phone when you came out of the bathroom ready to go to the pool. You told me to delete it but I didn't.'

Rebecca took back her phone and studied the picture more closely.

'So how has anybody got hold of that then?'

Andy retrieved the phone, clicked on to pictures and found the original amongst the Ibiza set from last year. Rebecca grabbed the phone and started flicking through them.

'Shit! What else is there?'

The only two photos that concerned her were from a few years ago before she met Andy where she looked very drunk on a night out. Andy leaned back in the chair and processed the information as best he could.

'So, who has access to your phone and could have uploaded a picture on to Facebook?'

'Nobody.'

'Might someone at work have done it for a joke? Or one of your friends maybe?'

'For a joke? What are you talking about? What sort of joke is it if someone takes your phone, goes through your photos and makes one of them public? Don't be ridiculous, Andy!'

'What about a back up? Do you back up your phone on a laptop?'

'Laptop? What would I be doing on a laptop?'

There was a penny-dropping moment for them both as they seemed to simultaneously arrive at the same conclusion, but it was Andy who spoke it out loud:

'It must be when your phone went missing. Somebody must have downloaded the information from your phone.'

'But we found the phone in the car. It can't be that.'
Again, there was a moment's pause before Andy said, 'I think that guy who came into the house must have taken your phone and copied the photos … and maybe everything on it. He must have taken it away to do that, which explains why we couldn't find it. At some point he must have brought it back and put it in the car where we found it.'

'You mean, everything on the phone: my messages, contacts, emails … everything?'

'Maybe. I better ring Cooper,' Andy said calmly as Rebecca buried her head in her hands.

★ ★ ★

Part of Laura Peterson's plan to take back control of her life was to get back to work. She had done reasonably well at school but, like a lot of her contemporaries had little idea of what she wanted to do by way of a career. Her choice of A levels was random, as was her decision to study history at Warwick University. She'd just imagined that a career would reveal itself to her and she would fall into it. But that never happened. The combination of becoming pregnant, a variety of part-time jobs and then meeting Charles had eaten away the years. Charles had suggested she give up her job at a local estate agency and she had agreed, thinking it might help their relationship and her desire for a second child. She realised she missed the job at the agency, where she had developed an easy style when showing houses and dealing with potential purchasers. Michael Black, the owner of the business had suggested that she think of qualifying as a surveyor and had offered his assistance with her training and the exams.

It had been five years since she had worked, but Michael was delighted to receive her call and had immediately said she could have her old job back, or even run a new branch they were opening in Cottingham. He explained that the new premises were perfect for them but he was short of experienced staff and Laura was the safe pair of hands he needed. She told him she was a bit rusty for that right now, but would love to come back for two or three days a week and see how things went. She was a combination of excited and terrified at the prospect but her confidence had to be rebuilt. She had to start believing in herself again and recapture her former spark.

Laura was sitting at home and working out how she would tell Charles of her planned return to work. The fact that she was worried about it was enough to tell her how steeply the relationship had declined in recent years. In fact, in the last few weeks Charles appeared less contrite regarding his behaviour towards her and more assertive about his control. He was, in any event, something of a control freak and even displayed signs of OCD about many things, such as the newspaper always being folded back into chronological page order; the TV controls being placed on the TV table, never the coffee table; the bed always being made in a certain way ... the list was endless. He seemed to like his wife being at home when he returned from work and, more than anything, the fact that she was entirely financially dependent on him. That was going to change.

Laura heard the front door open and realised it was Abi returning from school.

'Had a good day at school, Abs?'

'Yes, Mum! Just off to my room.'

'What about saying hello properly to your mother?'

'What was that, Mum?'

'Do you mind coming into the kitchen please?'

Abi walked in looking preoccupied but otherwise

cheerful enough.

'What did you say, Mum?'

'I asked if you were coming into the kitchen to talk to your mother.'

'Oh, Mum! I've got loads of homework to do and I thought I'd get straight on with it.'

'Oh my God! My daughter has been kidnapped and they've sent this stranger to me – someone who does homework and is conscientious.'

'Very funny Mum,' Abi grinned, 'You want me to get good grades in my exams, don't you?'

'Of course, but ten minutes isn't going to stop that happening. How about a hot chocolate and a chat before you go upstairs?'

'Okay, you smooth talker. Milk chocolate please, with marshmallows.'

'Deal. Now tell me about your day.'

Abi chatted easily about her day and how her friend Suzy was such a pain, gawping at Terry Mitchell, who is "such a lamebrain but thinks he's something he isn't." Terry, apparently, is "just a mirror monkey, always looking at himself like he's lush, when he's as sick as,"... Abi put two fingers to her mouth and pulled a vomit face, much to the amusement of her mother.

Hot chocolate drunk, Abi asked if she could go upstairs. When her Mum nodded, she jumped off her seat, hugged her and told her she was the best. How Laura loved her; she'd do anything for her, even staying with a man she no longer loved ... if she ever loved him at all.

Upstairs, Abi changed into her tracksuit trousers and a T-shirt and switched on her phone to check for messages. She smiled when she saw Harvey had sent a message half an hour ago and she opened it.

'How are you doing today? I had to close quickly last night as my folks came upstairs and I just knew they would be like, who are you talking to and stuff like that so I just closed. Are you there?'

'Hi Harvey! Back home from school now. You were telling me you were sure you were coming over here soon. Do you have a date?'

There was a slight delay before the response came back.

'Hi Abi, yes my folks say we are coming and might be there for like a month or something. They have like a million things to do and asked me if I wanted to bring a friend. I told them I didn't have any friends at home but I do have a friend in England.'

'So, what did they say?'

'They said that was great and you could come and stay with us for a while if you wanted.'

'That would be great but my parents might say no or say they want to meet your parents. They never let me go anywhere unless they know where I am. It's like being a prisoner.'

'What if we meet and my Mom calls them when you are with us and asks if it's okay then? It would be hard for them to say no when you were actually with us!'

'How would I get to London?'

'I told my folks where you are and they said we would come up and meet you. They are going to rent a car and drive around looking at stuff like castles and churches and old shit that old people like. I would rather jump in front of a train.'

'Harvey, you are funny! So, they will drive up here and we can meet somewhere, then your mum will ring my mum?'

'Yeah that's the plan. Then we can have some time together. I can't wait to meet you and see you rather than just words on a screen. Please say yes! I don't know what I'd do if I never got to meet you and I was in England.'

'You sure I shouldn't just ask my mum? She is pretty cool and I'm sure she would come with me and meet your parents.'

'No, don't do that. She will say no and then you couldn't get away. You said they don't let you go anywhere. They will say I am a total stranger.'

'You are not a stranger, Harvey, you are my best friend.'

'They won't see it like that.'

'Let me think about it.'

There was another delay before the next typing started.

'Maybe you don't want it as much as me, Abi. Maybe I have this wrong and shouldn't have asked. Forget about it, Abi. We will keep it like this and you won't get into trouble. Maybe that is for the best.'

'Don't say that, Harvey, you know that isn't right and you know how I feel about you. I love you and you love me.'

'Hey I don't know anymore.'

'I'll come, Harvey, I will, honestly, just give me the time and place.'

'That's great, Abi, I will be in touch and arrange it with you. Love you lots xx.'

'Love you too xx.'

The heavily tattooed hand stopped typing and the bald-headed man leaned back in his seat, picked up his phone and tapped a message:

'Agreement reached. Just need a time and place for the pickup.'

Chapter 26

Andy phoned Cooper straight away and for once he picked up immediately. Andy brought him up to date with the latest brick in the wall.

'Okay, but again we mustn't jump to conclusions here. You may be right about the phone, but it may be someone else or a hacker.'

'Come on, David! Do me a favour and give me some credit for intelligence. How much information do you guys need to do something? We are sitting targets here and your magic phone isn't going to save us.' Andy replied, anger and confidence rising in him. Truth be told, it was more frustration than anger; he wanted to do something but just had no real idea what.

'Andy, if I go and arrest Tasker on this and the other stuff we have on intimidation, there is simply no evidence that ties him in and the CPS will tell me that. We have to catch him or his associates doing something. Look, I shouldn't tell you this but we're tapping his phone and monitoring his calls and those of one of his men. If they make any reference to any of the things that have happened, we'll pick them up, I promise you.'

'What if I just tell them they win and I won't give evidence?'

'Then matters would be out of my hands, Andy and the CPS would look at the case and decide what to do. They could subpoena you to attend court and you'd have to come or face contempt of court charges if you didn't cooperate – maybe even perjury charges depending on what you said. Do you really want that?'

'I don't want any of this, David,' Andy replied bitterly.

'Do you want this thug to get away with it? Do you want him on the streets when the next one might be killed because we didn't put him away when we could?'

There was a silence whilst Andy thought about it. It was not so much the protection of some faceless future victim but the rage growing in him. A primeval desire to tackle this enemy despite his fear; a desire not to lose and forever live in the shadow of regret.

'Do something, David. Just do something.'

Charles Peterson was having a better day. He had met new clients at their home and immediately knew that the couple would like his sophisticated, easy charm. He noticed them looking at his Mercedes when he arrived at their large detached house and exchange a look with each other that implied this was the sort of man they were looking for.

Once he had greeted them at the front door and complimented them on their lovely home in such a desirable area, they were putty in his hands. He asked about their lives and the children as they drank fresh coffee and marvelled at the home-made biscuits. When the time was right, he pulled out some sketch plans for the large extension they were planning and they worked through some ideas. They told him he was just the man they were looking for, asked him to go ahead with some detailed plans and agreed a fee structure.

As Charles parked his car in the company car park, he held on to that feeling of success to enjoy it a little longer and imagined the chatty email that he would send to the managing partner, Angus Trevelyan, telling him about this profitable deal. It was with a jaunty spring in his step that he breezed into the office and greeted Mandy, the firm's attractive receptionist, flirtatiously. He was just about to bound up the stairs when Mandy told him that Mr Trevelyan had asked him to pop into his office when he arrived. Suddenly the elation of the morning started to drain away as he wondered about the reason for the summons. He fixed his game face, knocked and opened the door simultaneously and with a painted-on smile said,

'Morning Angus, I gather you were looking for me.'

'Ah yes, Charles, come in and close the door,' Trevelyan answered looking uncomfortable.

'Had a good morning so far Angus – just bagged that Alexander account for the extension and there may be more to come I think.' Charles blurted out the good news, which seemed to have less of an effect than he'd hoped for.

'Oh, that sounds promising, Charles,' Trevelyan answered absently before leaning back in his chair and clasping his hands together.

'The reason I wanted to see you, Charles, is we have had a formal complaint on the Parkinson account from last year. It seems they believe they were overcharged and now there is an issue with the works themselves, which they say are defective.'

Charles frowned.

'I thought that had all been resolved, Angus. There were murmurings at the end of the job, but I went through everything with them and they seemed satisfied.'

'Apparently not. They have gone to solicitors and we've

received a preliminary letter asking for our response to a list of complaints. I've been on to our lawyers, who tell me it is not a letter of claim but the next one will be. They say we need to inform our insurers who may appoint separate lawyers to deal with it.'

'So, what are they saying?'

'Well, you will need to take the letter and digest it in detail but briefly, they say our estimate of fees was 35k and the final bill was 55k yet the estimate was never altered. I have had a look at the file and that seems to be correct.'

'Yes, but there was extra work I needed to do and they know that.'

'That might be the case, Charles, but you and I both know we have to amend the quotation of fees in that eventuality and to confirm that in writing to the client. I can't see that we've done that.'

'But I am sure I did discuss it with them and sent something out.'

'Not according to the file, Charles. Also, they have a report from a surveyor, which says the electrical wiring does not conform with regulations and the under-floor heating has been incorrectly fitted, amongst other things. This was, of course, a fully supervised contract.'

'No, that must be rubbish, Angus. The wiring was done by Clarke and Fabour, who we've used before ... and the under-floor heating was working,' he added desperately.

'Well, I think you need to let me have your written observations on the letter and I will pass it on to the insurers. I will also formally respond to the lawyers, just to confirm we have done that.'

'I'm sorry, Angus; would you like me to deal with it?'

'No, I think I have to deal with it. Also, I should warn you they have made a complaint about you to the RIBA and they will contact you directly.'

'The Institute? Why have they done that?'

'They say they were misled, so that could be a conduct issue. We'll just have to see what the Institute says, but I imagine they will investigate.'

A darkness descended that would fester and grow all day.

Andy met his dad in the car park of the Sunnyvale Golf Club and they unpacked their gear.

'Not got one of those electric trollies yet, Dad? A man of your age needs all the assistance he can get.'

'If you want to give me assistance you can give me ten shots.'

'Ten shots? Why don't I just give you the pound now and we can go and have a drink? You can have three shots and even then, I'm being robbed.'

'Three? Well that's three more than I was expecting so it's a deal.'

Andy's woes began to fall away as he teed off on the first hole and concentrated on his friendly battle with his dad. It would take all of his concentration to play the game adequately and stop his father getting into his head in with the regular mental gymnastics they both used to put each other off. His father was a master of it and waited for the perfect moment to say something like, "That stance you took to drive on the last hole reminded me of how you used to look just after you'd wet yourself as a toddler. Of course, you stopped doing that when you went to college."

Or: "Still got that tendency to hook the ball to the left; wonder if your mum breastfed you too long ... or maybe not long enough."

After seventeen holes they were all square, despite the banter. His father stood on the 18th tee, lined up his drive and miss-hit it to the left into the trees. Andy smiled, lined himself up and followed with a perfect drive down the centre of the fairway.

'Looks like the pound is mine, Dad. Do you want to give it to me now and save yourself the embarrassment at the clubhouse?'

'Oh, I'll soldier on. You never know in this game ... can your opponent live with the pressure? That's always the question to ask.'

Andy watched his father wander around in the rough grass beside the trees and realised all of his own tension had gone, having spent just over three hours with a man he trusted completely – a man who was always on his side. Even the pressure of keeping up with the banter had melted away his stress elsewhere. His father had sensed the need to take him away from his troubles for a few hours.

'Found it!' Andy heard as he was about to leave his perfectly positioned ball to help his dad search for it. Instead he watched his father lean back and swing at a clump of grass that flew into the air. The ball shot out like a missile, clipped a nearby tree then bounced over the bunker, hitting the rake, which caused it to turn sharply right before coming to rest ten feet from the pin.

'Shit!' Andy cursed as he looked at a completely different situation. He calmed himself and hit a sweet-sounding shot which felt right on the money ... until it pitched into the bunker and stayed there.

'Oh, bad luck, son! You deserved so much better,' his father said with a wide grin.

It took two shots just to get out of the bunker and as Andy's father pocketed his pound, they walked to the clubhouse for a drink.

After a little family talk, Paul Connolly looked earnestly at his son.

'So, Andy, bring me up to speed on the case and leave nothing out. I want to know what's happening. Everything, and I mean everything.'

Andy thought about censoring some of the developments but he always sensed his dad could see right through him and would instantly know he was holding something back. And in fact, he wanted to tell him everything and he did, in detail.

'Wow! That is some story, son. How's Rebecca holding up?'

'Not well really. We just keep expecting the next thing now.'

'Do you trust this DCI?'

'Not really, but I don't have much option. Your lawyers aren't sure about him either but there isn't much they can do.'

'Do you feel you're at serious risk from this Tasker bloke? Do you think he might hurt you?'

'Well he stabbed somebody, didn't he? And that poor sod Gary just happened to be there. In my case, I might be the reason he goes to prison so, yes, I think he might, especially if he gets desperate.'

There was a moment's pause before Paul Connolly spoke again.

'When I first opened the garage, you and Laura were very young and I used to work most days. I knew if I could get the business right that I could give you the kind of things that I didn't have as a child. Your grandparents were great parents, but they always struggled for money so they just did the best they could. I wanted more, so I stretched myself financially and was prepared to put the hours in.'

'I remember that,' Andy replied. 'But we used to go to the garage sometimes with you and sit in the cars in the showroom ... it was cool. We loved the garage.'

'Yes, there were some great times but not everything was so rosy.'

'How do you mean?'

'We had been going for about a year or so and a local hard case came into the garage one day. Billy Dodds was his name and he came in looking at a pickup we had. I remember it clearly: we had it on the forecourt for £2999 and he offered me a grand for it. I thought he was joking but he came back the next day and offered me £900. I asked him to leave but he said he'd be back. When he did come back, I called the police but he wasn't bothered and when they arrived, he left. We started to get petty things like broken windows and wing mirrors smashed but the police never got him or any evidence.

'Anyway, one night he and one of his mates caught up with me in the street and said they would stop all the vandalism if I paid them £100 a week.'

'Protection money?'

'Kind of. Of course, they said it wasn't them, but they knew who was doing it and it would get worse unless they were looking after me.'

'So, what did you do?'

'Well, I was never going to pay them but I worried about you two and mum, and the business. Anyway, one of our early customers was Ted Lomax and one day he was in so I asked if I could have a word.'

'Is that the haulier guy?'

'Yes, Lomax Transport. I explained it all to Ted, saying I didn't know what to do, and I remember to this day what he said to me: he said there was no point me talking to Dodds because I didn't speak his language. Ted said he did, or at least knew people who did.'

'Shit! So, what was he offering?'

'Oh, he was careful not to offer anything specific, but said that he would help me to solve the problem.'

'And did you?'

'Not at first, no. But one night there was a knock at the door at home and a Polaroid picture of your school was pushed through the door. I picked it up and opened the door but there was nobody there. I knew it was Dodds or one of his mates but there was no CCTV in those days and no real evidence. Anyway, that was enough for me so I called Ted. I realised if I called the police, they wouldn't be able to do anything and then it might be a problem for me if I called Ted later on. I was out of my depth and I realised we were at risk. I was never going to pay those thugs anything but I didn't fancy waiting to see what they would do next. I was desperate and scared but my priority was to remove the threat hanging over all of us.'

'God Dad, I had no idea!'

'I've never told anyone until today and you mustn't either. Your mum doesn't even know.'

'Go on,' Andy urged.

'Well, Ted met me, I gave him the picture of the school that had been pushed through the door and he asked me to leave it to him.'

'Did he tell you what he was going to do?'

'No, and I didn't ask.'

'Did he ask for money?'

'No, well, not directly. He said there might be some expenses up the line but he didn't specify.'

'Expenses?'

'All I know, Andy is that I had a problem and I didn't know how bad it was going to be. There was a man who said he could solve it and I believed him.'

'So, what happened?'

'Maybe a week or so later, Ted popped in and said the problem was sorted. After that, I never had any more issues with Dodds.'

'What happened to him then? Is he at the bottom of the sea?' Andy asked, wide-eyed at his father's revelations.

'It was a couple of years later that I summoned up the nerve to ask Ted, when we were out having a drink. He told me that he was related through marriage to some proper hard-cases and in times of trouble he turned to them. There can be some dodgy characters connected to the haulage business and Ted didn't bother with lawyers or the police if he was threatened.'

'Were you not worried about Ted and what you were getting into?'

'Of course I was, but as I said, I was desperate. Ted is okay though. He has never asked me for anything but I would help him if he ever needed me. I wouldn't break the law or anything like that, but my door is always open to him.'

'You didn't say what happened to Dodds.'

'Oh yes. I hadn't seen Dodds around since that day and worried that something bad had happened. Anyway after a few pints, Ted told me that a couple of his "colleagues" shall we call them, caught up with Dodds one night and hung him over the suspension bridge by his ankles. They made it clear that the garage was off limits and the next time they would let go. That seemed to do the trick.'

'Blimey, Dad! You really were in the world of gangsters. Do you think they would have ... you know, dropped him the next time?'

'I don't know, son and I don't want to know, but horses for courses. I've spoken to Ted about you and he has made some enquiries about Tasker. He's a bad sort – unpredictable – and you need to be very careful. You may need to talk to Ted.'

'I don't know if it's gone that far yet. I think Tasker is just trying to intimidate me and although he's doing a pretty good job, I don't think I want to get involved in any retaliation or anything like that.'

'Okay, Andy, but I thought I'd tell you. Remember: not a word to your mum or, in fact, anyone else.'

'No, of course not, Dad.'

They walked back to the car park and Andy told his father he'd really enjoyed the game and appreciated the chat and the honesty. They hugged and Andy felt his dad hold him a little tighter and a little longer than usual.

Paul whispered, 'You take care, Andy. I love you, son.'
Andy just about managed to get the words out that he loved
him too.

He drove home and wasn't sure what to feel; his
father's revelations had really shocked him and, although he
empathised with his dad, such action was a step too far for
him at the moment. As he was mulling it all over, his phone
lit up on his dashboard and he saw it was Rebecca.

'Hi babe, everything all right?'
He thought he could hear her crying and it was a faltering
voice that responded:

'No, it's not. There's another photo of me and this time
it isn't from my phone.'

Chapter 27

Charles Peterson was also driving home and was in a thunderous mood. The worst days are those that you begin to enjoy and even allow yourself to believe are going to be really good all day, only for them to turn bad. Something about that change made the bad so much worse. If a day starts badly, you seem to develop a shield for the rest of the day. Then you can tell yourself things didn't turn out as badly as you feared.

Charles's early optimism had been knocked out of him and he felt an enormous pressure from the complaint against him and the claim against the firm. He imagined one or two of the partners meeting in private and speculating about his future, or secretly checking his files in search of further error. A good reputation takes years to achieve and can be lost in moments.

'Shit ... shit ... shit ... FUCKING SHIT!' he bellowed, banging the steering wheel with both hands and temporarily nudging the car towards the kerbside. The small relief the outburst gave him soon disappeared and he was again glaring at the road ahead and the two miles or so to home.

* * *

Hannah Connolly told the children to hurry or they'd be late for the party. She was already stressed about the invitation. What kind of a parent had a party at 5.30pm on a school night for ten-year-olds? Isabel was, of course, delighted to be invited by her classmate Cordelia; God, fancy calling your child Cordelia! It sounded like something out of a Noel Coward play. Then, worse than that, asking Ben if he would like to come but saying Phoebe was too young, meaning she had to come with them there and back. She wouldn't understand why she wasn't allowed to go in with her brother and sister, which would mean she'd be howling in the car and late to bed. Why were some parents so insensitive? Why had she not just said no, that she couldn't arrange things? She knew the answer to that. Since being a single parent, she had lost some authority. There was no second parent to back her up and the constant spoken (or unspoken) message of 'Daddy would have let us' danced around her troubled mind. There was also the constant image of her former husband having a trouble-free life of evenings out and no responsibility, whilst she was tied to an everlasting list of tasks and a lack of appreciation. The mental picture of Andy and his girlfriend in some pub laughing with friends was never far away. She imagined them hugging each other publicly and being accepted as a couple by people she once knew. She always found herself shaking that image out of her head, but it never stayed away for long.

Last week she had bent under pressure from her friends and had enrolled on a dating website, "Sophisticated Singles". She hated the idea and the name but Patty had told her it was brilliant and it was the site that had found her current partner Colin, who was fantastic. "Fantastic" was not the word that sprung to mind when she saw the picture of Colin, but Hannah knew she had to move on, or at least try to. Having registered, she was paired with six "ideal matches" and she felt physically sick as she flicked through the photographs and descriptions. The first was James Porterhouse and the description read:

'James is a 46-year-old fun-loving guy who was divorced three years ago and lives on his own during the week in an immaculate apartment in the fashionable district of Bramley Hill near Goole. James loves the theatre, walking with friends and fine dining. He has two boys aged 13 and 16 and they enjoy fishing with their dad as often as they can. James is in middle management, is a car owner and a non-smoker.'

Oh, how her blood ran cold as she read the description! And colder still when she looked at the photograph. James appeared to enjoy fine dining a little too much and Bramley Hill might have been fashionable fifteen years ago, but not so much now. Was the apartment a studio apartment or … a bedsit? The only plus was that he was a non-smoker. He was also a non-starter.

It was the last one that sparked some interest: Simon Drake.

'Simon is a self-employed financial advisor who has recently moved into the area from his former home in Oxford. Simon is 43 and enjoys most sports, but especially football and rugby. He played both sports until work commitments intervened. He has a ten-year-old daughter from his first marriage and, apart from spending time with his child, he also enjoys films, bistro-style restaurants and relaxing at home when he can.'

His picture was a major improvement on James's and Hannah rather hastily clicked Like on the page, knowing this meant her details would be passed on to Simon. She had felt physically sick again and even more so when the agency had telephoned to say that Simon would like to meet her. They asked permission to pass on her email and mobile details and she had said yes so quietly that she'd had to repeat it.

The following day Simon had phoned her and an awkward conversation followed. She was the one who was awkward and felt like running, but instead she had agreed to meet at the Imperial Hotel for a drink at 8pm on Wednesday the following week – if she could get a baby sitter. She had emailed Simon to confirm that the baby sitter was in place. It had seemed like a good idea then, but the days had since flown by and the date was now tomorrow night, which added to her stress.

'For God's sake kids! Will you get downstairs and into the car? Isabel, have you got the present for Cordelia? Ben, what on earth are you wearing? Phoebe! Where are you?' Hannah's temperature was rising as she herded the children into the car, checked all seatbelts were properly fastened and for the tenth time told them to stop arguing. Phoebe was looking as glum as only a four-year-old can as she clung onto her Teddy bear with such ferocity that the poor animal would have suffocated were it real. She had been promised a party with Mummy that the other two would envy, but she wasn't buying it.

★ ★ ★

'Hi Abi … you there?'

'I'm here, Harvey. Been waiting an hour for you.'

'Yeah, sorry about that. We're at the airport and this was the first chance I got to be on my own.'

'So, you are really coming over then? Your parents haven't changed their minds?'

'They are so uncool, Abi. Packing like forever and all kinds of lame stuff like you guys don't have drugstores in the UK. They even packed chocolate and I'm like hey they got chocolate in England folks, just chill out.'

'So when do you arrive?'

'Sometime in the morning, like real early and then a cab takes us to Chelsea. They have a soccer team, don't they? Some Russian dude owns it.'

'I think so but we call it football and I don't really follow it.'

'I'll get in touch when we get settled in. Then we can arrange for you to come. It'll be super cool.'

'Really looking forward to it, Harvey but a bit scared about my parents.'

'Don't be, Abi. We have been through all that – it will be fine. We can't let parents get in the way, can we? You know I love you, Abi and I need to see you and be with you. You know that, right?'

'Yes, I do, Harvey. I love you too. My mum's coming. Speak soon xx.'

Laura asked Abi what she wanted for dinner and received the usual answer of 'anything will do.' She reminded Abi to do her homework and not be on the phone all night to her friends. On her way downstairs, she heard Charles's car pull into the garage. She'd decided she wouldn't greet him at the door or pretend that everything was fine tonight. Hayley had phoned and said they must meet for coffee tomorrow; she needed to talk to her as she had some information but she'd tell her when they met. Laura speculated that perhaps Hayley had discovered Charles was having an affair or something like that. She hoped she was right, as that would give her the perfect reason for leaving – one that was easier to explain and maybe easier for all parties to accept. She was frightened of Charles but she felt some freedom in having told all to Hayley. Although she worried about how Abi would take it and what she would do financially, she was not prepared to be a victim anymore. Hayley had helped her re-discover some of her former self.

That fragile confidence began to drain the moment she saw Charles's troubled face as he came through the door and did not speak. She didn't acknowledge him on her way to the kitchen but once there shouted,

'I'm doing a pasta bake for Abi. Is that all right for you for dinner?'

'Yes, anything will do. I have some work to do in the study so I don't want any interruptions for the next hour or so.'

'Okay,' Laura replied with that familiar churning of the stomach.

★ ★ ★

Two hours? What are you supposed to do for two hours after you've dropped off your children at a party and have a four-year-old in tow? Bloody stupid woman having a party at that stupid time. Hannah had hidden her irritation during the handover of the children to Cordelia's mother. She even smiled to herself at how two-faced she had been; of course, it was no trouble. Phoebe's fine – she's even looking forward to undivided attention! Oh, how easily we all socially lie. Far from being fine, Phoebe was glaring from her seat in the back of the car and Teddy's head risked being torn from his body.

Still unsure what to do, Hannah had driven to McDonalds and appeased Phoebe with a Happy Meal, which had taken up half of the time. Mercifully, the first five minutes after restarting the car had been enough for Phoebe to fall asleep and release the grip on poor Teddy.

Hannah drove around to eat up time and wondered what she would wear tomorrow night on her date and what she would say. It had been so long since she had been on a date that she could barely remember what to do. Should she shake his hand or kiss his cheek? Should she wait for him to make that decision? What would she do if he was deadly dull or there were awkward pauses? Patty had told her not to go on about Andy and the break up, or the kids, or feeling low, but especially not about Andy. Patty said that she had been on a few dates and all they could talk about was their ex-wives and what shits they had been, or about their wonderful kids and how hard it had been for them and how much they missed them. Such a huge turn-off, Patty had said. Oh God, why am I doing this? What if he tries to kiss me after the drink? Maybe I should cancel and say the babysitter can't make it.

The angst and the mulling over of the following evening consumed the remaining time and Hannah joined the queue of mothers collecting noisy children from Cordelia's house. Isabel and Ben came running out with their party bags: plastic toys, cheap sweets and birthday cake, and ran to the car, ignoring their taxi-driver mother. Doors slammed, younger sister awakened and noise levels rising, Hannah drove home wondering what time she would manage to get the children to sleep tonight and if she would get any sleep at all fretting about tomorrow night. She parked on the drive and ushered the children inside without noticing the white van parked opposite, or the driver on his mobile.

'They're back now and in the house. All three kids and the wife. What do you want me to do?'

Chapter 28

David Cooper pulled up outside the chambers of Julian Mountfield QC in Park Place in Leeds for his evening conference with Marcus Tavistock and the CPS solicitor Gerald Hilsdon. Hilsdon had organised the meeting for a pre-trial discussion on evidence and review of the charges on the Tasker case, despite Cooper's efforts to delay it.

A list of fifty or so barristers on framed nameplates tastefully adorned the Georgian brickwork of the impressive entrance and Tavistock was tenth from the top. Of the nine names above him, six were Queen's Counsel and Cooper smiled, knowing two of them to be entirely useless.

As a young police officer, he had struggled to understand the archaic world of lawyers. Barristers could only be instructed by solicitors, rather than the public, and some solicitors could speak in all the courts but some could not or would not. Members of the Queen's Counsel were appointed in some weird system that sounded like a secret society to him. Anyway, he'd soon realised it was no guide as to who to use; some of these barristers were promoted to QC and then received little work as many solicitors were not prepared to pay the massive increase in fees. Some barristers never became QCs, but appeared more talented and expert than many who did. To the layman, the difference was barely noticeable in any real sense. The QC had a little lectern, which he placed on the bench in front of him and the junior barrister, who might be older than the QC, sat behind him. A weird world indeed.

Cooper was a detective constable when he first encountered Marcus Tavistock ten years previously and was giving evidence in a case that Tavistock was defending. Tavistock was portly, even then, but had an intimidating presence and a fearsome reputation. Cooper never lacked confidence and felt up to the challenge, but the barrister had ripped him to shreds in an hour or so of utter torture. He had played the room and the jury like a director making a film in which he was the star. He made some people laugh (when he chose to do so) and would then turn to raw aggression and cut like a knife. Cooper learned more in that hour than at any other time in his career. It never happened again.

Once inside the building, the receptionist told him that Mr Hilsdon had arrived and was with Mr Tavistock in conference room eight and he was to go straight up. Having arrived, he knocked and opened the door to see the 56-year-old barrister leaning back in his large red leather chair opposite Hilsdon, who had an array of papers spread in front of him.

'Ah! Do come in DCI Cooper. I hope you don't mind but we've made a start,' exclaimed the enthusiastic barrister.

'Yes, no problem. Hello, Gerry how are you doing?'

'Fine thank you, David. Take a seat,' answered Hilsdon, shaking Cooper's hand. Tavistock got up and gave a firm handshake, then Hilsdon began.

'So, David, I've just been going through the state of play on the Tasker trial. Marcus has seen the original statements and the various reports we have, as well as the background information. We need to look at the evidence and what we need to be doing before trial.'

Hilsdon had been with the CPS for a few years and although only in his thirties was nobody's fool and knew his own mind. He took his job seriously and had turned down one or two offers to join criminal practices in the private sector. He was not afraid of a challenge and whilst Cooper always felt he could work with him, he was careful how much he told him. Like a number of police officers, Cooper was suspicious of the CPS and often saw them as an obstacle to get over in terms of getting a result in court.

'Okay, where do you want to start?' asked Cooper.

'Well, let's start with the car Tasker was driving on the night. Have you traced it?' Tavistock enquired.

'No, I'm afraid not.'

'Nothing at all?'

'No. We had the description from Mr Connolly, which was pretty good as he's in the motor trade, but there was a delay in a proper search for it. Connolly didn't get the registration number so we couldn't use the camera recognition system to track it.'

'What about CCTV cameras in the area?'

'We drew a blank on that as well. We think the car was torched on a nearby industrial estate sometime later. It was a BMW that was burnt and there were signs of damage to the front panel but there were no forensics we could use. It was a stolen car, which we were able to trace from the chassis number.'

'Did Tasker have a BMW registered to him at the time?'

'No. He is notionally a car trader with two other people

so they have cars coming and going between them all of the time. The trading is probably a cover for his main business of drug trafficking.'

'Was there a blue BMW amongst his stock around that time?'

'I'm afraid there was a couple of weeks' delay in the enquiry on that one. We did trace a blue BMW but it was in pristine condition, which may be because it had been repaired, but there was no way of establishing that. We had an engineer check it and he said it may have been re-sprayed recently but Tasker's mate said he re-sprayed it before the incident as it needed work when he bought it a couple of months before. The previous owner couldn't help much either.'

'Pity you couldn't have found it straight away in its damaged state.'

'Take that up with the Home Secretary and get us proper resources,' Cooper replied firmly.

'Moving on, David,' Hilsden interceded. 'I gather we have a problem with Mr Newcombe.'

'Problem?' Cooper asked somewhat taken aback; he had not shared the information about the potential bribe.

'Yes. As you may know, Tasker is being represented by Jacob Newman in these chambers and he has indicated to Marcus that his client believes the description of him was given to Newcombe by one of your officers and that Newcombe will confirm that.'

'How would Tasker know what Newcombe may or may not say?' Cooper answered, the temperature rising.

'You tell us,' Tavistock asked joining the fray.

'Newcombe is frightened. Anybody would be when

they'd been nearly killed, and Tasker will try and intimidate him if he can. We're keeping an eye on him and warning Tasker to behave himself,' was Cooper's defensive response.

Hilsden intervened, trying to mediate in the uncomfortable atmosphere that was developing.

'We need a clearer statement on the ID. Maybe that can form part of his victim statement, describing the effect on his life since the attack'.

'We're looking into that,' Cooper responded, trying to sound neutral and disguising his irritation at two barristers from the same chambers chatting about evidence over coffee.

'What about the motor dealer? Where are we with him?' Tavistock changed tack.

'He's clear on his evidence.'

'And are you fearful of intimidation there, David?' Tavistock asked, referring to Cooper by his first name.

'We're keeping an eye on that as well.'

Cooper hesitated a little, whilst he calculated how much to say. The concern he had was the line he was walking: if he gave too much information, the CPS may drop the case altogether; if he held too much back, he could be looking at disciplinary proceedings himself. He compromised:

'There have been approaches to Mr Connolly and he has disclosed those approaches to us. We are working together to try and obtain evidence of the intimidation and bring other charges.'

Tavistock and Hilsden looked at each other without changing expression before Tavistock turned to Cooper.

'So, what's the nature of these approaches?'

'He's had a few phone calls warning him to be careful

and he's been offered some money.'

'Money for what?' Hilsden enquired, clearly wondering why he hadn't been told this before.

'No requests were made. He was told it was for "compensation" – for being used by the police to fit somebody up.'

'How much was he offered?' Tavistock asked.

'No particular amount, just compensation,' Cooper lied for no particular reason other than his mistrust of the cosy barrister arrangements he saw as a threat.

'Is Mr Connolly in danger, David?' Tavistock added in a softer tone.

'We're looking out for him and have provided him with a phone for emergency assistance. He also has my mobile number.'

'Are you worried for him, David?' Tavistock pressed, leaning forward and placing his elbows on the enormous mahogany desk.

'Not especially, but he is at some risk.'

'Keep a very close eye on him. We don't want a repeat of that unfortunate business with poor old Graham Todd, do we?'

Chapter 29

Andy arrived home having tried to imagine what sort of photograph of Rebecca had appeared on Facebook. He had thought of stopping the car to check before he got home but the traffic was fairly heavy and there was no obvious place to stop. Besides, Rebecca seemed to be in such a state, he thought he'd better get home as quickly as he could. He parked outside and walked quickly to the door, which opened before he got there. Rebecca had the phone in her right hand and showed him the picture as he stood on the front step.

'Let's go inside,' he said, gently placing his hand on her back to escort her into the house. Standing in the hallway, he looked at a grainy picture of Rebecca standing beside her car in a car park.

'Do you know where this is?'

'Yes, it's Sainsbury's car park.'

'Do you know when it was taken?'

'How would I know that for fuck's sake?' she fired back.

'You might remember when you went from what you're wearing in the photo.'

'What?' she exclaimed as she snatched the phone out of Andy's hand.

'Oh God, I don't know! Maybe last week or the week before. Looks like I'm wearing jeans, so I wouldn't have been at work but I don't know. Who's following me and why are they doing it? WHY ANDY? WHY?' she shouted.

'Calm down, babe. Let's have a drink and think about it.'

'Have a drink? Your answer to everything. We're being

followed and God knows what's going to happen next, and all because of you having that damned accident.'

'Look, Rebecca, it isn't my fault. What do you expect me to do?'

Rebecca let out a scream of frustration, threw her phone on the sofa and ran upstairs. Andy's instinct was to shout after her, but he knew that would lead to a furious row and he was tired of thinking, tired of arguing and tired of being afraid. He walked over to the drinks cabinet and poured himself a whisky and sat down, still wearing his overcoat.

The drink had no effect, as is often the case when it's most needed. It seems to take a bath full of alcohol to relieve stress or anxiety before an event or after a disappointment. Conversely, a thimbleful can seem to rob all sense when it's most needed.

Andy poured himself another drink and thought of ringing Cooper again, but he knew he would say he had to catch them in the act and, once again, put him under pressure. No, he would get Rebecca to close her Facebook account and that would at least solve the posts going on to her page. Although they had her contact details, so messages could start to appear anywhere. He was sure now that the phone details had been stolen and that Tasker had them.

Maybe the second drink was having some effect as he started to contemplate taking the fight back to Tasker. He pulled his diary out of his pocket and opened a notes page to write his list of counter attacks. Number 1 was allowing a trap to be set enabling an arrest, but he was still not keen on that. Number 2 was Ted Lomax and a vision of Tasker being held by his ankles over the suspension bridge. He was beginning to like that option but was afraid of the consequences. Did something like that not make him the same as Tasker? Truth to tell, he had started having visions of shooting Tasker in the head or running him over but they were fantasies. Number 3 was meeting with Tasker and facing him, but what would that achieve? His problem had no solution. He couldn't back out of being a witness as that might lead to criminal charges against him but he couldn't avoid risk to his safety either.

A new determination was developing in him; he could no longer tolerate the idea that Tasker and the people who worked with him would get away with it. He had a real anger fuelling him now: Tasker was a disease, a cancer in society that eats away at the fabric of normality and threatens law-abiding people who just want to go about their lives. How could he assist him get away with his crimes or his lifestyle? He would love not to be in this situation, but he was and he wasn't prepared to lose everything because of this evil man he had accidentally met.

One final thought flitted across his mind: Graham Todd – the man stabbed in the other crime involving Tasker that he'd read about. What had happened to him? He must try and find out.

★ ★ ★

Hannah finally got the children to bed after hearing the whole story of Cordelia's party from Isabel and Ben. Cordelia had insisted on winning the pass the parcel game after being eliminated twice, then, during musical chairs, her mother had returned a chair and told everyone it was Cordelia's special day so she should be allowed back in. Having won the prize, Cordelia had ripped it open and then thrown it to the ground, disappointed it was only a box of jelly babies. Ben had asked if he could have them but Cordelia had said no. Hannah felt like suggesting that the next time, they went to Cordelia's house she would give them a gun and they could shoot her and her mother but instead found herself making excuses for the behaviour and saying how nice it was for them to be at a party. She smiled at the deceptions she created to try and say the right things to her children and how nice it might be to tell the truth.

The day had been very draining for Hannah and the job of being a single parent was always much more challenging when there was no back up at home. Andy always took the kids to parties and seemed to have endless patience with the children and the parents. He was always cheerful when he returned and not bothered if there was a meal ready or if they ordered a take away. She was so exhausted; she had done neither and the absence of food had depleted her energy even more. How she yearned for those days when she had a voracious appetite and was worried about gaining weight. Now she had a poor appetite and her mother thought she was 'painfully thin'. Even when she did have a big meal or a few extra drinks, she didn't seem to gain the extra weight. If anyone else told her that she looked tired she might well look for that gun and shoot them. Who decided it was all right to tell somebody they looked tired?

Now sitting quietly on her own, she thought again about her date with Simon Drake tomorrow night and immediately started to feel her face flush. Perhaps she should call him and cancel. She would just say it was too soon for her – maybe some time in the future would be better but she could hardly expect him to wait. Perhaps she could say she'd met someone. Well, he would hardly believe that, would he? They only spoke the other day. She threw her head back against the headrest of the chair and closed her eyes. She knew that anxiety and regret was sweeping into her again and another night of interrupted sleep was on the cards. But she was totally unaware of the white van outside, which had started up and driven slowly away. It would return tomorrow now that instructions had been given to the driver.

★ ★ ★

Laura had finished the preparation for the meal and shouted for Abi to come downstairs to eat. She went to the study door and could barely bring herself to even enquire, but heard herself say,

'Charles, I'm about to serve up. Do you want to join us or shall I leave some in the oven for you?'

She realised she was developing a disconnected, formal tone to her voice when talking to Charles. She thought it sounded like a cross between Margaret Thatcher and John Major. It was not deliberate, but she was unconsciously hiding her anger and hatred with the tone. Yes, it was now hatred and when she allowed herself that thought, the feeling grew within her. She knew she had to tell Abi what was happening and then make her escape with her daughter, but she had no plan and, at the moment, nowhere to go. She also knew that Charles would not be shaken off easily; in fact, she feared she may never get rid of him. The thought of solicitor's letters, arguments and Abi's disappointment made her feel cold and clammy but she had to find the strength; she could no longer tolerate this man.

'I'm tied up, so leave something in the oven,' was his curt but welcome response. At least they could eat in peace.

Abi chatted away over dinner about school and friends, and even played with the idea of telling her mum that she had a special friend she was going to meet. Harvey's warning about the danger of telling her parents was the only thing that stopped her from sharing her plans.

Laura too was at a roadblock when it came to sharing information. She started a few sentences, designed to lead to her admitting things were not good between her and Charles and she was thinking of separation. Abi and Laura glanced at each other several times, trying to summon up the words to divulge something of great importance, but for some reason, were unable to move forward.

The decision not to confide in each other would have dire consequences for them both.

Chapter 30

Rebecca had calmed down a little by the next day and had closed her Facebook account, something she found surprisingly difficult to do. She had followed Andy's advice and sent a message to all her contacts saying she feared her phone had been hacked and to be wary of any messages they might receive. She also changed her number and informed everyone. She had however, failed to spot one contact in the list: Amanda Kelly, her longstanding friend. Amanda's genuine number was under the name Kelly Amanda and a casual glance would fail to notice the different number. If she'd seen it at all, she would have assumed it was a repeat of her friend's name – a double reference – and if she had noticed the different number, she would have concluded it must be an old one. It was neither. She had just alerted the thief of her new number.

★ ★ ★

Hayley had wrestled the whole drive home with the information she had received about Charles Peterson. At first, she thought about driving straight round to the house and confronting him in front of Laura. She ruled that out straight away; Abi would probably be there and she could see how upsetting it would be for a teenager. The second idea was to see Charles on his own, but what would she achieve? He would deny it all and tell her to mind her own business. Should she tell Laura's brother and father so that they could protect her, or make her see sense? She had promised Laura she wouldn't do that. She realised that her only option was to speak to Laura on her own, make her see that she had to leave and face the consequences of doing it. She was settled on that course of action – it was just a question of how to arrange it.

But as she pulled into her garage at home, doubts began to emerge which encouraged her to think it through a little more. She thought about her cousin, Amy, who had ignored all the information she had been given by her and her friends about her husband's cheating. Amy had sought help from the family and her friends about how unhappy she was but when help was offered, she had bound herself more tightly to the cheating husband and attacked those who criticised him. Hayley had fallen out with Amy in exasperation, as had others, and she was now isolated and still living with a cheating, possibly abusive husband. Hayley simply couldn't understand how a woman could suffer any form of abuse from a partner and stay; it seemed a form of denial and a fear of the alternative – a thought process that was alien to her and she would have thought that Laura would be the same. Hayley decided she had to be careful and think this through before she approached Laura.

* * *

Charles had finished reading the letter he had been given by Trevelyan and had made notes in his own defence. His mood had not improved as he realised that some of the points were strong and that action of some sort was likely. He tried to find explanations for the errors or oversights and concluded that he was not being given enough support at work or at home. The best leads at the office were given to that infernal arse, George Pilbury, who played golf with Trevelyan. Then there was the new partner Gloria Chamberlain who had a first-class honours degree and boy, did she let everyone know about it. She had gathered her own work since becoming a partner and was obviously a big favourite now. She was far too smug for Charles's liking.

Then there was his home life: Laura could see he was under stress, but she persisted in winding him up or being cold to him, despite everything he had given her and all he'd done for her daughter. He had treated Abi as though she was his own, despite the fact that some other man had been inside Laura with his filthy sperm and she had not had the sense to take precautions. Images then filled his head of Laura lying on a bed and another man lying on top of her. They were both groaning and writhing about, then changing positions as she willingly let him do anything and everything to her – his own wife.

Laura had cleared away her and Abi's dinner plates and was settling down to watch TV. The entire time, she was playing over in her mind the conversation she was going to have with Charles. She had reluctantly settled on a plan to stay, but on certain conditions and her heart thumped inside her chest as she rehearsed how she was going to present her terms. Initially, she had postponed her plan when she had seen the mood Charles was in, but then she had found some of her long-lost confidence and decided to confront him tonight. This was the last-chance saloon: he either accepted the terms or she would tell him she was leaving and file for divorce. Her mouth dried again at the thought but she knew she would just have another sleepless night if she left it any longer. She walked back into the kitchen and poured herself a glass of white wine.

A little after nine o'clock, Charles left his study and went straight to the kitchen.

'Is that you, Charles?'

'Yes, I'm just going to grab something to eat.'

'Can we have a chat first?' she replied, heart racing.

'Not tonight, Laura, I'm preoccupied with work.'

Digging deep, Laura got up and marched unsteadily into the kitchen.

'I'm afraid there's something we have to discuss,' she said nervously as Charles took out leftovers from the oven.

'What is it now for God's sake?' he replied without looking at her.

'We need to talk about how things are going to change here … one way or the other.'

'What do you mean by that?' Charles replied, uncharacteristically calmly.

'You know what I mean. I'm prepared to give our relationship another chance but it is the last chance and things must change dramatically … and I mean dramatically.' Laura surprised herself with her defiant composure but took another sip of wine to replace lost moisture in her mouth.

'Look Laura, I know things haven't been right but I'm under pressure at work and need to sort a few things out. I may even need to move firms, but I can't do that right now. I will change and our relationship will change, but I need time.'

'Well, you have to agree to counselling about your anger and your violence. One more and I am out of here. Do you understand?'

There was a pause, a stand-off almost, as they both looked at each other as prize fighters might whilst searching each other out for weaknesses and planning the next move.

'You're right Laura, it has to stop and I have to change and be a better man – a better husband and father to Abi. You know I love her and want to be there for her. You know, that don't you? You must do. We'll have a proper dinner on Friday and sort all of this out, I promise. In the meantime, I need to concentrate on this piece of work I have to do.'

Laura had imagined several outcomes to her ultimatum, but had not considered this one. She was ready for violence, ready to defend herself and to flee, but this measured contrition was totally unexpected and it wrong-footed her.

'Well, all right,' she said meekly. 'We'll talk about it on Friday, but no excuses or delays. I mean it, Charles. Oh, and I'm going back to work. I've been offered my old job back; well, actually a better job, but with my old boss and I am going to do it. That is non-negotiable, Charles. You understand, don't you?'

Charles nodded. 'We'll talk everything over on Friday, I promise. Now, I'm going to take this food into the study and get on, if that's all right with you.'

'Yes, of course. But remember Charles, I mean it.'

'I realise that, Laura. I really do,' he replied, leaning forward and kissing her lightly on the cheek before heading back to his study.

Laura wasn't sure how to react but sto
kissed her. Once he'd gone, she felt a sen
her nerve in confronting him and the fact t
a solution was in the process of being foun
even be able to preserve things, not have to ~~upoci Abr~~ and
admit to her family and friends that her marriage had failed.
Perhaps there was hope after all.

Charles opened the study door, placed his plate on the
desk and whispered, 'fucking bitch'.

★ ★ ★

Rebecca had just finished her call with her mother who
had phoned from Spain. She was concerned about what had
happened to cause her daughter to change phones and warn
people about rogue messages. Rebecca had told the whole
story to gasps and squeals from her mother.

Her mother made no secret of the fact she did not
approve of her relationship with a married man. She had
blamed Andy for the affair and advised her daughter to find
a nice single man who had no baggage. Largely because of
that, mother and daughter had suffered a cooling of their
relationship. And although her mother usually returned to
the UK twice a year, there had only been one visit this
year and she had stayed with Rebecca's Auntie Marjorie
in Dorset. That had irritated Rebecca further – her mother
didn't get on well with her sister Marjorie but had preferred
that to meeting Andy. She usually spoke to her mum once
or twice every few weeks by phone but the calls were

ᵥays short. This was different and Rebecca drew strength from her mother's genuine concern for her.

As Rebecca replayed the conversation in her mind, particularly the tearful expressions of love for one another, her phone pinged with a new message. She smiled, expecting a reaffirming text from her mother but when she saw the message, it was from an unrecognised number. Her smile dropped away as she read it:

'Saw you go into your house this afternoon Rebecca. Those light blue jeans really suit that lovely body of yours. Hope to see you soon xx.'

Chapter 31

There was a universal tension in the air the following day, for so many people and for so many different reasons. The common denominator was a feeling that something was imminent; the series of circumstances affecting their lives had boiled up to a point where something was going to happen – something significant, bringing to a head the questions, dilemmas and imponderables that had been floating around of late.

Hannah had been nervous all day. She had reached for a phone several times to cancel tonight's date but still hadn't managed to make the call. She was paralysed on the high diving board of life and scared to jump, but unable to turn around to walk to the stairs taking her back down. Back to where? Back to a life of sadness and regret, of feeling cheated of a life she had, a peace she had lost. She loved being a mother, but did not want to be defined by it. She was a woman who happened to be a mother but did not want to become purely a checker of homework, provider of meals, taxi service and the constant sole source of discipline, then abuse from the very children she loved. She wanted to buy clothes, dress to impress, to feel attractive and attracted to somebody else. The thought of somebody other than Andy frightened and daunted her. She was so much older than when they had first dated and somehow her emotional connection with dating was stuck in that era – as though she should be dating someone of the age Andy was when they met. She knew that was illogical, but felt that someone of forty was too old.

Now the time had come. Hannah had tried on almost every piece of clothing she had during the two hours she spent getting ready. Underwear was graded as either too sexy or too matronly. Why was she worried, she mused – she had no intention of her date seeing her underwear, still less helping her out of it. But she needed to feel good and confident and so chose some silky pants and a matching bra. Looking at her slim body, she did feel good and eventually chose a knee-length, fitted dress she had bought a few weeks ago to cheer herself up. She looked good to the extent that Isabel asked her if she was going to a party and, if so, could she come too. With a pang, Hannah wished she was taking her daughter with her.

The taxi arrived on time and having kissed the children goodnight and given her number to the babysitter for the fifth time, she was off. Hannah reminded herself of the advice not to go on endlessly about her ex and her children and practised in her mind some conversation topics away from those subjects. As she did, she felt her temperature rise and a droplet of perspiration trickle from her right armpit into the fabric of her dress. That's all I need, she thought, to look like a sweaty cow when I meet him. The thought caused her to laugh out loud and when the taxi driver looked in his rear-view mirror, she pretended to be looking at her phone.

At the restaurant, she paid the driver, took a deep breath and walked in. Hannah was shown to her table in the corner where Simon Drake stood upon seeing her, smiled and, extending his right hand said,

'Hi! You must be Hannah. I'm Simon and it's lovely to meet you.'

There was something about him that put her immediately at ease. He hadn't gone for an awkward kiss or not known what to do. He seemed polite and friendly. He was dressed in smart jeans, an expensive shirt and a casual jacket. His hair was greying, but had a modern cut without trying to look too young and he was quite good looking.

'Nice to meet you, Simon. I'm sorry but I am out of practice at this, so please bear with me,' Hannah replied, surprising herself with her honesty but her instinct told her this man was someone she could be relaxed with.

'Oh, don't worry, Hannah. I'm so rusty at this, they'll probably hear me creaking at the next table!' he replied which had them both genuinely laughing.

The conversation was unforced and they ordered a bottle of Sancerre as they chatted and glanced at the menu. Hannah felt quite hungry and ordered a pate starter and the rack of lamb before she had time to think about the process of eating it. Perhaps she should have ordered something easier to eat. At the end of the meal she looked at her plate, clean apart from the stripped bones, and realised she must have managed but she had been caught up in the conversation. She wondered about the advice she had received beforehand.

'Oh Simon, I hope I haven't been going on about my kids and my ex.'

'No, not at all. I asked you questions about them and you asked about my daughter but don't worry – you didn't go on about them. I imagine you have read the books about not doing that when dating,' he grinned.

'No, it was a friend who warned me about that,' she smiled back. She couldn't remember what Simon's details with the dating agency had said.

'Sorry, Simon, I asked about your daughter but not your ex. What's the situation there?'

'My wife died, Hannah.'

'Oh my God, Simon! I'm so sorry. I should have remembered that from your profile,' she said blushing in genuine embarrassment.

'No need to apologise: I didn't let them include it because it tends to produce all kind of reactions from "he must be looking for a mother for his daughter" to "never go out with a widower – you'll be up against a saint.", And so I prefer to leave it off the profile and just discuss it when it comes up.'

'Do you mind me asking how she died?'

'Not at all. It was a car accident five years ago. One of those moments you can't anticipate or control. A drunk driver hit her when she was coming home from a friend's house. She was dead by the time I got to the hospital.'
Hannah's eyes clouded in sympathy.

'That must have been so hard for you and your daughter.'

'It was. I think I cried for about two years but you have to pick yourself up and catch the threads of life. One day, I decided I was not going to be sad for the rest of my life; Sally wouldn't have wanted me to be. Life is for living, Hannah. Now how about another bottle of wine?'

Rebecca had been waiting for Andy to return home.

It had been her day off and she had been shopping with her friend Karen until around four o'clock, when she came back to the house, just before her mother rang her. The text from the unknown number had really spooked her. She was still wearing the light blue jeans mentioned in the text and the fact that the text referred to her going into the house this afternoon meant that whoever sent it was there a short time ago. They might even be there still.

She had run to the door after the text came and locked and bolted it. She even pulled the curtains closed in the front room that faced the street. For the last hour, she had been mulling over what to do, when she heard Andy's car pull up. Half a minute later, he came through the door.

'You home, Rebecca?' Andy shouted.

'In here,' she replied, without getting up from the armchair in the living room. Andy walked in, saw her strained look and sat down on the sofa opposite her.

'What's the matter love?' he asked gently.

'Look at this text I got this afternoon,' she replied, passing over her mobile.

Andy took the words in.

'Shit! Who do you reckon it is?'

'It's one of them isn't it? Drysdale or Smith or whatever their real names are – maybe even Tasker himself. They're letting us know we're being followed and they can get to us at any time.'

'I'll ring Cooper now' Andy said, decisively picking up his phone.

'What's the point? He'll just say it could be anyone and that they can't be sure enough to arrest anybody,' Rebecca replied, weary resignation evident in her voice.

'Well, what do you want me to do?' he enquired.

'There's nothing you can do, is there? We're just sitting ducks waiting for them to strike, aren't we?'

Andy knew instinctively that Rebecca had something in mind, some plan of action. He knew her well enough to know that she was no sitting duck and wasn't going to just wait around.

'What do you want to do?'

There was a moment's delay as she shuffled in her seat, crossed her legs and leaned back.

'My mum rang today because of the phone thing. She's really worried about me. I told her everything, although she doesn't know about the text because that came after I'd spoken to her.'

'So, what does your mum want you to do?'

'She wants me to go and stay with her in Spain for a while; take myself out of the firing line.'

'And what do you want to do?' Andy asked calmly.

'I said no. I don't want to leave you alone while this is all going on, but I am really scared Andy and after this text, and these bastards hanging around our house, I really don't know.'

Andy thought for a while and stayed calm. On one level, he was disappointed that Rebecca was considering it. He couldn't help but feel that Hannah would have rolled up her sleeves and they would have fought everything together. But Rebecca wasn't Hannah and although it was unfair to compare them, it didn't stop him doing it. And if she did go, it would be one less thing for him to worry about, that was for sure.

'Maybe you should go. You'd be safer there and you could spend some time with your mum. After all, she's never going to come here, is she? And even if she did, it wouldn't make you feel any safer. Why don't you check the flights and see what's available.'

'But I don't want to leave you on your own. Why not come with me?'

'You know I can't do that. I have the business to deal with and the kids to think about. I might even be a bigger target over there. Better that they think we've broken up, then you're less of an interest to them.'

'We aren't though, are we?'

'Aren't what?'

'Breaking up.'

'No, of course not! But let them think that.'

There was nobody watching the house at that moment. They had moved on and were now watching somewhere else, ready to make their move.

Chapter 32

The bill was delivered to the table and Simon Drake immediately pounced on it.

'Let's split the bill, Simon, I would prefer that ... really I would,' Hannah said leaning forward.

'I'm an old-fashioned guy, Hannah; I wouldn't be comfortable sharing the bill. It's my treat and, to be honest, I've had a terrific evening,' he said holding her gaze.

'Well, that's very kind of you, but my treat next time,' she replied smiling.

'Will there be a next time then?' Simon enquired, leaning forward. Hannah had spoken without thinking and it was just the standard response she would automatically give in response to an act of generosity, but this was a date. She thought for a second.

'Well, who knows? Looks like I'm committed now, doesn't it?' she flirted, much to her surprise.

'Sounds like it to me!' he replied placing his credit card on the bill.

Hannah had enjoyed herself and was a little merry by the second bottle of wine but wasn't drunk. She had stopped drinking a little while ago and had switched to water, wanting to stay in control of her faculties. She felt she did want to see him again and at least tonight she had felt young again and desired – she liked the feeling.

'Can we share a taxi home?' Simon enquired when they went to collect their coats.

'We go in different directions I think, but let's walk to the taxi rank together,' Hannah replied as they walked the few hundred yards to the rank. She thought about linking his arm but decided that was too forward at this stage. When they arrived, they had a short wait until it was their turn and when they approached the available taxi, Simon opened the rear door and gestured her inside as the gentleman he appeared to be. As she passed, she kissed him on the cheek and said she would ring him. Like a teenager, she felt the rush of excitement as the door closed and she waved goodbye. He waved back and got into the next waiting cab.

The children had played the babysitter up: Phoebe had awoken and insisted she have her mum come and read a story to her but eighteen-year-old Rachel had managed the situation well and read several stories before Phoebe's resistance was exhausted. Ben had told Rachel that his mum had said he could watch anything he liked on TV, including a horror film on Channel 4, but Rachel had said no. She even called his bluff and said she would ring his mum if he wished. Ben, having thought better of it, had declined. Isabel had been the easiest to look after but Rachel felt she had thoroughly earned her money tonight. The taxi pulled up and Hannah opened the front door quietly.

'How have they been, Rachel?'

'Oh, not too bad, Mrs Connolly.'

'Please call me Hannah. You make me sound so old! "Not too bad" sounds like they weren't very good.'

'They are lovely kids Mrs ... sorry, Hannah. The money is great for me anyway with Uni coming up so please don't ask anybody else.'

'Don't worry, Rachel, no chance of that. Your mum will miss you when you go and so will I,' Hannah answered whilst pulling the cash out of her purse.

Rachel walked to the front door but turned just as she reached for the handle.

'Oh, somebody called when you were out.'

'I bet you couldn't find the phone because it's never in its holder.'

'No, they knocked on the door.'

'Knocked on the door? Who was it?'

'He said his name was … hang on a minute, I made a note in my phone. Yes, here it is: Terry Balderstone. Said he had been asked to come around and quote for some electrical work.'

'Never heard of him. You didn't let him in did you?'

'No, he didn't ask to come in either but he had a white van and I think there was somebody else with him … you know … in the van. Anyway, he said he would call later when you were in.'

'Thanks, Rachel.'

Hannah was perplexed. She had no need for an electrician and what time of night was that for one to call? She thought about ringing Andy but it was late and she would think about it. Instead, she made herself a hot drink and went up to bed.

Andy and Rebecca had gone on to the Internet and found a flight to Spain for the next morning. Initially Rebecca thought that was too soon but the next convenient flight was three days later and they both realised it was better if she went sooner rather than later. Once the Genie had escaped the bottle; that Rebecca would rather be out of the firing line than tough it out with her partner, it was difficult for either of them to work up any enthusiasm for her to stay. They both felt it and there was a cooling between them. As much as they pretended it hadn't happened, they both knew it had. They went to bed, each uncertain about approaching the other for a last night of passion and ended up settling for cuddles and a night of fitful sleep.

★ ★ ★

It was 3am when the move was made. There is something about three o'clock in the morning that seems to attract those embarking on dark deeds.

Arnie Gallagher was a man with a long criminal record. He was 39 but his shaven bulbous head, tattooed neck and large frame made him look 50. Criminal convictions for burglary, robbery and violence had meant that he had spent as much of his adult life in prison as out of it. Prison was an occupational hazard for him; the only life he knew was crime, either as part of a criminal gang or freelancing for others. He did not deal drugs himself, but often worked for those who did.

He was a night-time villain as his appearance meant he could not hide in plain sight. His job tonight was to break into the house, giving his partner for the night access to it. He had been given details of the locks on the doors and windows. The rear sash window appealed to him as it was poorly maintained, had no secure lock and was hidden from the street. In the stillness of the early hours and the pitch-blackness away from street lighting, he had got into position and inserted the thin metal wedge in between the wooden frames to force open the catch. It was stiff, so he widened the gap and used the thin hacksaw blade to cut carefully through its fragile metal. After a minute or so, the released piece fell quietly on to the bottom sill. He was then able to pull open one of the frames to allow access. The window creaked as he did so, but he was surprisingly delicate at these tasks for such a big man. A large wrench lay at his side in case he was disturbed. His tightly fitted rubber gloves allowed free movement of his fingers without the risk of leaving prints.

Once fully opened, he signalled 'Tatie' forward. James Tate was a much smaller man and, at 27, younger. Known to everyone as Tatie, he also had a long list of convictions but his were drug related in the main. He had done his fair share of thieving, but dealing in drugs of any sort was his preferred game. He didn't like this job but he had no option as he owed the bosses money and in his business, you either paid or lost body parts. Accepting the job was a no-brainer.

The absence of a burglar alarm meant once inside they didn't need to worry about ringing bells and security lights. Using small torches, they wandered into the living room looking for the family photographs and frames they had been told to take, as well as mobile devices and laptops. Two family pictures were picked up and stuffed into the canvas bag, then they moved into the kitchen.

The Mac Pro was open and still plugged into the socket as they approached it. They took it, along with the plugs.

There were no mobiles and Gallagher whispered to Tatie, suggesting he creep upstairs to see if they were easily visible. A whispered argument followed as Tatie wanted to get out but Gallagher told him to get on with it. He grasped the wrench more tightly and indicated that he'd deal with anyone coming at them or use it on Tatie, if he didn't get his arse up the stairs. The pair gingerly made their way to the staircase and the first stair creaked loudly, causing them both to stop and switch off the torches. Silence followed and Tatie's small frame and cat-like balance prevented any further noise. On the fifth step from the top Tatie put on his torch, immediately illuminating a figure standing on the top step looking straight at him.

'Who are you?' said four-year-old Phoebe Connolly wearing her nightdress and clutching her teddy bear. She showed no alarm and appeared to have just woken up. She stared at him in her natural childlike innocence. Tatie was, for a second, frozen to the spot ... but only a second. He turned and bounded down the stairs slightly behind the bulky figure of Gallagher, who was already making for the window.

Hannah Connolly slept like most parents, almost as though a sixth sense operated through slumber enabling her to listen for any noises that might relate to the children. She woke suddenly as she heard footsteps and realised one of her children was up and about. Lights on and scrambling out of her room, she hurried on to the landing, saw Phoebe and realised immediately that someone had been in the house. Finding a tiger-like courage, she jumped two stairs at a time and ran towards the open window, flicking on the lights as she went.

In the kitchen, Hannah pulled out the largest knife from the rack and searched the house room by room, ready to stab anyone who appeared and threatened her 'cubs'. Still shaking, she rang 999, when she was sure whoever had broken in had fled. The white van was already speeding on its way, false plates making it hard to identify. Tatie was on his phone to his boss.

'We got in. You never said nothing about kids being in the house! You never said nothing about that.'

'What did you get?'

'Photos and a laptop.'

'Any mobiles?'

'No … we were rumbled and had to do a runner. You never said nothing about kids in the house,' Tatie repeated indignantly.

'Did they see you?'

'Yeah.'

'Good. Bring me the stuff and then fuck off.'

★ ★ ★

Andy took Rebecca to Leeds/Bradford airport for the 7.45am flight. They talked as if nothing unusual was happening and Rebecca raised the question of summer holidays to test the water as to where they stood. Andy said they could look online when she got back but it would be nice to have a break. They kissed affectionately when she was about to go through the departure gate and Rebecca was a little tearful as Andy waved goodbye. Back in his car he saw three missed calls from Hannah. He rang and she breathlessly explained the night's events. He asked several times if she was all right and how the kids were.

'The police said there have been burglaries in the area recently,' Hannah stated, making it sound like a question.

'Yes, could be,' Andy answered.

'But you don't think it is?'

'No, I don't but I will sort this, Hannah. I promise you that. I'm on my way round now.'

'Take care, Andy. Please take care.'

'Will do ...'

Andy sat for a few minutes mulling everything over. He went to the recent calls list and pressed one of them.

'Gosh, this is early for you! Are you just getting up or going to bed?'

'Hi Dad ... I think I need to speak to Ted Lomax.'

Chapter 33

Andy drove to his old house and had coffee with Hannah and the children, who he cuddled making sure they felt safe. Hannah had hugged him when he arrived and as he left. She appeared calm and strong.

The drive back home was unpleasant for Andy – his head was spinning with the recent developments. Rebecca leaving was one thing, but there was no doubt now that his children were at real risk and anything could have happened to them. For the first time he felt real anguish at not being at their side as he felt he should be. He was not there to protect them or reassure them that everything was going to be all right. He wondered if he could give that reassurance anyway; he was so out of his depth and seemed to be at the mercy of people who could do what they liked and might be capable of anything. That train of thought had started in his mind and he could not seem to switch it off as his imagination filled his head with images of horror. The rage, deep and compelling, was burning within him. Once again, he imagined going into Tasker's home and shooting him in the head or beating him to death with a baseball bat, or of finding the men who'd gone into his children's home, and spraying them with bullets. He had no access to firearms and no experience using them, but the rage disguised his fear and confused his powers of reasoning. The world felt a very unsafe place; suddenly the things he had taken for granted were painfully vulnerable. He sat outside his house for a few moments and stared out of the front windscreen whilst he tried to find some composure, but he really wanted to scream and let out all the pent-up angst within him.

When he showered later on, he kept his head under the spray in the hope that it might clear his mind or wash away some of the images his brain was conjuring up. Although it didn't achieve that, he at least felt fresher and ready for his day. As he was dressing, he saw that he had missed a call from his dad and, still wearing his towel, he returned the call.

'Hi Dad, just missed your call. I was in the shower.'

'Okay, Andy, we're meeting Ted at The Fox and Hounds at Barchester at three this afternoon.'

'We? Are you going to be there as well, Dad?'

'Only to introduce you – then I'll leave you to it.'

'You can stay if you want to.'

'No, Ted wants to talk to you on your own.'

'Why's that then?'

'Not sure really, but he's deep is Ted. I imagine he needs to feel he knows you, be a bit more comfortable with you. Maybe he thinks I would talk too much.'

'Well, he'd be right about that!' Andy tried to lighten the conversation but for once his dad ignored the opportunity for banter.

'I hate these people, Andy. I really do. I ... it's just that I ... anyway, let's see what Ted says.' Andy's father changed tack: 'Have you spoken to that DCI?'

'No, not yet. Why?'

'I would wait until you have spoken to Ted, that's all.'

'Okay, Dad, but I imagine he'll know about the break in by now.'

'Probably. Anyway, I'll see you at three and don't be

late. Ted hates that. So do I, as a matter of fact.'

'I won't be late Dad.'

'Okay, son. Take care now. You know I worry about you, always have, always will; you and your sister.'

'I know, Dad. And you know we love you.'

'Now don't you get soft on me. I love you too. Remember: don't be late.'

Andy wiped his moist eyes at the end of the conversation, got dressed and drove into work but checked every car in the street, as well as everyone in front and behind him on the journey.

He arrived at the garage and was not in the mood to share recent developments or to talk about Rebecca. Instead he sent an email to all staff.

Morning everyone. Just to let you know that Rebecca won't be in for a couple of weeks as her mum is ill and she has gone to her house in Spain to look after her. We'll be a little short handed in the sales team, but think of the opportunities to steal her leads whilst she is away! If there are any specific enquiries that need her input, then just let me know.
Thanks,
Andy.

He felt that should be enough to keep the conversation light, although Andrea was bound to ask what the illness was, so he just had to make sure his story was consistent. He rang Hannah to tell her Rebecca was on her way to Spain but he told her the truth.

'God, Andy! What's going to happen next?' Hannah

asked, concerned but not panicked.

'There's a guy called Tony Billings coming around this evening to see you. He's from Trent Securities and we are going to have every security device going fitted: CCTV, full alarm systems and front door cameras. You know, the ones where when somebody rings the bell it sets off an app on your phone so you can see who it is.'

'Can we afford all of that, Andy?'

'Don't worry about it. We need it and I need you to feel safe. Anyway, the main thing is it is a deterrent.'

'Okay, whatever you say. Are you having the same at your place?'

'No, I'll have a better one.' There was a moment's delay before they both laughed. It had been a long time since they shared a joke.

'Anyway, I have a meeting this afternoon and will come round straight after, if that's all right with you.'

'Yes. Once I've picked the kids up from school I'll be in.'

'Okay, see you later.'

'Oh, Andy ... one other thing.'

'Yes?'

'Oh ... never mind. I'll tell you when I see you.' Hannah thought she might tell him she was seeing someone but changed her mind. Somehow the timing didn't seem right. She would tell him another time.

Andy counted down the minutes until meeting time. Barchester was a small rural village with just one pub and was about twenty minutes away. Aware of his dad's warning, he gave himself an extra twenty minutes to get there. As he pulled into the car park, he saw his father's car and smiled; his dad was always early for everything.

The pub was a typical old village pub, where the smell of beer met you at the door and the dimly lit interior was divided into a public bar, lounge area and a snug. Very basic food was served in all areas but Andy noticed that the snug door was closed and assumed his father was inside. He opened the frosted glass door and Paul Connolly got up from his seat immediately to greet his son. The man sitting opposite him also got up and turned to face Andy.

'Andy, let me introduce a good friend of mine, Ted Lomax. Ted, this is my only son Andy; thank God I didn't have any more boys!'

Andy smiled and shook the hand of this man he had been imagining for a few days. He was more or less what he had expected: he was in his mid-sixties, around six feet tall, powerfully built with a full head of steel-grey hair. He wore an overcoat, despite the weather being mild and had the face of a man you would cross at your peril.

'Hello, Andy. Nice to meet you. I've heard a lot about you.'

'Well if it was from my dad, can I ask you to ignore most of it?'

'Aye, you sound just like him!'

Andy went to sit down but Ted's large right hand extended as an open palm indicating he should wait.

'Just before we go any further, can you get your phones out and switch them off. Not silent, but off and, if you don't mind, I'll need to look inside your jacket and pat you down, just to be sure.'

Andy hadn't expected this and really didn't know how to respond but fought his instinct to make a joke. Instead he handed over both his phones after switching them off and let Ted search him. Ted felt inside of the jacket pockets and patted his shirt and trousers with both hands whilst looking him square in the eyes.

'Sorry, son, but I don't take any chances. I know this pub and they know me so I don't need to worry about the place but I do need to be sure there's no chance of anyone hearing us or us being recorded.'

'Sure. I understand,' Andy replied but he was shaken by the experience which underscored just how uncomfortable he felt and how worried he was about exactly what he might be getting into. Was he jumping out of the frying pan into a fire?

'So, Andy, your dad has given me some details of your trouble. I understand they broke into your wife's house and frightened the kids. Are we sure it was them?'

'Pretty sure. But let me tell you everything and then you can tell me what you think.'

Andy proceeded to tell the whole story and, seeing some of his father's expressions, realised his dad was also hearing some of it for the first time. Ted nodded throughout the tale and when Andy finished, he leaned his large frame into the back of his seat, glanced at Paul and then spoke.

'Well, son, I would say it was them at your house and they would be looking for personal items to show you they had them and could get to you. Maybe someone would come up to you in the street or in a pub and show you a picture of your family or the house. Or if they got a computer or phone, they could share some of that information to get into your head. Aye … I would say it was them. Now Paul, why don't you leave your lad with me to have a little chat and you go back home to that lovely wife of yours.'

Paul Connolly rose, shook hands with Ted and his son, and then left them to it.

Lomax asked Andy if he wanted a drink, ordered himself a pint of bitter and gave a signal to the barman that they were not to be disturbed or overheard. The barman seemed to understand and moved away before confirming that nobody else would be going into the snug while they were there. Sitting back down, Lomax undid his overcoat revealing a surprisingly expensive looking tweed suit underneath that exuded a certain old-world charm.

'That is some story son and I know your dad is worried about you. He had a word with me a couple of weeks ago and I made my own enquiries. I'd heard about this Tasker character before but he never crossed my path so I thought I better find out some details about him.'

'So … my dad asked you to look into it?'

'No, he just asked me what I thought; if I had a view, but I wanted to be sure before I said anything to him or to you.'

'Who do you ask about something like this?'

'Well, you don't need to know that now, do you? I have plenty of friends or associates who know a thing or two and we look after each other. Some are family; some are even better than family, if you know what I mean.'

Andy didn't know what he meant and nearly asked if there was a traveller connection but thought he might inadvertently cause offence so he decided just to listen.

'Here's the thing Andy: Tasker is scum; proper grade A scum and he lives a life you will not understand. He's not frightened of the law or the police or normal things. He's had some convictions in the past – nothing serious – but he has done plenty of serious things and, so far, got away with them.'

'Do we know how?'

'Aye, he likes to brag amongst his set that he has a copper in his pocket and therefore a free pass. He reckons that most times nothing happens when he comes on the radar, but when he's arrested, his inside man queers the pitch for him and he gets off scot-free.'

'Is it Cooper?'

'We don't know who it is and even that arsehole Tasker isn't stupid enough to name him, but there's something going on that's for sure.'

'What is he likely to do to me? Or the kids? Or anybody for that matter?'

'He is bad enough to do something son, no point in me dressing it up. If it was a choice of going away or hurting you, he wouldn't think twice.'

Lomax wasn't telling Andy anything he hadn't already thought himself, but the confirmation from someone else hit him like a hammer blow. He could feel his face reddening as his body temperature rose.

'So ... what are my options then?' he asked in desperation.

'You can ask the police to protect you but they're short-handed, aren't they? Also, until we know who the inside man is – if there is one – we wouldn't know who you could trust.'

'I have asked Cooper, but how can you protect against an attack you can't predict? Cooper says Tasker isn't stupid enough to do something directly.'

'I think he's wrong there. He is dangerous and reckless enough or he wouldn't be in the situation he's in, would he?'

Andy frowned, frustrated.

'What are my other options? Should I just not cooperate with the police and take the risk of legal action? At least my family and I would be safe.'

'I have to say, I wouldn't do that either son. I told you, Tasker is scum. He would think he owned you then and who knows what he would want? He may leave you alone but he knows you have a business and cash. I think he would want to hang on to you.'

'What do you suggest?'

'If it was me, son, I would take the attack to him.'

'I'm a car dealer, Mr Lomax! Not a gangster. What can I do?'

'There are people who would do it for you... you know that. It's simply a question of what they would want and whether you are willing to give the instruction.'

There was an uncomfortable silence as Andy pondered the obvious question and how best to ask it. He had never felt so out of his depth as he did in this moment where his danger was all too real but he was being given what appeared to be the Devil's choice.

'Mr Lomax, can I ask you–'

'Call me Ted, everyone does,' Lomax interrupted.

'Okay, Ted, thank you. I need to ask what you're

offering … you know … exactly what we are talking about here.'

'I think you know but okay, I'll spell it out. There are people who will deal with Tasker for you. You see son, you don't speak his language or understand him but they do. You were unlucky to come across him but we can't pretend you didn't. They will either hurt him really badly or dispose of him permanently – for a fee. And of course, there are no come backs.'

'Oh my God! I don't think that I could do anything like that. Can't they just frighten him? You know, make him realise that he has to stay away or something … something bad might happen … something like that?'

'No, that isn't the way these things work, lad. You send him a frightener and he has to respond to it or he loses face. If you threaten him, or somebody does so on your behalf, he must then attack you to show he isn't afraid and that he has big bollocks. That's his world. If you enter his world, you have to challenge him. It's deeds not words that he needs.'

'I just don't think I could, Ted … I mean, I couldn't live with myself or –'

'Okay son, just think about it. But don't discuss it with anybody, including your dad. The fewer people who know the better. If you want to go ahead, I'll arrange for you to meet someone, somewhere safe and then it is up to both of you. I would put aside some cash over the next few days if I were you, so there's no money trail back to you. That way, you have options.'

'What sort of money?'

'Maybe twenty grand.'

'Is that all it costs for a life?'

'I told you son, he's scum. Besides, I think that's with a discount,' Lomax winked.

A dark and troubling new chapter had been opened up for Andy.

Chapter 34

Charles Peterson had worked all night on his file and the letter of complaint his firm had received. He had gone through all of his messages and emails to find any communication with his clients and was exhausted. He did however, manage a breakthrough with an email to the clients, which informed them there would be a price hike as a result of their recent changes to the design. He had even sent a text to Bradley Allen in accounts, asking him to sort out an amended statement for the clients. The chance to apportion blame elsewhere was emerging and had temporarily renewed his energy as he worked on his approach. He would tell Trevelyan that he accepted full responsibility for not checking that Allen had prepared an amended estimate and brought the account up to date, and that he had learned a valuable lesson. This was executive shorthand for 'It's not my fault, it's the fault of someone below me who cannot do their job properly'. It just might work and get him off the hook.

The next morning, he woke after a disrupted night's sleep. His dreams were troubled and he felt an acute sense of danger in his well-ordered world. The risks at work were very real and his optimism in his exhausted state last night had partially drained away during the night. He felt as though he was a half-charged battery and he was very much on edge. As Laura was in the shower, he heard her phone ping with a message. He picked it up and saw it was from Hayley. He opened it and read it:

*'Hi Laura, I must see you urgently to talk about you know what.
I have some information for you that you must hear. Ring me asap
Hayley xx'*

The last thing Charles wanted was Hayley sticking
her nose into their lives and his strong instinct was the
message related to him. Was this why Laura had given him
an ultimatum? He deleted the message and put the phone
on silent.

At breakfast Abi shifted in her seat and looked at her
mother to try and gauge her mood. She decided to test the
water.

'Mum ...'

'Yes, Abi.'

'Can I arrange to meet a friend after school?'

'Which friend?'

'Oh, nobody you know but it would only be for a few
hours?'

'So, who is this friend?'

'It's somebody from school?' Abi lied spontaneously in
a bid to get a definite maybe as an answer. In her head, she
thought if her mother got used to the idea of her friend
being somebody local, she might give the go ahead and she
could be told the truth later. Anyway, the plan was Harvey's
mother would ring and smooth things over. Abi didn't want
her mother making her sound too young and treating her
like a child ... especially when it came to Harvey.

'Is this a boy, Abi?'

'Yes, it is. Why?'

'So, you have a boyfriend you haven't told me about.

What's his name?' Laura quizzed gently.

'His name's Harvey and he's just moved into the area,' Abi lied again, pleased that this was, at least, partly true.

'Where has he come from then?'

'Not sure Mum, but can I meet him after school?'

'No, you cannot, Abi. We've never met him and we would need to know more about him and where you were going.'

'Well I know him really well. Don't you trust my judgement?' Abi added raising the stakes a little.

Laura extended an olive branch.

'Bring him round to the house and then we can meet him'

'What, so you can make him feel uncomfortable?'

'No! So we can see who you're spending time with.'

'Oh, you're impossible! Just forget it,' Abi snapped.

'Abi don't speak to your mother like that. She's just trying to protect you. There are some very strange people out there, you know?' Charles absently added, taking a break from his own troubles.

'Yes, well Harvey isn't one of them. Let's change the subject.'

Laura smiled, both at the support and the irony of her husband's comment. Abi regretted raising the subject and thought how right Harvey had been about not asking for parents' permission as they always said no. He was right about putting them in a position where they had to say yes. She knew that now and would say no more about it to them. She got herself ready and was off to school.

After Abi left, Charles checked Laura's phone while she cleared away the breakfast dishes. Three missed calls from

Hayley and another text.

'Hey Laura, pick up please I have tried you three times and really need to speak to you.'

Charles coloured with concern. What was this about and how might it affect his plans? If he had to tell Trevelyan his wife had left him it would just add to the suspicion that he was losing control of his life and lessen the chance of support from the partners. He just could not let that happen. Laura was his wife; she had committed herself to him as he had to her. She just had to stop provoking him and show more understanding, then they could go back to where they had been before. It was her fault she couldn't see how her coldness affected him; her lack of understanding of the pressures he faced. She was important to him in that she was an attractive wife – part of a family he could be proud of and talk about to his partners and staff, as well as clients. Divorce was for people who weren't in control; who had no understanding of what you need to do to make things work. In short, it was failure; failure to make a relationship work and he was not going to have that on his record.

An image of Laura arm in arm with another man came into his head and then her kissing him, Abi running to him and calling him Daddy. No, no, no that will never happen. He quickly shook the images away as Laura came back in.

'I'm working from home this morning, Laura,' he said, thinking on his feet. It would give him time to think about how to deal with Hayley and the messages.

'Okay. I have a few things to do and a couple of calls to make,' she replied.

Charles sent a text to the office to say he was seeing a client and wouldn't be in until the afternoon. He went on to the diary system on the firm's internal system and entered a fictitious name for a 10.30 appointment. Now, what would he do about Hayley? Maybe her message wasn't about him but how could he find out? He could hardly ring her and ask, and he had now crossed a line by deleting her texts. He felt the walls closing in.

'Have you seen my phone, Charles?' Laura shouted from upstairs.

'No, I haven't.'

'Can you ring it and see where I left it?'

'Will do.' He pretended to ring even though her phone was on silent in his pocket.

'Can you hear it anywhere, Laura?'

'No. Where can it be?'

'No idea.'

Charles had to know about Hayley so he went into the downstairs cloakroom, opened Laura's messages and clicked on Hayley. Laura thought her phone was secure but Charles never let on that he knew her password. He even made a show of not being able to open her phone to throw her off the scent. He regularly checked the phone without her knowledge, to see who she was talking to and looked for names of men – men who might be sniffing around his wife looking for their chance. He had never bothered to look at calls or texts from other women – especially that bloody cow Hayley but now he was interested. He flicked back to read the history and found an exchange.

Really worried about you and thinking about what you need to do.

I really don't know and there is Abi.

You know my view on that.

I do.

He felt an anger rising as all doubt was removed by the next text:

He won't change sweetheart, you know that.

There was no reply but that evil fucking cow was trying to prise his wife away. What had Laura told her? How bad did she make it sound? His normal tactics of denial and apportioning blame elsewhere deserted him as he thought of public shame and ruin. What to do … what to do? Whatever it was, he had to think quickly.

At her break time Abi found a quiet corner to herself and went on to Snapchat with that usual tingle of excitement. She sent the first message.

'Hi Harvey, have you missed me?'

A moment's delay then a reply:

'Are you still at school? Yes, I've missed you but wasn't expecting to hear from you until later.'

'I know but I can get out of school at 2pm today. We have a supply teacher in and I told him my mum was collecting me to take me to the doctor's – she'd sent the note in weeks ago. I'll tell mum by text that I'll be staying back at school, then your mum can ring her like we planned.'

'Cool.'

'So, can I meet you at the town clock at 2.30 today instead of Friday? Is that okay with your mum?'

'Sure, that would be great! I'll tell Mum. She's really looking forward to meeting you.'

'I can't wait, Harvey xx.'

'Me neither xx.'

There was a brief pause then Harvey wrote,

'Hey, Abi, Mum asks if you know the car park at the back of that supermarket behind the clock.'

'Does she mean Aldi?'

'Yeah, think so.'

'Yes, I know it.'

'She says can we meet you there as she knows how to park in that one ... doh!'

'Okay, what car will you be in?'

'Buzz me when you get there and we'll come to you.'

'Will do ... love you xx.'

'Love you too xx.'

Chapter 35

'Still can't find my phone!' Laura shouted as she wandered around upstairs.

'I've looked everywhere down here. I'm just about to make a coffee, do you want one?' Charles shouted back. Just then Laura's phone vibrated in his pocket and he pulled it out to see a message from Abi.

'Hi Mum. Staying at school with a group until six. One of the mums will drop me off after it finishes. Is that okay? xx.'

Charles couldn't check with Laura without alerting her to the fact that he had her phone. And so he replied:

'Yes, that's fine, Abi. See you later. Love Mum xx.'

He returned the phone to his pocket and shouted again,

'Did you want a coffee, Laura?'

'No, I haven't got time' Laura replied. Charles could hear the footsteps of stiletto shoes and made his way up the staircase.

'Are you going out?' he said, as he located her coming out of the guest room.

'Yes, I told you I had some plans.'

'What plans?'

'I'm meeting my old boss at the new office for a chat,' she answered firmly. This was a new Laura or maybe the old one reborn. She had a busy assertive look about her, a look of being assured and determined. Charles felt the urge to challenge her, but his mind was whirling in a desperate attempt to seize control of the various situations surrounding him. He wanted to say he had not agreed to her returning to work but instead chose a more conciliatory tone.

'I thought we might have lunch together today – have that chat you wanted,' he said in a tone that in recent times had become unfamiliar to Laura. She hesitated at the apparent warmth of his approach before gathering her thoughts.

'Well, that might have been nice, but I've arranged this meeting now so I am afraid I can't.'

'Can't you ring and re arrange?'

'No. Sorry Charles, I can't just drop people at a whim; a whim of yours,' she replied sensing usual service was about to be resumed.

'Okay, but we have a lot to talk about. There are some things happening and some people who would like to see us have problems,' he replied in desperation.

'What things? And who are these people you're talking about?' Laura answered sternly.

Charles was in unfamiliar territory. Not only did he feel a lack of control, but he was being met with a firmness he had not anticipated and was struggling to know how to react. He could feel anger welling up in him, but he was also acutely aware of the risk of losing his temper.

'Some people at work would like to get rid of me and … and … that friend of yours, Hayley, is up to no good, I'm sure of it.'

'Hayley? What on earth has she got to do with anything?'

'She'd do anything to break us up, that's all. She's so jealous that you're married and have a child whereas she can't keep anyone for five minutes. She would love things to go wrong between us and God knows what she might say to make that happen.'

'What are you talking about, Charles? Hayley isn't

jealous of anyone, least of all me. You're talking nonsense. I have to go,' she added brusquely before brushing past him. Charles turned quickly and grabbed Laura's right arm firmly but not aggressively.

'Look, Laura, you don't know her, really you don't. People have told me things about her that I have never mentioned to you purely because I didn't want to upset you. Bad things, mean things. I just …'

'LET GO OF ME,' Laura growled with a threatening glare.

'You need to listen to me,' Charles pleaded but kept hold.

'Let go of my arm now.'

'I will when you calm down.'

'Let go of me, you bastard or I will leave and never come back,' Laura spat out the words slowly and deliberately, totally wrong-footing her husband who, in a panic, moved to grab her left arm. It was like trying to control a horse that was bucking and braying and the move was a mistake. Laura pulled her left hand away, clenched her fist and stuck him full force in his chest. The blow was not painful but was totally unexpected and when her arm recoiled to strike again, he moved his free arm to protect against the blow. Laura swung but also pulled her trapped right arm to free it and, in so, doing lost her balance. When Charles twisted his body to try and hold on to Laura's right arm and avoid her left fist, he caused the overbalancing Laura to fall backwards against the bannister. Laura's back hit the wooden bannister hard. As she tried to turn to grab it, her legs became tangled and she fell heavily down the first flight of stairs, landing with a sickening thud on the half landing. Charles watched as though it was happening in slow motion. He saw his wife's shocked face as she hit the bannister, the registering of pain in her expression and then the ugly tumbling of arms and legs before her head hit the skirting boards and she came to a groaning rest. Charles stood open mouthed for what seemed like an eternity before he jumped down the stairs.

'Jesus Christ, Laura! Oh my God! What has happened? Please, please ... oh my God!' he screamed as he reached her. She was unconscious and making a gargling noise. Charles was terrified. She was breathing though, yes, still breathing. Thank God for that, he thought as he searched for his phone. He remembered he still had Laura's phone in his pocket and in his rising panic he fumbled for it to ring the emergency services. Still shaking, he saw five more missed calls from Hayley. Shit ... shit ... shit ... what am I going to do? He sat down beside his stricken wife and put the phone down. He needed to think.

'Just off now, Mr Andrews,' Abi said to the very young supply teacher as the clock ticked round to two o'clock.

'Ah yes, is your mother here?'

'Yes, she just sent a text saying that she is in the car park.'

'All right then, Abi. See you tomorrow,' he said while preparing notes for class.

Abi skipped out and went into the female toilets to change out of her school uniform, which she stuffed into her bag, and into her jeans and top. She applied her lipstick, combed her hair and then she was off. When she arrived at the Aldi car park and looked around for Harvey – she would know him straight away from his photo – she expected he would be there to meet her. She had been nervous and excited about the meeting but now she was here, she was even more nervous. Maybe he wouldn't like her. Perhaps she had sent him the very best photos of her. Maybe she should have spent more time getting ready. Her heart was pounding. Where was he?

Her phone pinged and she pulled it out of her bag to see it was a message from Harvey. She had given him the number but he said he didn't have a phone in the UK yet and would give her a number when he saw her. The number was a new unrecognised number but she had seen the first line of the message and she knew it was him. She opened it fully.

'Can't believe it but we are here. Mom had to go to the toilet but we are the white BMW, Reg TS17 AHJ in the car park. If you get there before we get back, just wait for us.'

Abi checked the cars and right in the corner she saw the white BMW. She walked over to check the number plate and sure enough it was the one. She looked into the car as she approached, hoping they were sitting in it but nobody was there. A young mother with her two children was loading up her shopping in the car opposite, as her children fought with each other and her. Eventually, she managed to get them into the car, reversed and they were gone leaving just the empty cars. Abi went to send a message and leaned against the white car paying no attention to the black van alongside her. The side door of the van slid open as Abi was typing her message and, although she was preoccupied with the task, she half turned in the direction of the noise. The move was quick, decisive and efficient. A strong tattooed left arm grabbed her waist whilst the right hand held a cloth over her mouth. In one move, she was inside the van and the door was closed. Instinctively, she flung her arms upwards and tried to scream but the cloth muffled the noise. As she tried again, the chloroform took effect, her eyes closed and she sank into a turbulent deep sleep.

Charles could hear the quickness of his own breathing as his heart pounded at an escalating rate. He jumped to his feet from kneeling alongside the body of his prone wife and then dropped back down to search for blood and signs of life. He was now in a blind panic and on the verge of screaming as he fought to think. His hands were trembling as he stroked Laura's head and then leant down close to her face to check she was still breathing. Ring for an ambulance – yes – that's what I must do. Ring them, but what do I say? What will Laura say? What if she says I pushed her? I didn't push her; she just fell but what if she says that's not true? What if the police arrest me and the partners find out … or it appears in the press or on social media? Oh my God, what a mess! What should I do?

The thoughts continued to spin as though the information centre of his brain was overloading and spitting out theories and facts, which were cascading like snow flurries. A dark thought emerged in the middle of them: if Laura died, then nobody would know anything or accuse him of anything. He would say she overbalanced on the stairs; she was rushing around and was late for a meeting and he heard a crash and found her. Who could contradict that? Also, he would be the subject of great sympathy from his partners, all of whom would attend the funeral and offer him the support he needed. Even the clients who had complained would feel uncomfortable and surely withdraw the complaints. Abi would be distraught, of course, but he would rise to the challenge of being her father and would be the main parent, not someone who had to watch what he said. Or someone who knew that the looks exchanged between mother and daughter meant he was not a real parent with real authority.

His pulse quickened as the dark thoughts engulfed him. He put his right hand on Laura's cheek and felt the warmth of her skin as he stroked it slowly before edging his hand to her mouth. He could feel the heat from her gentle breath as the palm of his hand touched her slightly opened lips. He moved his hand upwards so that his thumb and forefinger encircled her nose and applying a little pressure, his hand closed both of Laura's nasal passages. That act caused an unconscious movement of her lips to compensate for the lack of oxygen. His hand had almost taken on a life of its own as the palm pressed down a little further, finally completely covering Laura's open mouth. His eyes were now wide and frightened at the sight in front of him, at the deed he was contemplating and the consequences of it. Regardless, his hand did not waver or move from its position.

Chapter 36

Charles was now shaking and tears were forming in his eyes as his hand began to extinguish life in another human being – his partner, the woman he had committed himself to. There was the beginning of an unconscious struggle as Laura's body fought to clear her airways and preserve her existence. The struggle was uncoordinated so that there were no conscious natural reactions of flailing arms and legs to repel an attack. Instead there were only head movements and groaning in a failing attempt to breath and then a relaxation as those attempts failed.

Charles felt his temples pulsating and his heart pounding as the tears began to fall and his face contorted with the enormity of the situation. In that moment of anguish, he let out a cry as he pulled his hand away and desperately tried to think. How could he do this? How could he commit murder? Here, in his own house. Yet what option did he have? Laura would inevitably now leave him – God knows what Hayley would say and he might be arrested. Laura would find another man, if she hadn't already. Yes, that was it: she had been acting strangely lately; she must be already seeing somebody; sleeping with them; letting another man use her body for his pleasure. She would try and take him for all she could get: sell the house, go after the savings and the pension scheme… take everything to go and be a slut with some other bastard living off his money. His hand returned to Laura's mouth and nose but this time, it was fuelled with anger.

Abi awoke from a bad dream. It was a nightmare, in which she was being chased by wild animals, and she was running for her life against the deafening noise of beating drums, but her legs wouldn't work properly. She tried to scream but no noise came from her mouth as the animals gained on her. Now that she was waking up, her senses were dull. She felt exhausted; even opening her eyes was difficult. It felt like her eyelids were heavy weights and she could only hold them up for a second before they closed again. When she did force and keep them open, she realised she had a cloth around her mouth, just under her nose. As she attempted to touch it, she found that she couldn't move her arms and realised her hands were tied behind her back. She screamed as loudly as the gag permitted but the noise was muffled and disguised the abject panic that her eyes betrayed.

'Shut up and you won't get hurt,' a harsh male voice instructed her. Abi kicked out and again attempted the scream. In the darkness, two firm hands grabbed her shoulders and shook her.

'I said shut up and you won't get hurt. Do as you're told or we'll put a hood over you.'

Even in her terrified and disorientated state, Abi registered the worse nightmare of a hood covering her entire head and stopped screaming but started sobbing. She was lost, afraid and totally without any life experience to draw upon. She wanted her mother more than at any time in her life. Through her tears she realised she was in a room somewhere and it was in darkness. There was light filtering under the door and the man who had spoken to her opened that door which flooded the room temporarily with light, before he left and closed it firmly. In that short time, she had seen a bed, two chairs and a picture on the wall – a coastline and ships. She stared at the door for a period she could not gauge, before it opened again and a man dressed in a suit stood in front of her, illuminated by the light behind him. He wore dark brown shoes with the suit, white shirt and no tie but the figure was one of menace because he wore a black balaclava over his face.

'Hello, Abi. I know you're scared but I'm not going to hurt you. We have you here because we need something from your Uncle Andy and when he gives us what we need we'll let you go. Nod your head if you understand me.'

Abi nodded obediently but understood nothing.

'Now, I'm going to take that nasty gag off your mouth but you must promise to behave or I will have to put it back on. Do you understand?' he added, rather like a friendly teacher trying to win cooperation.

She nodded again. The man undid the gag and Abi could smell his aftershave as he bent over her.

'Okay, that's better isn't it? Can I get you a drink of water or cola or something?'

'Water please,' she answered looking straight at him but trembling uncontrollably.

'All right. I'm going to put the light on and I'll be back in a minute with your drink. You just need to behave nicely, then nothing will happen and this will be all over before you know it,' he added before switching on the light and leaving, closing the door behind him.

Now that the light was on, Abi could see she was in a medium-size bedroom, which was decorated in a masculine way with pale blue walls and only the one picture she had glimpsed previously. There were no shelves or ornaments, just a table and the two chairs she had seen. The table had magazines and three used coffee mugs on it. Where on earth could she be and why was she here? She slowly began to realise that Harvey did not exist and she had been lured into a trap that she had willingly walked into and tricked her mother into believing she was still at school. She had no idea how long ago she had been taken or what time it was now.

The door opened again and the man brought in a tray which he placed on the table. On it was a bottle of water, some biscuits and a slice of chocolate cake.

'Now then Abi, I am going to take the ties off your hands and I want you to sit at the table to have your drink and snacks, but I've locked the door so there's no point in running. I know you're scared but this mask is for your protection – to make sure you can't see my face and we hope to be letting you go soon. If you make a fuss, we'll have to tie you up again and use the gag, which we don't want to do unless you make us. Do you promise you'll behave?'

'Yes,' Abi timidly replied while considering her options of running or screaming for help. She was unaware of the text that had been sent on her phone to her mother:

'Hi Mum, Carrie's Mum is picking us up and says I can stay at her house tonight. Is that okay with you?'
Equally, she had no way of knowing they had received a

reply her mother would never have sent:

'Yes that's fine, Abi. Enjoy yourself!'

The combination of events that can lead to or avert disaster can be planned but sometimes, they just accidentally fall into place. How could those holding Abi have possibly known that the girl's mother was unconscious and it was her stepfather who answered the text. It suited him perfectly – he didn't want Abi coming home and was involved in a struggle of his own.

The message alert on Laura's phone had caused Charles to remove his hand from his wife's mouth, interrupting his developing plan. Having returned the phone to his pocket, he steeled himself to try again to complete what he felt was his only way out. As his hand moved slowly into position over Laura's face and mouth there was a hammering at the front door.

'LAURA! IT'S ME – HAYLEY!' came the shout. Charles jumped to his feet and stood staring at the door.

'LAURA! I KNOW YOU'RE THERE BECAUSE YOUR CAR IS HERE. PLEASE – OPEN THIS DOOR!' Hayley shouted after the next round of knocking.

'I'm not leaving until you do,' was the quieter addition.

Charles jumped to the side and out of view in case she opened the letterbox and saw him. What could he do now? He brought his hands to his face to muffle the anguished sounds that were escaping from the back of his throat.

There was a short silence and a brief moment of hope that she had gone, but then he heard footsteps as Hayley made her way around the building to the back door. Charles moved to the kitchen door to see what she did and knelt down out of sight to see which way she went. He watched Hayley walk past, then double back and place her cupped hands to the window. She leaned forward to peer in. Charles stayed low and still, jumping when Hayley knocked loudly on the kitchen door.

'LAURA! YOU NEED TO ANSWER THE DOOR.' In his increasing panic, Charles scurried to the under-stairs cupboard and took out a claw hammer as he tried desperately to form a new plan. He had to shut this bloody woman up somehow.

Abi ate the chocolate cake as her teenage instinct kicked in and anyway, she was hungry. She gulped the water as the chloroform had dehydrated her, and she stared at the man in front of her the whole time. He stood in silence. Once she had finished, she wiped her mouth with the back of her hand, looked around the room and returned her gaze to the man.

'So, what do you want with Uncle Andy then?' she asked with surprising composure considering the circumstances.

'Nothing for you to worry about, but he'll be here soon.'

'Uncle Andy's coming here? Where are we?'

'You are a clever little thing, aren't you? I'll clear away your plate and glass and I'll come back when we have some news.'

'Can I have my phone then?' she asked hopefully.

'No. And don't push your luck,' was the firm reply.

'Laura, if you don't open this door I'm going to break in!' Hayley shouted through the letter box in the back door. As Charles moved away, he saw his next-door neighbour out on the front lawn beginning to take an interest. In desperation, he moved into the kitchen and unlocked the door with his left hand whilst keeping the hammer in his right hand, hidden behind his back. He had no plan but as he opened the door, a spontaneous one emerged.

'Oh, thank God, Hayley! Laura's just fallen down the stairs – she's out cold.'

'What? Have you called an ambulance?' she demanded tartly as she brushed past him and rushed to the staircase.

'I was just about to when you knocked. I was trying to make sure she was all right – you know, comfortable,' he blundered, placing the hammer on a kitchen shelf.

'Oh, Christ almighty, Laura! Are you all right?' Hayley pleaded as she reached her friend and felt for a pulse.

'CALL FOR A FUCKING AMBULANCE NOW!' she bellowed at Charles who immediately complied.

'Also, get a pillow for her head and some water in case she comes round.'

Charles made the call and did as he was told in getting the pillow and a glass of water.

'Do you want anything, Hayley?' he asked meekly.

'Yes, a gin and tonic with ice and lemon … what do you think?' she spat back.

'Sorry, I'm just in shock,' he mumbled.

'You're in shock? How long has she been here?'

'It had just happened when you arrived. I heard a stumble – I was working in the study and came out to find her like that. I think she had a business meeting or something so maybe she was rushing and tripped up.'

Hayley did not reply but continued to try and soothe her friend. Charles paced from room to room until he heard the sirens of the approaching ambulance. A couple of minutes later, two paramedics walked quickly to their patient and heard the same story from Charles. Oxygen was prepared and that unique monologue from medical practitioner to patient began as Laura started to groan.

Having ensured there was no spinal nerve damage, Laura was loaded on to the stretcher and Hayley instructed the paramedics she was going with them in the ambulance. As they reached the door Hayley let them go on a few paces before turning to Charles.

'You better not be behind this or I'll make sure you fucking pay for it.'

'What do you mean?' Charles answered, looking suitably indignant.

'You know what I mean. Where's Abi?'

'She's staying at a friend's house.'

'Good. Well at least she's safe,' came the final ironic barb as Hayley made her way to the ambulance.

★ ★ ★

Andy was walking back to his car in Sainsbury's car park when a vehicle pulled up alongside him. The rear passenger seat window opened with a buzz of its electric motor.

'Hello, Andy, long time no see!' said the smiling

passenger, whom he recognised as the man who'd offered him the cash at the garage.

'Hello … Mr Smith … that was your name, wasn't it?'

'Get in, Andy.'

'No thanks,' he replied whilst feeling for the phone Cooper had given him.

'I wouldn't use that if I was you,' said Smith, holding up his own phone. A picture of Abi tied and gagged filled the screen.

'You wouldn't want this little girl to get hurt, would you?'

Without another word, Andy got into the car.

Chapter 37

Sitting in the back of the car, Andy struggled with a range of emotions. He felt the now familiar fear he had encountered several times since the incident with Tasker, but now it was mixed with anger and a steely determination to do something about it; to rid himself of the plague that had descended on him. He also felt vulnerable, but it was tinged with frustration that the police seemed unable to protect him or those closest to him. Added to the mix now was his disappointment in himself for not protecting Abi. He had never even considered her at risk; it was his own children, his ex-wife and his current partner he had felt the need to protect. Instead, these evil creatures had pounced on his niece.

He had been relieved of both of his phones by Smith, who smiled knowingly when taking the phone given to Andy by Cooper. That phone had been handed to an accomplice in the car park before they'd driven off.

'What have you done to her?' Andy demanded of Smith, who was casually gazing out of the window.

'Just sit back, Andy and be quiet,' Smith replied without turning. As well as the thickly set driver, there was also a front seat passenger: a man in his thirties with a tattoo of a snake on his neck that wound its way up to his shaven head. There was a palpable sense of menace in the car.

'You better not have hurt her,' Andy said in an unconvincing way, despite his anger.

'Or what?' Smith turned to reply. A smile played around his lips.

'You'll find out you bastard,' was the response but this time with real hatred.

Smith turned to look out of his window again but then swung around effortlessly and punched Andy in the solar plexus. The blow came without warning and was delivered with professional precision and effect. Andy's diaphragm was temporarily paralysed, rendering him immediately breathless. He gasped to recover the function as his brain registered the intense pain.

'Now sit back and shut your fucking mouth,' Smith ordered as the bald passenger turned to see if his assistance was required. It wasn't. Any doubts as to the kind of people Andy was dealing with had been removed completely and permanently.

After another ten minutes or so, the car pulled on to a deserted industrial estate and Andy was bundled out of the seat by the front-seat passenger, who opened his door and grabbed him. Smith opened the boot of the car and the bald man pushed Andy into it, folded his legs inside and slammed the boot lid shut. There seemed little point in resisting or shouting for help. Andy made the decision to lie there and wait as the car pulled away.

It was so dark that Andy became disorientated and claustrophobia was beginning to bring back his childhood asthma, a condition he had not suffered in many years. Visions of depleting levels of oxygen and his constricting throat combined with the overwhelming smell of fuel. The inclination to scream was almost overpowering but he managed to resist it. Instead he concentrated heavily on controlling his breathing. When he had calmed a little, he thought about revenge of some sort, at some stage. They would pay; he would make sure of that, and if they had already hurt Abi, he would find a way to make that payment sooner rather than later.

Hayley sat outside Ward 15 at the General Hospital waiting for an update. The staff nurse had told her that Laura was severely concussed but had regained consciousness and they were carrying out precautionary scans before admitting her to the ward. Hayley had told the nurse she was Laura's sister, to avoid the argument about staff only speaking to family members. She was determined to be there when her friend was brought on to the ward and to make sure she found out from Laura what had happened. Charles had arrived at the hospital and wandered off to get a coffee as Hayley made no attempt to disguise the coldness she felt towards him. After a little over an hour the staff nurse returned.

'Just to let you know that your sister is on her way to the ward. We'll observe her over night and the doctor will see her in the morning. The scans look normal but she's had a nasty blow to the head so we just want to be sure,' she said in a reassuring tone.

'Oh, that is good news. Will I be able to see her?'

'Yes, she'll be in a room on her own; room seven, I think. Anyway, you can see her when she arrives,' she said with a smile.

A little while later the porter pushed Laura in a wheelchair towards the ward and Hayley got up to rush across and hold her hand.

'Oh, Laura I was so worried! How are you feeling?'

'I'm fine,' Laura replied. 'I'm just so embarrassed to be pushed around in this chair. I told them I was perfectly capable of walking but they insisted. Silly really.'

Once Laura was settled in the bed in room 7 and the nurse and porter had gone, Hayley dived in.

'So, what happened?'

'I don't really remember to be honest, Hayley. Charles was working at home and I was going out to meet my old boss but the rest is just a blur.'

'You can't remember how you came to fall down the stairs?'

'No. I remember getting ready and Charles being worried about his job or something at work – he wanted to talk to me or have lunch with me, I don't really know. The next thing, I woke up here.'

There was a pause as Hayley mulled things over.

'Did he push you Laura?'

'Why do you ask that?'

'You know why.'

'Oh, come on Hayley! You can't really think he would push me down the stairs!'

'Why not? He took a long time to answer the door and a bloody long time to ring for an ambulance. He also had a look about him when I came in … something dark. Do I think he is capable of doing it? Yes, I do.'

'Hayley, that's a terrible thing to think!' Laura answered unconvincingly.

'How well do you know him, Laura?'

'Better than you know him,' she answered defensively.

'Maybe not,' Hayley answered.

She proceeded to tell the whole story of her trip to Leeds, the meeting with the ex-girlfriend and the background of a man capable of stalking and violence. A dangerous man whom women couldn't get rid of, were menaced by. A potential monster. Laura listened intently and fought her instinct to defend her husband, partly because she recognised the description. Years of wanting to see a picture she preferred, as opposed to the one in front of her had taken its toll. She was weary and began to draw strength from her friend. After all, Hayley was entirely on her side; she wasn't going to be deflected from her task of total support.

'How do you know this is all true?'

'Why would they lie? Anyway, you know it is true, don't you? Your own life with him shows you that.'

At that moment the door opened and in walked Charles with two coffees.

'Darling! You're awake, thank God for that!' he said putting the cups on the bedside table and leaning in to kiss his wife. She turned away coldly accepting the kiss on her right cheek.

'What a scare you gave us! But the doctor says you will be fine and should be home tomorrow, all being well.' Charles added with a slightly overenthusiastic tone.

'Where's Abi?' Laura enquired, changing the subject.

'Staying with a friend,' he replied.

'Which friend?'

'Carol or Carrie … something like that.'

'What? You don't know who it is?'

'Yes, I spoke to her mum and everything's fine. It's nothing to worry about and anyway, it's just as well she doesn't know you are here.'

His lies and deceit had taken on a momentum of their own. His mind played with the texts on Laura's phone and his answers in her name; the explanations that may be required in the future, but for now, any old lie would do to remove pressure.

'So how's she getting to school tomorrow?' Laura asked.

'Her friend's mother is taking her.'

'But what about fresh clothes?'

'I'll sort that out when I get home, darling. Don't worry, it's all under control.'

Andy had controlled his breathing and repelled the panic attack. He needed patience and a calm head; his priority was Abi's safety and he knew he had to control himself as he thought of the possible demands that might be made. If they were going to kill him, surely he would be dead already and Abi wouldn't be captive somewhere.

He felt the car come to a halt and heard muffled voices before the sound of a garage door being pulled open grated through the stifling air. The car moved forward slowly and he heard the garage door being closed. After a few seconds the boot was opened and he squinted at the light flooding in. When his eyes adjusted, he looked up to see two figures either side of the car.

'Okay, out you get,' one of them said, as they both

got hold of him and lifted him on to the garage's concrete floor, where he stood unsteadily, trying to straighten his clothes. Smith and another man were seated at the back of the garage and an empty wooden seat faced them. Smith pointed to the chair and smiled.

'Have a seat, Andy. We're going to have a little chat.'

Chapter 38

This was reality for Andy. He no longer had to imagine the kind of people he was involved with, or the situations he might find himself in. He had been abducted, assaulted and forced into the boot of a car after being confronted with a picture of his abducted niece, bound and gagged. These were real deal criminals ... gangsters ... whatever you wanted to call them, and they were capable of extreme actions, extreme violence, maybe ever murder.

'So, Andy, here we are and you only have yourself to blame,' said Smith, unblinking and unsmiling. He continued after a short pause.

'I mean, we made you a very generous offer that any reasonable person would have taken and then we'd be out of your life and you'd be free to rip off those poor customers of yours as much as you like but no, you had to be difficult, allow our friend to get stitched up, and for what? Here you are and you've made us involve your pretty little niece. This is your fault and it's up to you to put it right.'

Andy felt like an actor in a TV drama as he sat on the uncomfortable wooden seat surrounded by these thugs. They hadn't tied his hands, they weren't (yet) beating him with baseball bats, but the setting seemed to be the same. He was frightened, but a survival gene was working away within him: all his senses were on full alert as he plotted and planned his every move, trying to regard this as the ultimate sales negotiation for which he might have some skills to help. Only this time he wasn't negotiating multiple car sales or a bank loan, but his and Abi's safety and freedom. He thought carefully about both his answer and its tone. He had to appear in control and as if he had something to offer.

'Where's Abi?'

'She's safe, don't worry about her.'

'I need more than that. How do I know she hasn't been hurt?'

'You're not in a position to negotiate, mate. She's fine and will stay that way if you do as we tell you. Do that and everyone gets to go home.'

'What do you want?'

'Well, Andy, you are going to do a bit of acting and if we are satisfied with your audition you might just get a little reward. Now, Big Tony over there has an envelope for you and you're going to open it while Peter films you. There's three grand in there and you are going to count it and tell him you want more.'

Smith got up from his seat and moved to the back of the room where he picked up a sheet of paper and handed it to Andy.

'These are your lines … learn them.'

Andy looked at the sheet, which was remarkably professional in its preparation. His lines were set out clearly, as were the responses he would hear. He saw the plan immediately: it was designed to make him look like he was extorting money for telling the truth about Tasker. He was to say that he had already received £5000 and this was another £3000, which he had agreed to, but now he wanted another £10,000, otherwise he would tell the police the attacker was Tasker, despite the fact he now knew it

302

wasn't. The others in the 'scene' would protest Tasker's innocence, eventually refusing the attempted blackmail and Andy would reluctantly agree.

'Do you really think anyone will believe this shit?' Andy said in a general observation whilst reading the sheet.

'You had better hope so. Anyway, you will take the three grand and keep it in your desk at work until the charges are dropped. Then you can keep it.'

'I thought the offer was ten grand,' Andy said, playing along.

'It was, but we've had expenses since then, so just be glad of the money you will get ... and that your family will be safe.'

'What happens to the film?'

'The CPS will get it just before trial. They'll lose their nerve and drop the case.'

'What, and bring one against me?'

'No, they won't do that because you'll tell them we made you do it and they won't know if that's true or not.'

'What about Abi?'

'What about her?'

'She will tell the police what happened.'

'No, she won't.'

'What makes you so confident?' Andy answered as the adrenaline pulsing round his veins swelled his own confidence.

'We have some photos we've taken of her that she won't want on the Internet. Plus, she came to us to meet her internet boyfriend she was keeping a secret from you all. It's best for her to forget the whole thing and get back to normal. The two of you can come up with something to tell her mum. After all, you don't want us calling again, do you? I hope you appreciate how good we're being to you; you could both just disappear and never be found. Is that what you want?'

When Abi tried the door at the back of the room, she found it was an entrance to an en suite bathroom, which quashed her plan to ask to use the toilet and make a run for it. But run where? She had no idea where she was or how long she had been there, but was now worrying about her part in all of this: she had lied to her parents about what she was doing and been tricked into deceiving them. She thought about all of the warnings she'd been given about grooming and how she had ignored them all, believing Harvey was real. Why were these people interested in her and Uncle Andy?

The trembling had stopped and she hadn't cried for a while. She was focused instead on the trouble she would be in at home and the danger she might be in now. How she longed for the safety of her bedroom, the noises of her home, the security of her family. She sat on the bed, drew her knees up to her chin and tried to think or, at least, keep the demons in her head at bay.

Andy decided to play along with the charade. There were several takes of the money changing hands as he was urged to be more convincing. Even when he had been, the scene was shot again as the video showed the person Andy was talking to. Only Andy could be in shot and he had to look like he was unaware he was being filmed. Eventually, the men seemed satisfied and Smith spoke again.

'Right, that will do. You now go back to your garage and put the cash in your top right-hand draw and lock it. Understood?'

'Okay. What about Abi?'

'We will bring her to you when you get home tonight. And we'll return your phones. You will be under observation the whole time, so no funny ideas about being a hero or getting your friends in blue to help, is that clear?'

'But her mother is going to be looking for her. I can't control that and she might have gone to the police already.'

'Her mother thinks she's at her friend's house so isn't expecting her until tomorrow. Better that she knows nothing about this and it stays a secret between you and Abi. Remember, we know where you all live.'

Andy nodded fearfully.

'Good. You won't be warned again, Andy. This is it for you now. Stick with it and you and yours will be fine. Do something stupid and people are going to get hurt ... badly.'

Smith turned to the others, nodding towards the boot of the car and this time, Andy climbed in without assistance. As the boot lid closed, he knew he was powerless for now and desperately hoped that Abi would be dropped off later that night.

Andy tried to time the journey on the assumption he was being taken to the garage. He could not see his watch in the pitch blackness of the boot and again had to fight his claustrophobia, but when the car stopped, he estimated the drive was around twenty minutes. The boot lid opened and he was back on the industrial estate, where one of his own cars from his garage was waiting for him.

'How did you get this car here?' he asked one of the two thickly set, vacant-looking thugs standing beside him.

'You need better security at your garage, mate,' was the reply as both men laughed.

'Now get in and off you go like you were told.'

Andy did just that.

He saw no sign of being followed and realised that only he would be seen on the security cameras back at the garage. As he disarmed the alarm system, he locked the door and made his way to his office, slumping down at his desk. He took the brown envelope from his jacket pocket and placed it in a desk drawer as instructed. Andy noticed his clothes had a vague smell of diesel from the car boot and he leaned back in his chair to mull over everything that had happened and what he might do next.

The fear had gone and been replaced with a seething, burning, overpowering rage. He wanted freedom from these monsters who had so easily slipped into his life, threatening those he loved. But most of all, he wanted revenge. He had changed. He was now a pressure cooker on full power, only held back by his concern for Abi.

Chapter 39

Andy drove home, poured himself a stiff whisky and sat in the semi-darkness of his kitchen waiting for news. There were three messages on his home phone, one from Rebecca asking him to return her call and two from his mother saying she had tried him on his mobile but couldn't get hold of him. He couldn't face ringing either of them at the moment; he didn't want to be distracted from getting Abi back.

He wasn't sure how long he'd been sitting there waiting but the second whisky had caused him to doze off into an exhausted but unsettled sleep. He was disturbed by his house phone ringing and didn't recognise the number. It must be them, he thought as he answered.

'Hello.'

'Andy, is that you?'

'Yes, who's this?'

'It's David Cooper. Why aren't you picking up on your mobiles?'

'Oh, hi. I seem to have misplaced them.'

'What both of them? So where have you been tonight?'

'At home mainly.'

'So how come the tracker on our phone has had you driving all around town all night?'

'I don't know. Maybe somebody has taken it. I haven't seen it for a few hours.'

'Are you all right, Andy?'

'Yes, fine – just a bit tired, that's all.'

'Can I come round to see you?'

'Can we leave it until tomorrow? I'm tired and I have somebody here,' he lied.

'Okay, but I wanted to tell you that we picked up Jamie Tasker today. He's been remanded in custody until the trial.'

'WHAT?' Andy screeched, immediately regretting the obvious show of emotion.

'I thought you'd be pleased!' came Cooper's response.

'No ... no ... I'm ... just surprised that's all. How come you were able to do that?'

'I would rather have told you face to face, but we've arrested him on further charges of attempting to pervert the course of justice and some drug-related offences.'

'What was the first one?'

'Perverting the course of justice. We have evidence of him interfering with witnesses other than you so we believed we had enough. We had a special hearing before a judge today.'

'How did he take it?'

'I think you can imagine. His lawyers put up a fight but he ran out of options and is now safely tucked away.'

'Okay, David, thanks for letting me know.'

'No problem. You sure you're all right, Andy?'

'Yes, yes ... fine. Thanks again.'

As Andy replaced the phone, he put his head in his hands and then let out a stifled scream. What did this all mean for him, and more importantly, for Abi. She was now in even greater danger. How would Tasker react to his arrest? Would he blame Andy and punish his family? It was around midnight that Andy heard his letterbox creak and the noise of something dropping on the mat. He was still in the kitchen and stiffly got up from his seat, pulled out the largest knife from the rack and walked very slowly towards the door, his right hand tightly gripping the handle of the knife. If anyone appeared in front of him now, he was ready to strike. He didn't put on the hallway light, but let his eyes adjust to the darkness before moving towards the door, where he saw a padded package lying on the mat. When satisfied that nobody had gained entry to the house, he put the knife down, picked up the parcel and opened it. Inside he found his two phones and a piece of folded paper, which he took out and opened to read.

'THE DEAL IS OFF.'

He leaned against the door and slumped to the ground. What should he now do? Should he call Cooper? He didn't know what was the best course of action. He switched on his mobile and saw he had twenty-seven missed calls and twelve texts. Some of the texts were from his mother, who never texted him so he opened her last message.

'Andy, where are you? You're not answering the phone or texts. Please get in touch.'

He flicked to the first text from his mother,

'Just tried ringing you. Laura has been taken to the General Hospital with concussion and your dad and I will be there'

He immediately rang his mother who picked up on the second ring.

'Andy where have you been? We've been so worried!'

'Sorry, Mum, I lost my phone and I've been out all day. How's Laura? What happened?'

'Oh, she says she is fine. She thinks she fell down the

stairs but they are keeping her in tonight, just to keep an eye on her.'

'Are you still at the hospital?'

'No, we came home about an hour ago, but Hayley is staying with her and insists that Laura either comes home to us or goes to stay with her until she's better. We'll be there at eight o'clock tomorrow morning and the doctor will decide on his rounds if she's well enough to be discharged.'

'I'm sorry, Mum … about the phone, I mean.'

'Don't worry about that. Just as long as you're okay.'

'Thanks, Mum … love you.'

'Love you more,' she replied and Andy could hear the smile in her voice.

He put the phone down and sobbed in misery and helplessness.

After a passage of time he lost track of, he pulled himself together. Wiping his face with his handkerchief, he took a deep breath then found the contact on his phone he was looking for before. He pressed call and it was answered within three rings.

'Hello … good job I'm a light sleeper.'

Andy looked at his watch and realised it was nearly 2am.

'I'm sorry, Mr Lomax, I hadn't realised the time.'

'Ted, please.'

'Sorry, Ted … I didn't realise it was so late. I really need to talk to you.'

'Must be urgent son. Meet me at the Bellingate Services in an hour.'

'Are you sure that's okay at this time of night?'

'Aye … no problem.'

Andy washed his face in an attempt to remove signs of his distress and vulnerability and thought about what he had been drinking. Being over the limit was the least of his problems but the way things were going, he felt he was bound to get stopped. Although not hungry, he ate some apple pie from the fridge to soak up any remnants of alcohol. He had no option but to drive and in a long list of problems, driving over the limit was well down the list. He came out of the house into the cool night air, checked for anyone watching him and set off.

He pulled into the services and was surprised at how many people were around at that time in the morning. He looked around and saw Ted sitting in the corner in his trade-mark overcoat. As he approached, Ted stood and shook his hand warmly.

'Okay son, tell me what's happened. Don't leave anything out now.'

Andy told Ted everything about the abduction of Abi, his own abduction and journey in the boot of the car, the violence and the threats, and the revelation that Tasker had been arrested. Throughout the story Ted Lomax listened silently, never taking his eyes off him.

'So that's it, Ted. What the hell am I supposed to do now?'

'I did tell you that you didn't speak their language, didn't I? Now you've heard how different that language is and seen what a different world they live in.'

'Yes, I realise that but what do I do?'

'I have to admit, I'm a bit worried about the little girl. It's a big thing to have taken her rather than just make a threat. I get the bit about breaking into your old house and frightening the kids and your ex-wife but actually taking a kid ... well that's something else.'

'How do you mean?'

'Well kids are very unpredictable; you can never be sure what they'll do or say. They can never be certain that she'll say nothing if they release her. And if they get caught, kidnapping comes with a long stretch.'

'What do you mean "if they release her"?'

'I don't mean anything, son, but these animals think in terms of cost. There may be little difference between sentences for kidnapping and murder, so if murder gives them a better chance of escape, they'll consider it for sure, especially now Tasker is inside.'

Andy felt all the saliva disappear from his mouth and his temperature soar as his face reddened. He had thought these things, of course, but this was a man who knew this sort of criminal and here he was saying it out loud.

'Shit, Ted! I'm really scared now. Do I call the police?'

'No,' Ted replied firmly. 'You might force their hand. One thing I need to get my head around is who came up with the idea of taking the girl. You see, a lot of these thugs have got kids themselves and kids are normally considered off limits. Touch a kid and get caught and you're a nonce – a target for everybody else inside. It's bad enough being locked away, but nonces have no life. The best they can hope for is solitary or being put in with real nonces. I just don't get it.'

'Isn't it just leverage against me?' Andy asked, his desperation increasing.

'Maybe, but there are other ways. Look son, you're

going to have to leave this with me to make some enquiries, find out what's happening, then I'll come back to you.'

'Can you find out? I mean, how?'

'Leave that to me. You go home, then go to work as normal. Ring me if anything happens or if you hear from them, but don't call the police for the moment.'

'Okay, Ted … you know best.'

'Aye. I do lad.'

Chapter 40

There was no sleep at all for Andy that night as he arrived home. He finally gave up and drove to the hospital to see his sister, all the time his mind flooding with horrific images of his niece and no idea what he would say to Laura when it became clear Abi was missing. He parked his car and made his way to Ward 15.

As Andy came out of the lift he looked to his right and saw his mother and father sitting outside the ward chatting away normally. He stood for a second to drink in the scene of familiarity. His parents were so easy in each other's company and were always first on the scene at any family event or crisis, bringing to it a calmness, control and affection. In stark contrast, he felt like a walking time bomb, dragging chaos and potential devastation into matters already out of his control. His parents turned as he walked towards them and his mother Molly got up and hurried to give him a hug. He needed it so badly.

'Hi, Mum, how is she this morning?'

'We don't know yet but they said she had a peaceful night when we rang first thing.'

'Still no idea what happened?'

'No, not really,' she said turning away as if concerned her face may betray an emotion.

His father took his mother's place and warmly hugged his son before placing his hand on his cheek and smiling.

'Glad you're here, son; your mum has been worried.'

'Where's Charles?' Andy asked, trying to conceal an edge of sarcasm.

'Oh, he's on his way here before he goes off to work,' his mother replied.

'Yeah, right.'

'Now then Andy, don't interfere, especially with things you don't know about,' was her censorious reply.

Just then, the ward doors opened. Charles trotted along the corridor and joined the group.

'Hello, Charles,' Andy's mother said warmly.

'Hello, Molly, any further news?' Charles asked, concern furrowing his brow.

'She had a good night apparently,' came the slightly less warm reply as they moved into the ward. The family was wondering why Laura's husband hadn't bothered ringing the hospital. Andy could barely disguise his contempt and suspicion, which elicited a scowl from his father.

Laura was sitting up in bed but still looked pale. Her mother told her how much better she looked, as a mother would, and Paul and Andy both gave her comforting hugs. Charles was last in the line and was again presented with Laura's cheek when he stopped to kiss her. She still couldn't remember the events of the previous day, but her instinct was negative when it came to her regard for her husband.

They all indulged in the usual hospital chitchat: how friendly the staff were; the weather outside, which was worth missing. Andy sat on the side of the bed and took his sister's hand. He asked how she felt and if she remembered what had happened. Charles realised that he should be sitting there but he felt like an outsider in this company.

After a few minutes Laura turned to Charles.

'Did Abi get off to school okay this morning?'

Charles felt sweat dampen his armpits.

'Yes, she did darling.'

'How do you know?'

'I rang her this morning and she was already on her way. Her friend's mother was taking them.'

'Did she have fresh clothes?'

'Yes, I took some round.'

'This morning?'

'No, last night.'

Andy had turned his full attention to Charles. He knew was lying about the clothes and talking to Abi … but why?

'Did you tell Abi I was in hospital?'

'No darling, I didn't want to worry her. I'll collect her from school and bring her here if they keep you in, but hopefully you'll be home and you can tell her yourself.'

That seemed to settle Laura but Andy stepped in,

'Is her friend that one who lives on Cantwell Drive in the big house with the wrought-iron gates?'

'Yes, that's the one' Charles lied, relieved at having his story seemingly corroborated.

After another ten minutes or so of stilted conversation, Charles said he had to get off to the office. He avoided the chance of rejection from his wife by blowing her a kiss and waving goodbye to everyone else.

'I'll walk you to the car, Charles. I have to move mine anyway,' Andy said, then told his family he'd be back in ten minutes.

The two men walked briskly to the car park and Andy asked

Charles what he thought had happened to Laura. He got the same explanation Hayley had heard earlier – she'd been rushing for a meeting and fell. As they turned the corner into the underground car park, Andy took hold of Charles's left arm and swung him round.

'What the fuck is going on?'

'What?' replied a genuinely startled Charles as he pulled his arm sharply away.

'You didn't speak to Abi and you didn't deliver any clothes to anyone.'

'What are you talking about, you maniac?' Charles stuttered.

'Why are you lying?'

'I don't have to put up with this. You've lost your mind!' Charles said, as he turned to walk away. The pent-up anger of the last few weeks and the anxiety about Abi had created an overload in Andy; the pressure cooker was about to explode. He instinctively grabbed his brother in law's left shoulder and pulled him against the wall. Charles, also acting instinctively, raised his right forearm and connected with Andy's chin, sending him sprawling to the floor. Andy quickly sprang to his feet and drove his right fist into Charles's abdomen, doubling him over as the air gushed from his mouth. Andy was now lost in rage and brought his right knee up into Charles's head. He fell against the wall and slid down it. Unable to breathe, he couldn't prevent Andy from grabbing his throat.

'Listen to me, you fucking shit. I know you haven't talked to Abi. I made up that address and the description of the house to see how far you would go with your lies. If I find out you are mixed up in this, I will fucking strangle you, do you hear me?'

Andy's fingers tightened around Charles's neck but he heard a loud shout echo across the car park.

'Hey you! What are you doing? I'm calling the police.' Andy turned and saw two middle aged men making their way towards them. One of them was opening his phone. The last thing he wanted was the police here, so he stood up and hurried off. As he did so, he heard Charles call after him.

'Mixed up in what?'

Back in Ward 15, Andy had composed himself and was relieved to find security weren't after him. He had told his staff he would be late and was in no hurry to leave his sister. At about ten o'clock Laura's phone rang and she saw it was Abi's school.

'Is that Mrs Peterson?'

'Yes, it is.'

'Oh, hello Mrs Peterson, it is Emily Cruikshank here. I'm the deputy head of the school and I'm ringing to ask why Abigail hasn't attended this morning.'

'But she was being dropped off by one of her friend's mother. I'm sorry but I'm in hospital at the moment. Are you sure she isn't there?' Laura said, her distress and confusion rising. Her response sounded inane, even to her.

'Quite sure, I'm afraid. Do you want me to speak to the other parent?'

'My husband made the arrangements. Do you mind if I speak to him and ring you straight back?'

'No, that's fine. I'm sure you appreciate we have to follow up these things.'

'Of course. Thank you for ringing.'

Laura turned to her family in alarm and told them about the call as she started to dial Charles's number.

'Don't ring Charles, Laura,' Andy said calmly.

'Why not? We have to find out where Abi went to last night – why she isn't at school.'

Andy got up and walked to the door to close it so they wouldn't be overheard.

'I know what's happened to Abi and we have to be very careful, very careful indeed.'

In Pemberton Maximum Security Prison, ten miles outside Hull, Jamie Tasker was settling into his second day of custody. As he moved away from the food hall, he brushed past his target, who placed an envelope in his hand without making eye contact. Tasker seamlessly dropped it into his pocket mid-stride. Back in his cell he opened the envelope to find the mobile phone he had rented in return for drugs. It was a pay-as-you-go with just enough credit for his calls. Checking there was no one around outside of the cell, he dialled his first number which was answered on the third ring.

'Yeah, who is this?'

'It's me… get rid of the girl.'

Chapter 41

Laura had taken the news surprisingly calmly to begin with as she questioned her brother on the detail, seeming more concerned by her mother's alarmed expression. But whatever natural narcotic had produced that calmness was now beginning to wear off and Laura started to tremble, as though the temperature had dropped ten degrees.

Andy sat on the bed to hug his sister and that released the first wave of sobbing. Andy held on tightly and Paul comforted his wife who also moved into action. Molly Connolly was always strong and in control and seemed capable of dealing with any crisis. She had a natural warmth about her, which made her popular with almost everyone she met, but she was nobody's fool and would tackle any problem head on. Despite her horror at the news and the feeling of rising panic, she had moved into matriarchal mode to protect her family. The first indication of this was to politely send a nurse (who had come to take Laura's blood pressure) packing.

'Just give us a minute love, while we sort out a little domestic matter.'

Then she stood at the foot of the bed and took full control.

'Now then, listen everybody. We have to pull together here, and in the same direction. So, as I understand it, Abi has been kidnapped to make sure Andy tells the police what this Tasker creature wants him to. As long as he does that, we get her back. Is that right?'

Andy nodded at his mother and Paul and Laura just stared on, knowing not to interrupt.

'So, Andy is going to do just that, but Tasker is in prison now and we don't yet know what that will mean. Ted Lomax is on it now and will find out what's going on. He tells us not to involve the police for now as we can't be sure if this DCI is part of it. Have I got that right?'

This time all three of them nodded.

'So, we can't take any risks with poor little Abi, can we?' As Molly said that, her eyes filled up with tears and her chin momentarily trembled. She quickly recovered.

'I think we have to let Ted have a couple of days and your dad can stay in regular touch with him. I trust Ted and he'll know what to do with these low lives. If Cooper is bent, we can't take the risk of telling him anything at this point. Andy, you just sit tight and see what happens. Laura, you must pull yourself together until we get our girl back. What does Charles know about all of this?'

Andy told them of his conversation with Charles; he left out the fighting but included the lying. This set Laura off crying again but this time, they were tears of rage.

'Okay Laura, you're coming home with us when they let you out of here and we'll decide what we're going to do. Charles wouldn't hurt Abi and he can't possibly be involved in this. We'll have words about him though, just not today. Is everybody clear?'

Everyone nodded again and Paul got up and hugged his wife who smiled.

'Now, I'll go and find that nurse and then a loo.'

Molly marched out of the room like a commanding officer, signalled for the nurse to go in and found the ladies toilet. Once inside, she opened the first cubicle door, sat down and sobbed her heart out.

Laura was discharged late in the afternoon, and her mother and father collected her and drove her to her house to pack up clothes and personal items that filled the boot and back seat. They then took her home.

Molly rang Charles to say they wanted to look after Laura at home, to keep an eye on her because of the head injury and, of course, it made sense as he was working. She said they would collect Abi and just see how things went with Laura's recovery. Charles felt he had to agree but sensed no hostility from his mother-in-law, which gave him some relief. Molly also spoke to the school to tell them that both mother and daughter had a virus and therefore would be staying with them for a few days.

Andy rang DCI Cooper and asked for some details about Tasker's arrest. He was told that he had resisted but they'd expected that and so gone in mob-handed. Cooper asked if he wanted him to pop round and discuss anything, or if anything was troubling him, to which Andy replied no, he felt reassured and would just wait for further news.

Paul had several discussions with Ted, both in person and on the phone. Ted told him that he had put feelers out and was beginning to make progress, but on no account were the police to be involved; the delicate nature of these sort of discussions could not withstand anyone being arrested or suspicions being raised.

After their last meeting, Ted had said goodbye and was walking away when Paul grabbed his coat sleeve, causing him to turn back in surprise. In a shaking voice Paul said,

'Don't let anything happen to my little granddaughter, Ted. I just couldn't bear it. I … I … '

'I know, Paul. They get into your soul, don't they? I have grandchildren myself. I'm on it, don't worry.'

An eerie lack of activity followed for everyone involved, where the sound of clocks ticking or the TV playing to an absent audience replaced conversation and normality. Waiting for news was a slow and painful game. The only thing that stopped them going mad was the pretence of calmness and normality they each felt obliged to display. Anything else – a show of the real fear and panic – would spread like a disease through the family. Each member of the Connolly family played their part in that pretence, as they awaited news over which they had no control.

Abi was asleep on her bed. She had been given a McDonalds cheeseburger and fries a while ago but she wasn't particularly hungry and more out of boredom than anything, she had curled up on the bed. Her sleep was disturbed as she heard the lock to her door being turned. She presumed her plate was being collected but when the door opened there were two men wearing hoods, neither of which appeared to be the man she had been talking to. As they walked towards the bed, she moved to get up but the first man grabbed her, lifting her by the shoulders to her feet. She began to scream but felt his thick right hand cover her mouth. His left arm held her tightly against his body as the other man moved in. She kicked the second man sharply on the right shin and he yelped before pulling her jumper clear of her right shoulder, showing her skin. Abi's eyes were wide open in horror as she saw him pull a syringe from his pocket. She felt the sharp pain of the needle enter her arm. Within seconds she felt a numbness throughout her body, and her brain was filled with lurid pictures. Finally, she lost consciousness and slumped on to the bed into total blackness.

It was the early hours of the following day that Jamie Tasker was awoken by a noise outside of his cell. He was in solitary confinement until a permanent cell was allocated and he had delayed that process with some bribes to give himself extra time to organise business. He was feeling quite relaxed about his situation and the insurance policy he had in place. He imagined he'd be back home soon.

He heard a noise like a door being unlocked, then footsteps retreating. He was thinking of going to check but dropped off to sleep again for a few seconds. Suddenly the metal door of his cell was thrown open and he glimpsed three figures rushing towards him in the darkness.

Tasker jumped out of the bed but the first figure thrust his right knee sharply into his groin causing him to crumple to the ground. As he did so, the other two kicked him in his ribs, expelling all the air from his lungs. As he gasped to refill them, he was pulled up and held by two of the figures as the third pushed a sock into his mouth and then wrapped tape around his head to keep it in place. Three thick leather belts that had been fastened together were tied around the internal bars of the Victorian window over the bed as

Tasker was dragged back towards it. Two more knee blows to the groin prevented any more resistance as the force of the three men pulled him to his feet, then on to the bed. They wrapped the other end of the belts around his neck creating a loop and a fourth belt was used to tie his hands behind his back. They yanked the bed away and, with it gone, Tasker hovered two feet from the ground. Two of the men held his legs and pulled with all their might.

★ ★ ★

It was around 2am that Andy went to bed. He didn't feel tired or at least, not in the general sense. He was filled with adrenaline, anxiety and rage, all of which prevented the normal changing down of gears to a restful sleep. He went to bed hoping that would happen.

Paul and Molly Connolly were asleep through simple exhaustion, and Laura, back in her own room, was fast asleep, helped by the sedative her mother had slipped into her hot chocolate. A new day was about to dawn. It was a day the family would never be able to forget.

Chapter 42

Andy thought he was awake as he planned imagined conversations to come with Cooper, his sister and various other people. He only realised he was asleep when his phone rang and woke him up. He quickly came to his senses and grabbed the phone to see it was Ted Lomax.

'Hi Ted, is everything all right?'

'Can I pick you up in twenty minutes from yours?'

'Sure … where are we going?'

'Don't know that yet but I'll explain when I get there.'

'Okay. I'll be ready.'

Ted pulled up outside of Andy's house in his Range Rover, a private plate on show: 'TL 55'. Andy couldn't help valuing the vehicle at just short of a hundred grand (when new) and another ten grand for the plate. He shook his head at his inability to switch off the motor trader in him. Andy opened the passenger door and jumped in. It occurred to him that Ted never looked any different as he settled into the journey to wherever it was they were going. Ted exuded his usual expression of calm authority mixed with silent menace. He was evidently a man not to mess with.

'So, where are we going, Ted?'

'The Marsden Estate, just outside Goole. I haven't been given the address yet so keep an eye on my phone as we drive.'

'Who are we meeting?'

'Now that I don't know. My man rang me to say he was in touch with someone who could help us find Abi. He didn't say whether we were going to talk to him or where they're holding her.'

Andy looked nervous.

'So … there's just you and me?' he asked apprehensively.

'For now, yes. Depends what I'm told when we get there.'

Andy's chest felt tight.

'God you're a cool one, Ted. What if it's a trap?'

'A trap for what? They already had you and let you go.' Ted dismissed the idea with a wave of the hand. 'And why would they want me? If they do me any harm, well … let's just say that would be a mistake. A big mistake.'

Andy realised that Ted genuinely had no fear. He himself was used to playing roles: a boss or salesman, a dealer but he always had a nagging doubt he could be found out. Ted, in contrast, seemed to have no self-doubt or fear as he drove towards the unknown.

'What do you expect it to be?'

'I really don't know, lad, but I know there are some scared people out there. I just hope the girl is all right,' he replied.

The two men sat in silence for the rest of the drive.

On the outskirts of Goole, Ted pulled into what appeared to be a large housing estate of former council-owned properties, which looked like they had been built in the 1950s. There was a stillness about the place at that early hour of the morning and they sat and waited. After a few minutes Ted's phoned pinged with a text and he reached for it in an unhurried fashion.

'Okay son, we're going to 64 Pilkington Avenue,' Ted said as he punched the details into his satnav.

Six minutes later, they pulled up outside of a semi-detached house. The front garden was overgrown and the windows and doors were in dire need of painting. Ted got out and Andy followed without asking if he should; Ted's confidence was infectious. There were no lights on in the property and Ted turned the door handle without knocking. The front door was open and he carefully moved inside and switched on the hall light. The place wasn't as bad as Andy was expecting; it was recently decorated and tastefully furnished.

They moved into the living room, which was tidy but unoccupied, as was the dining room and kitchen. Ted signalled that they should go upstairs and they did so with measured steps, in case the owners were still in bed. Ted put his right hand in his pocket and kept it there, making Andy think he must be holding a weapon of some sort – maybe even a gun – so far out of his normal life had he strayed. As they reached the first door upstairs, Ted pushed it open and they both saw what appeared to be the master bedroom. It was empty. The family bathroom was next door, then a box room, which was being used for storage. The final door had a key in the lock, which was unusual as it was on the outside. Ted tried turning the handle but the door was locked. Andy held his breath; he could feel his heart thumping as Ted unlocked the door. As he pushed it open, the shape of a bed loomed out of the darkness. He switched on the light and could see that someone was in the bed.

There was no movement though and whoever it was in there was covered by the bedclothes. Andy made to rush forward but Ted extended his arm and held him back.

'Just be careful, lad,' he whispered. 'We don't know what we're going to find. This might be a crime scene. Let me have a look first.'

Ted moved towards the bed and gently pulled back the duvet. The person underneath did not move. Andy rushed forward,

'Jesus Christ, Ted, it's Abi! Oh my God they've killed her!'

Chapter 43

Andy had fallen to his knees, but Ted gently moved the body, feeling for a pulse in her neck.

'She's alive, son. I think she might be sedated. Let's get an ambulance and get the cops in.'

Andy moved forward and turned Abi fully around and hugged her in her unconscious state as his tears of relief and illogical guilt flowed freely. Through the tears he whispered in her ear,

'I'm so sorry that I wasn't there and didn't protect you, Abi. I'll never let anyone hurt you again, I promise.'

Ted rang 999 and twenty minutes later the ambulance and local police arrived. With blue flashing lights everywhere, the formerly sleepy neighbourhood was now well and truly awake. Andy had telephoned Laura and then his parents, all of whom were struggling to take in the news that Abi had been harmed but was now safe. The emotions of all of them were too raw and too deep to express. There were no screams of delight, just tears and confusion, before the family set off for the hospital where Andy said he would meet them.

Andy travelled in the ambulance with Abi. The paramedics began to get some response from her and she finally came round. She looked confused and scared, until Andy moved forward and she grasped him round the neck.

'I knew you would save me, Uncle Andy! I knew it!' she sobbed.

Ted Lomax told the police he had received an anonymous tip off that Abi was at the address and the police informed him they would take a detailed statement later. He urged Andy to get into the ambulance – he would call and see him tomorrow at the garage.

At the hospital there was much hugging and crying as the Connolly family closed ranks and sat around Abi's bed. Abi apologised for lying to her Mum about Harvey but was reassured she wasn't in any trouble. The anxiety of recent days was replaced with unadulterated pleasure and relief. For all of them, the pure joy of the moment was the ultimate narcotic.

It was a couple of hours later that DCI Cooper arrived. He was surprisingly very good with Abi, speaking to her as though she was a friend of his family. He asked details in a matter-of-fact way and regularly punctuated his responses with wide-eyed exclamations, which encouraged Abi to talk.

'Well that is some story, Abi and you have been very brave. I'm going to make sure you get plenty of rest and won't be bothered by the men in uniforms. When you're feeling better, I'll come round and see you at home and we can have another chat. You're safe now, that's the main thing.'

Andy walked him to the lift and Cooper turned to him.

'Do you know who supplied your friend with the address?'

'No, I don't.'

'Would you tell me if you did?' Cooper asked with a wry smile.

'Why not … you are a police officer, aren't you?' Andy returned the smile.

Cooper made to get into the lift but then stepped back.

'Oh, by the way, Jamie Tasker won't be troubling you again.'

'Why's that then?'

'He was found hanged in his cell this morning.'

'What?' Andy asked, a shocked expression wiping away any residue of humour.

'Yes. So, you won't need to be a witness after all … well not on this case anyway.'

'He hanged himself?' Andy asked in disbelief.

'Well, either that or he had some help. We're looking into it,' Cooper responded, whilst scanning Andy's face for any reaction.

'I'm sorry, David, I don't know what to say.'

'There is nothing to say really. You take care, Andy.'
They shook hands and Cooper left.

The next day Andy told the whole story to his open-mouthed staff and was just finishing when Ted Lomax walked in, still wearing his overcoat. Andy ushered him into his office as the staff gazed at his guest as if he was a cross between a superhero and a mafia Don.

Andy ordered coffee, then asked Ted to fill him in on what had happened. Ted's response was characteristically vague.

'Some people I know reached out to others for information. That led to the word being spread, so it was just a question of waiting after that.'

'And then what?'

'Well, it seems your friend Tasker was not a popular boy. When people heard he had kidnapped a young girl, that was a step too far – people were prepared to talk.'

'And somebody gave the details of where Abi was?'

'Maybe. I'm guessing some of it, but Tasker's card has been marked for some time apparently. He was a hot-headed yob who took too many risks. In the end, his men realised his unpredictability could damage them all and one of them gave the information as to where we'd find Abi. They'd been ordered to get rid of her but instead they sedated her to keep her quiet and told bigger beasts where we could find her. They then did a runner.'

'Those bigger beasts, are they the Baldwin brothers?'

'They might be, son but you don't need to be involved.'

'But I am involved.'

There was moment's delay whilst Ted organised his thoughts.

'Okay, but I don't want any of this repeated. Understood?'

'Understood. Absolutely,' Andy added.

'The Baldwin brothers are vicious criminals but they operate in their own world so you're unlikely ever to come across them. Tasker was a chancer who upset them and was living on borrowed time. He was on a charge of knifing somebody but the case was dropped.'

'Yes, I read about that. He knifed a guy called Graham Todd who didn't turn up at court or disappeared or something. Cooper was involved in that case and might have been helping him, I gather.'

'Cooper wasn't helping him. Cooper was looking for a conviction but Todd was persuaded to disappear on a promise that he would be rewarded in more ways than one.'

'How?'

'Todd was stabbed in an argument about drugs and the Baldwins didn't want that played out in court, plus they probably had other plans for Tasker.'

'Why?'

'The Baldwins have a sister called Marjorie and she married a drug runner: one Graham Todd so, as you can see, it was a family matter.'

'Oh, I see. So, did the Baldwins have Tasker killed in prison?'

'I don't know son and I'm not about to ask. But the guys working for Tasker got spooked and are on the run from the Baldwins, who both have daughters. There's a code about that sort of thing. I would rather be on the run from the police any day than those two.'

Andy hardly dare ask the next question.

'So, am I likely to get a call from the Baldwins?'

'No, that's been sorted.'

'You mean they've been warned off?'

Ted laughed. 'You don't warn off the Baldwins ... not unless you want to be sticking a mirror under your car every morning before you start it. No, some friends of mine have said that you and yours are no threat. That's the end of it.' Andy hesitated, trying to take it all in.

'What about the three grand? What do I do with that?'

'Oh, that's all yours, lad. Nobody is going to ask you for that.'

'Ted, I can't thank you enough. What can I ... what do we owe you?'

'Nothing son, just glad to help,' Ted said getting up and signalling the end of the conversation.

'I hope I haven't offended you, Ted – it's just that we're so grateful.'

'No offence taken, son.'

Andy couldn't help himself,

'Ted, can I ask why you're helping us?'

Ted hesitated then turned and walked back to his seat.

'Okay, I'll tell you. About thirty years ago I had a cousin who was a bit younger than me and always in trouble of some sort or other, but he was basically a good lad. Anyway, he couldn't hold down a job, so when his girlfriend got pregnant, he decided he had to do something. One day he wandered into your dad's garage and enquired about a van that was on the forecourt at £495. Your dad asked him what deposit he could give and he said he had saved £50 and he would need to pay for the rest on HP. Your dad asked why he wanted it and he told him he wanted to start a window cleaning round to provide for his new family. Anyway, he couldn't get any credit but your dad asked him to bring his girlfriend round so he could meet her. So, the next day, that's what he did and your dad said he would sort something out. He told them the van was no good for them though – it only had the two seats and they had a young one on the way.'

'What did he do, put them on to a cheaper one?'

'No, he sold them a better one for £1000.'

'Always looking for the deal, my dad!'

'Not really, because your dad bought that van in an auction and I know that because I bid against him.'

'How much did he pay? About £500?' Andy said with a grin.

'No. £1000. He took a £50 deposit off my cousin and loaned him the rest interest-free until it was paid off. You see son, your dad wanted to meet the girl to see if the story was true. Once he knew it was, he wanted to help them get on their feet. He doesn't even know that I know about it and he's never mentioned it to me. My cousin is Davy Archer and he now has four vans and a commercial window-cleaning business. He always offered to do your dad's windows for free but your dad always insisted on paying.'

'Wow, I didn't know that!' Andy said, slightly chastened.

Ted got up to leave but as he reached the door, he turned once more.

'You see son, my cousin asked me for help but I said no. He didn't even ask your dad for help but he got it. Your dad's a good man, Andy; that's why I wanted to help him, and you.'

Ted hesitated for a second before adding 'Mind you, don't you go telling anybody or they'll think I'm going soft.'

Andy grinned. 'Your secret is safe with me, Ted. Thanks again.'

Chapter 44

THREE WEEKS LATER

Things were getting back to normal for all of those involved: Rebecca had returned from Spain and Andy was fighting any negative feelings about her leaving him to fight alone. But truth to tell, he didn't really know if they would still be together this time next year. He had developed a much easier relationship with Hannah and, although it had crossed his mind to try and reopen that relationship, she had told him she'd started seeing a new guy called Simon that she thought he would like. That was something else he would have to get his head around.

His own children thought the whole story was fantastic and had wildly exaggerated tales for their friends of murderous intruders in their house being chased off by their ferocious mother, who knew no fear. Their tales about cousin Abi being kidnapped by the Mafia and rescued by their dad made Andy sound like James Bond.

Abi herself had cemented her already deep connection with Uncle Andy and spoke to him almost every day. After she was released from hospital, Andy had gone to see her at his parents' house and pulled an envelope from his pocket.

'In true gangster style, Abi, I have £3000 here and I've decided it's yours by way of compensation for your recent ordeal. I realise that giving it to you now would be a mistake and turn you into a lunatic, so I'll hold on to it and you can spend it bit by bit. Your mum has agreed to you having £500 now and we are going on a shopping spree just for you next Saturday.'

Abi squealed in delight, then asked, 'Is this dirty money, Uncle Andy?'

'Dirty money?' Andy laughed. 'Don't ever let your granddad hear you say that. He'll have it off you!'

DCI Cooper paid a call on Abi shortly after she came home from hospital and took her statement, before going to see Andy to give him an update. After the usual small talk, he got down to business.

'We don't really know what happened to Tasker; the post-mortem was inconclusive as to whether he did it to himself or was murdered. I knew him and can't believe he would top himself but, for now, we have no evidence and the case remains open.'

'What about Gary Newcombe?'

'What about him?'

'Are you charging him? We both know they got to him.'

'No, there will be no charges. It must be in the public interest and how can it be? Gary was just a victim all the way through.'

'So ... that's the end of it?'

'More or less. Oh – my sergeant has been suspended and is under investigation. I shouldn't really tell you this but it'll be public soon.'

'What has he been up to?'

'Supplying information to felons. Allegedly,' Cooper was careful to add.

'So, he was bent?'

'Not exactly. He was old school, that's all. He gave information in exchange for information to keep the scum off the streets and away from schools. He thought he was doing the right thing.'

They said their goodbyes and Cooper, once again, paused by one of the new cars in the showroom, stroked the roof and turned to wink at Andy.

Laura had settled in at her parents' house and told Charles she wanted a divorce and wouldn't be returning home. She was flooded with texts, emails and flowers, as well as visits to the house, where a friendly but firm Molly refused Charles entry.

Abi had confirmed she knew there were problems and that she could live quite happily without her stepdad, especially as she was convinced he'd thrown her mother down the stairs, even though Laura never did recover her memory of that day.

It was late one Friday afternoon that Charles Peterson answered his internal phone to be told his father-in-law was in reception and wanted to see him. He said to tell him he was waiting for his next appointment but as he put the phone down, his door opened and Paul Connolly walked in.

'Hello Charles. I thought I would pay you a little visit so we can have a chat.'

'Oh, hello Paul. The receptionist should have told you I'm expecting a client so we might have to meet later.'

Paul didn't miss a beat.

'Well, your client will have to be patient.'

Charles looked perplexed; his father-in-law had never been difficult with him in the past or shown any sign of aggression.

Paul continued pleasantly. 'So, how are things going for you at work, Charles?'

'Fine, thank you. Look Paul, what's this about? If it's about Laura, then I'm sure we can work things out between us. I doubt very much she would want you or Molly to interfere.'

'Oh, Laura has no idea that I'm here, neither has Molly.'

Charles shifted uncomfortably in his seat.

'So, what is it?'

'You're right that it's about Laura and the end of your marriage. I want to talk to you man to man, so to speak.'

Charles sighed and made a big show of looking at his watch.

'Then I'm afraid I'm going to have to insist we discuss this another time, Paul. I'm not prepared to keep my client waiting.'

Paul smiled politely.

'I tell you what Charles, why not ask Angus Trevelyan to join us. I saw his car in the car park and I know him pretty well from the golf club. Plays off thirteen, you know? A real bandit, as I always tell him, though he does tend to slice his drives. Anyway, I'm sure he would be interested to hear about you hitting my daughter.'

The mood in the room changed instantly and colour flooded Charles's face as he responded instinctively.

'What are you talking about? That is an outrageous

thing to say. I don't know what Laura has been telling you but that is a lie,' he barked.

'Laura hasn't told us anything. You might be able to fool me, but not Molly. She noticed a couple of bruises more than a year ago and then again in the summer. She knows her daughter like no one else and could read it in her eyes. We have both watched you when we've had dinner together, and especially at Christmas. I wanted to say something sooner, but Molly said we had to wait until Laura was ready to leave you.'

Paul's face hardened.

'To be honest, I have wanted to come round here with a baseball bat, but I kept the peace.'

'No Paul. Believe me, you have it all wrong, truly you have,' Charles stuttered.

'No, I don't Charlie boy,' Paul replied calmly. 'But it stops here. Today. From this day forward, there will be no more texts or emails or visits. You will stay away from Laura and Abi, and you will instruct a lawyer and go through with the divorce. Laura will settle for half of everything: half the value of the house and half of your investments. She won't be seeking any maintenance from you or part of your pension. She's a bright woman who can earn her own money and she's part of our family, as is Abi. We will look after them.'

Charles's face coloured with fury.

'You can't tell me what to do, Paul! Who the hell do you think you are? And who the hell do you think you're talking to?'

Paul looked at him for a few seconds before leaning forward to speak.

'I am talking to a woman beater. The lowest of the low. Hayley has spoken to some of your ex-girlfriends so we now know exactly what you are and who you are. I really don't know what goes on in that head of yours, Charles, but I can promise you this: you will not trouble us again.'

'Are you threatening me?' Charles said, disarmed by Paul's air of cool menace.

'Yes I am and I'll tell you how.'

Paul stood up and walked slowly around to the rear of his chair, leaning on its leather back as he composed himself.

'A couple of years ago I had a cancer scare. They found a tumour and they treated it – said I should be fine. Anyway, a few months ago, I felt things weren't right so I went back for tests. I didn't want to worry Molly so I didn't tell her – or anyone for that matter. I went back to get the results and they told me it had come back, only this time it's brought all of its mates along and so, for me, everything is short term. They can't say for sure, but six months to a year is what they reckon.'

The shock of the revelation prompted Charles to respond.

'Oh Paul … I'm so sorry.'

'Don't give me that shit. The only reason I'm telling you this is so that you'll realise I'm serious. When that arsehole Tasker stepped things up with Andy I was introduced to a man and I paid him twenty grand to kill Tasker. I didn't say anything to anyone; I just took the necessary action to rid my family of a threat. Anyway, as it turned out, someone beat us to the punch and took him out. My man offered to refund fifteen grand as he hadn't done the job. It was like I was taking a second-hand car back but with a discount.'

Charles had not blinked through the last incredible revelation and his mouth was beginning to open involuntarily as Paul continued.

'So, when I realised you must have had something to do with Laura's fall, and when I found out what you are really like with women, I told him to keep the money and you became the target. You try and own women; you won't let them go and then you frighten the hell out of them. Well, not this time sonny. Not this time.'

Charles tried desperately to regroup: 'I don't know what you've been told, but it's all lies. That Hayley is a bitch, she...'

Paul held a hand up to silence him.

'Save your breath, Charles. You're wasting your time. Anyway, I'm giving you a chance: no further contact, sort things out as I have asked you to do, and nothing happens. But the contract stays in place now and after I've gone, just in case you return to old habits.'

'What's to stop me going to the police?' Charles asked, unconvincingly.

'Be my guest. I'll just deny it and we'll have you investigated for assault – get statements from your former girlfriends. And of course, I'll make sure that all this firm's clients are aware of exactly who you are. I doubt your partners will want to keep you once that becomes common knowledge.'

Paul walked calmly towards the door, unlocked it and then turned around slowly.

'Do yourself a favour, son: move to another town. You have no future here and if you interfere with my family, you'll have no future at all. And that is the solemn promise of a dying man. Oh, and by the way, Hayley is now family. I am telling the family tonight about my condition…not looking forward to that'.

Paul looked at the ground for a second to compose himself before adding,

'Anyway, I'm happy knowing I have put protection in place, even from the grave. Goodbye Charles.'